PROSPERO'S DAUGHTERS

Recent Titles by Sally Stewart from Severn House

APPOINTMENT IN VENICE
CASTLES IN SPAIN
CURLEW ISLAND
THE DAISY CHAIN
FLOODTIDE
LOST AND FOUND
MOOD INDIGO
POSTCARDS FROM A STRANGER
A RARE BEAUTY
ROMAN SPRING
A TIME TO DANCE
TRAVELLING GIRL

PROSPERO'S DAUGHTERS

Sally Stewart

This first world edition published in Great Britain 2005 by
SEVERN HOUSE PUBLISHERS LTD of
9–15 High Street, Sutton, Surrey SM1 1DF.
This first world edition published in the USA 2006 by
SEVERN HOUSE PUBLISHERS INC of
595 Madison Avenue, New York, N.Y. 10022.

British Library Cataloguing in Publication Data

Stewart, Sally
Prospero's daughters
1. Granddaughters - Fiction
2. Grandfathers - Fiction
3. Artists - Greece - Corfu Island - Fiction
4. Corfu Island (Greece) - Fiction
5. Love stories
I. Title
823.9'14 [F]

ISBN-10 : 0-7278-6319-3

Typeset by Palimpsest Book Production Ltd.,
Polmont, Stirlingshire, Scotland.
Printed and bound in Great Britain by
MPG Books Ltd., Bodmin, Cornwall.

One

On a bitter afternoon in January the High wasn't looking its best, and, empty of undergraduates because Hilary Term hadn't started, it was empty as well. The students were often tiresome and untidy, but Oxford seemed lifeless without them.

Anna walked away from the solicitor's front door, head bent against a flurry of sleety rain. A passer-by loomed up in front of her and she side-stepped to avoid him, then halted altogether. The lit window of an art gallery shone through the gloom beside her, seeming to insist that she notice what the proprietor had carefully placed there – a painting that blazed colour and warmth enough even to defy the bleakness of the afternoon. But there was something even more unexpected about it as well: it was very familiar. Hanging in her grandmother's drawing-room at home was an almost identical street scene of graceful houses coloured the same glowing mixture of rose and umber and terracotta.

Half-inclined to go into the shop, she saw the bus she needed pull up at the kerb, and ran to climb aboard it instead. Half an hour later she was looking again at her own painting when the door opened and her mother walked into the room. Anna smiled at her, surprised to realize how fond she was of a largely absentee parent. Nicola Rasini seemed, at least, a woman to be relished when she *was* there – still beautiful and, although she hadn't sung in public for at least ten years, even now the brilliant performer she'd long ago become; just to watch her entrance into the room was a pleasure in itself.

'Not much more of our weather,' Anna said, seeing her grimace at the rain slashing against the windows. 'According to today's forecast it's sunny in Rome, and you'll be back there by tomorrow evening.'

'For which, my darling, Heaven be praised. The Oxford climate has got worse, not better. God knows what it does to the vocal chords of any singer mad enough to come here.' She watched her daughter now occupied in lighting the fire and intent on the job of coaxing it into flame. 'Come back with me,' she said suddenly in a different tone of voice. 'I don't like leaving you here alone. We've laid your grandmother decently to rest – it's time for you to make a fresh start, and you could begin by getting rid of this morgue of a house.'

Anna squatted back on her heels, still watching the fire but hearing in what her mother had just said an echo of past unhappiness still not forgotten or forgiven. Nicola Curtis, as she'd been then, had escaped as soon as she could. Study in London, a brief marriage to an Italian opera-singer that, apart from producing a daughter, had been disastrously unsuccessful, and finally the blossoming of her own career – through all the tumultuous years Nicola had never learned to like her own mother, or quite forgiven herself for leaving her child to grow up with Lavinia Curtis in Oxford.

Anna turned to look at the woman she'd had so little chance to get to know. 'I don't hate the house as you did, rather too Victorian-Gothic though it is! And I even grew fond of my grandmother. We learned to understand each other and, in her own strange way, she was kind to me – kinder than she ever was to you, I think.'

It was likely to be the end of the conversation; in Anna's experience so far, Nicola had never been inclined to delve into a past she clearly reckoned was better left unvisited. But now, perhaps because Lavinia Curtis was at peace – though probably not, her unforgiving daughter would estimate, in paradise – she seemed ready to go on talking.

'We both had an unnatural upbringing, you and I – no

father present and a distinct shortage of parental love,' she commented slowly. 'I can blame Lavina partially at least for mine, but yours was all my fault. I chose a selfish, vain and rather stupid man to be your father – I'm glad to say that since then, like most singers apart from myself, he's got very fat!'

Anna grinned at the note of self-satisfaction in her mother's voice but then grew serious again. 'What happened to *your* father? I know that mine wasn't cut out for family life and very soon took off, but all Granny would say about her husband was that he was killed in the war, quite soon after they were married. She seemed to suggest that it was only a brief interlude . . . something she could scarcely remember . . . but I had the feeling that it wasn't really the case.'

'Far from it,' Nicola said definitely. 'She never got over his death, but it wasn't just grief. She stayed angry because he'd died unnecessarily, and jealous because he'd loved Greece and his friends there more than he loved her – or me, for that matter, but she wasn't so bothered about that.'

The room had grown dark, only lit by the flickering firelight, but Anna didn't move to switch on lamps in case she disturbed her mother's rare willingness to talk about their dysfunctional family life. 'Tell me what else you can about my grandfather,' she suggested quietly. 'It seems sad not to know.'

Nicola gave the little shrug acquired from living so much among Italians. 'Lavinia didn't encourage questions, but once – I think she was unwell and feeling sorry for herself – she did suddenly begin to talk. My father had been a brilliant Classics don, much sought after by all the daughters of his fellow-academics because he was also very handsome. She, Lavinia Singleton, had been the one to snaffle him.'

'Nothing unexpected about that,' Anna pointed out. 'She was beautiful – I've seen photographs of her as a young woman.'

'Certainly she was, and also clever and talented – a very fine pianist among other things. But instead of having a home of their own they shared this house with Lavinia's parents – a pernickety, rather obnoxious couple who lived far too long in my opinion. That was her first mistake. The second was to expect Steven Curtis to become a different man. He couldn't stop loving Greece – its history, language, people – but Lavinia didn't believe in sharing; he was only supposed to belong to her. He'd been there as usual in the summer of 1939 but then war was declared. He came home and they were married early the following year. She was always convinced that he married her because he'd lost the girl he'd wanted in Greece. But in spite of that Lavinia got pregnant and I was born the following year. By then, of course, France had fallen and ordinary contact with the Continent was at an end.'

'Grandfather wasn't young by then,' Anna said thoughtfully, 'at least, surely not young enough to be called up to fight.'

'Lavinia's view entirely. But Steven insisted on volunteering as soon as the Italians invaded Greece. He said they needed people like himself who knew the country and the language. The Army taught him how to jump out of an aeroplane and handle a gun, and a gentle, scholarly Englishman went off to share his Greek friends' war. Lavinia never saw him again. She became a teacher herself and slowly grew into being the embittered, hard woman who blighted my childhood; but God was merciful and gave me the talent I could use to get away.'

This time Anna didn't prompt her mother – the story was now complete enough, and it explained what had been so difficult to make sense of before. She got up to pour the white wine that Nicola expected as an evening apéritif, but halted in front of the painting above the fireplace.

'A strange thing happened this afternoon,' she said suddenly. 'As I left Mr Melksham's office I passed the window of an art gallery in the High. In it was a painting just like this one. I was trying to see whether there were the same initials in the corner when the bus came along and I jumped on it. The houses look Venetian to me, but you'd expect them to be bordering a green canal and they're not. I asked Granny about the painting once and it was the only time she got really angry with me – said it was just something quite valueless my grandfather had come across in a junk-shop.'

'It's somewhere in Greece, not Venice,' Nicola said slowly. 'That's where Steven's friends lived. I've no idea who "N.K." was, but it was probably his sister who Lavinia spent so much time hating. She even remembered the girl's name – Athina. Strange to think that they must *all* be dead by now . . . so much anguish just ended in dust and ashes!' She switched on the light beside her chair, dispelling the shadows in the room. 'Don't look so sad; it all happened a long time ago. Forget the past now, Anna, and forgive me for being such a selfish cow of a mother by coming to stay with me in Rome. I'd like you to, because I'm lonely without my darling Enrico; but for once I'm thinking of you as well. You're too thin and tired . . . I think a change of scene would be good for you, not to mention a nice handsome man or two!'

She sounded unusually sincere, and Anna thought she probably *was* lonely, despite a host of friends. No one had taken the place of her long-time companion Enrico Caetani, who'd died the previous year. She'd never been talked into marrying a second time, but the impresario much older than herself had not only taken her career in hand but become her true friend and lover as well.

'I'd like to come,' Anna agreed, 'but not straightaway, if you don't mind. I'll probably keep the house, and the nice tenants I've got upstairs, but there's still a lot of clearing-out to do. Apart from that, I've a deadline to meet and an impatient publisher beginning to nag. Granny wasn't ill for long, but I haven't got much work done for the past month or two. Let me keep Rome and the handsome men for a visit in the spring.'

Nicola nodded, aware that her daughter, however lightly

built and delicately featured she might look, was not for nothing a chip off Lavinia's unyielding block. Anna still had her Italian father's name, but she was like him only in the dark eyes and brows that went so unexpectedly with her fair English hair.

'You've become more successful than I realized,' Nicola commented, not attempting to get her to change her mind. 'I saw your last book in Rome before I left, translated into Italian. You didn't tell me that was going to happen.'

'I expect my name helped,' Anna suggested with an apologetic smile. 'Perhaps I ought to think of becoming Anne Racine in France, just to help sales along there!'

She thought it wasn't much of a *bon mot*, but her mother was smiling again, and they could consider as closed a conversation that had raked over the past Nicola still found painful. They didn't speak again of Lavinia, and it was only when Anna had waved her mother's taxi away, *en route* for the airport the following day, that she remembered something else that might have been mentioned in their conversation of the previous afternoon.

She'd been taken as a guest to dine at High Table in Balliol College some months before her grandmother died. In the course of the evening she'd found herself in front of the College Roll of Honour – heart-rending columns of names for the 1914–18 war, saddening but with far fewer names than for what followed twenty-five years later. There she'd read the name of Steven Curtis and heard herself say proudly to the man she was with, 'He was my grandfather . . . I'm sorry I never knew him, or even anything about him; it was a subject that Granny chose not to discuss.'

Her companion's reaction had been surprising at the time. 'Well, you can forget that showy chap Lord Byron, and Rupert Brooke as well – we have our own Greek legend here in the person of Steven Curtis. But I never realized he was anything to do with you – is Rasini a pen-name that you prefer to use?'

'It's my father's name,' Anna said rather shortly. 'He

didn't give me anything else, being an Italian opera-singer who made a very brief appearance in my mother's life.'

'Sorry – a *faux-pas*, I'm afraid, Anna; forgive me, please.'

She'd smiled at him, and unknowingly completed his undoing. 'Well, *I*'m afraid I sounded like my grandmother just then – it's exactly how she would have spoken!'

Yes, she *should* have remembered to tell her mother about that little incident – Nicola would have relished it for several reasons.

Three days later Anna returned to the solicitor's office to settle the final details of Lavinia's estate. She'd known Victor Melksham for as long as she could remember because he was one of the few men her grandmother had been prepared to trust. He was probably more aware than anyone else now of the peculiar history of the Curtis family, and Anna knew that any advice he offered would be disinterested and good.

When the official matters had been dealt with and his rimless spectacles laid aside, he smiled at her across his desk. 'I'm glad your mother was at least able to attend Lavinia's funeral.'

Anna heard the faint note of irony in his voice and smiled back. 'You mean you thought she mightn't bother! It's true she doesn't like Oxford even now, and the visit didn't last longer than it had to; but at least she came. She thinks I ought to sell the house – wipe the Curtis slate clean and start again; but I don't feel inclined to do that, at least not just yet.'

'For any particular reason?' Mr Melksham enquired.

Anna considered the question for a moment, aware that it was the one she'd been putting to herself.

'No reason that you'll recognize as businesslike and sensible, but I have the feeling that something's been left unfinished there. I could sell the house to someone else but I'd be taking the problem with me; that wouldn't wipe the slate clean.' Her dark eyes looked gravely at the lawyer. 'I'm sorry you didn't know my grandfather any more than I did.

It's as if Granny built a wall of silence around his memory, with a sign on it that said, "Keep out; trespassers will be shown off the premises".'

Victor Melksham nodded, knowing that what she said was true; he'd stubbed his own toes more than once against the rock-hard prejudices of a client who, generally speaking, seemed to dislike the rest of the human race. Her only exception to that rule as far as he knew was the girl facing him now – Lavinia Curtis had grown to love *her* at least; it was something to be said in an embittered woman's favour.

'You're right, Anna – I didn't join the firm until long after the war had ended, but my uncle knew your grandfather. Uncle Will left behind a commonplace book when he died and I made a point of glancing through it again last night. I thought I'd seen something you might like to have, and I finally found it.' He opened a drawer of his desk, and took out a photograph that he placed in front of Anna. It was a small portrait of a fair-haired, sensitive-faced young man, faintly smiling at whoever had held the camera.

'He looks nice,' she said after a while, knowing that it was the right word to use about Steven Curtis even if it sounded inadequate. 'We talked about him for once when my mother was here – she didn't know very much either, but Granny *had* given away the fact that he'd been dropped into Greece in the war and died there.' She picked up the photograph and put it carefully in her bag. 'Thank you for letting me have that. I'll take it to Rome when I go to visit my mother.'

Victor Melksham then decided to ask the question that had been bothering him. 'Am I right in thinking that she doesn't mind about Lavinia's will? I don't believe your grandmother was trying to create ill-will between you by excluding Nicola – she just wanted to be sure that you were taken care of.'

He waited for Anna to answer, and was relieved by the firm shake of her head. 'There's no ill-will, in fact no problem at all. My mother would rather die than live in the house again. She's happy where she is, and in no need of money.

I asked her to take whatever she wanted but she just laughed; her sumptuous apartment in Rome doesn't need anything North Oxford has to offer!'

'I'm glad . . . I rather like your house as it is,' the solicitor said unexpectedly. Then he reverted to the beginning of their conversation. 'I'd like to know how successful you are in writing "finis" to the Curtis story. Keep in touch, please, Anna.'

She promised that she would, thanked him for all his kindness and then let herself out into the cold, damp morning air. This time she let a bus go by, and went instead to look again in the art gallery's window, but it was differently arranged now; the centre-piece was a modern abstract vision of something she couldn't identify; it bore no resemblance to the joyous painting she was looking for.

She pushed the shop door open and walked in, to be greeted by a young middle-aged man who introduced himself as the owner, Rupert Whittaker, and asked how he could help her.

'You've changed your window display,' she said diffidently. 'When I walked past a few days ago there was a different picture there . . . a street scene of lovely Mediterranean-looking houses. Do you have it still in the gallery?'

She received a sharper glance this time, as if it hadn't been the question he expected. Then the dealer shook his head. 'That painting was sold, I'm afraid . . . yesterday. I wish I could show you something else by the same artist but, alas, I cannot.' He hesitated for a moment, trying to place the girl in front of him – she was too simply dressed to be very wealthy, surely, and too young to be an experienced dealer hoping to snap up a treasure that he didn't know he had. But the art world was a cut-throat business, and appearances were often not what they seemed. 'The painting was bought by a gallery-owner from Paris,' he finally admitted. 'The man was an expert, I'm glad to say, who was very excited by what he found here.'

'Because he knew the artist?' Anna asked, suddenly hoarse with excitement. 'Could you tell me, please, if it was signed?'

She'd been too intense, she realized, sounded too anxious for an unknown customer who'd just walked in from the street. The man in front of her answered with a cool question of his own.

'May I ask why you want to know? It can scarcely matter when the painting now belongs to someone else.'

Anna heard the chill in his voice, and smiled an apology. 'I'm sorry . . . I should have explained. It only matters because my grandmother owned a painting that looked very similar – the same scene, same colours, same technique even . . . chaotic daubs of paint at close-range that resolve themselves into something ordered and beautiful when you stand back. She died without telling me the artist's name – the painting is only signed with the initials "N.K."'

'And . . . where is this painting now?' It was Rupert Whittaker's turn to try to sound unconcerned, but although he failed, Anna was in no state to notice.

'I have it at home . . . it belongs to me now.' She saw and suddenly understood the eagerness in the dealer's face. 'I'm afraid it's not for sale. The painting's involved in some family history that I need to sort out. I was just hoping that you could at least tell me who "N.K." was.'

'Until yesterday I couldn't have done so . . . now I can,' said Rupert Whittaker carefully, disappointed but now anxious to be helpful. It was by no means unknown for the owners of something valuable to quickly change their minds about disposing of it.

'The artist was a man called Nikos Kladis . . . a Greek obviously. The French expert who came here has known his work for some time, and I'm afraid that my own ignorance merely confirmed his certainty that we're a race of barbarians who will never catch up with him and his compatriots!'

Anna dragged Whittaker back to what concerned her most. 'Did the Frenchman know if Nikos Kladis is still alive?'

'He admitted that he wasn't sure, but he thought it very

unlikely. The paintings began to change hands soon after the war, but Kladis himself has never materialized. Artists rarely choose to hide their light under a bushel, and the more likely explanation is that he was working in the thirties and didn't survive the war years in Greece. Sad, also; because he was an extraordinarily gifted painter – quite exceptional in fact.'

Anna nodded, sadly contemplating a dead end. Then she thought of one final question. 'Would you be allowed to tell me who brought in the painting you sold? Perhaps *they* had some connection with Nikos Kladis if the Frenchman is right in thinking that ordinary art-lovers over here haven't heard of him yet.'

Mr Whittaker forgave her for imagining that even English art-lovers would be ordinary and, after a moment's thought, agreed that he could at least telephone the seller and ask. He pattered away to a cubby-hole beyond the gallery and returned a few minutes later with a piece of paper in his hand.

'Mrs Carstairs said that I could give you this; but I'll warn you that she didn't sound eager to be helpful. Can you be . . . be cajoling if you ring?'

Amused in spite of herself by the note of entreaty in his voice, Anna promised that she would try.

'And would you be kind enough to let me know if you find out anything about Nikos Kladis? I should dearly like,' Mr Whittaker added wistfully, 'to be able to tell Monsieur Bouchard something he hasn't been able to find out for himself.'

Anna agreed, too, that this was very understandable, and allowed herself to be escorted to the door, where she thought they parted as the best of friends.

Two

Mrs Carstairs, willing to be helpful or not, had to be left undisturbed for a while. Anna ignored the pictured face of her grandfather lying on her desk – looking reproachful, she couldn't help thinking, whenever she caught sight of it – and went doggedly on with more urgent tasks. There were printer's proofs to be returned to her publisher, and the accumulated clutter of Lavinia's long life to be sifted through before it could be safely discarded. But one evening after she'd tiredly refused an invitation to dine out and then regretted it, she suddenly picked up the telephone and rang the number Mr Whittaker had given her.

The not-so-young voice that answered sounded crisp almost to the point of rudeness, and Anna's quick apology for being a nuisance didn't do much to soften Mrs Carstair's insistence that the call was pointless in any case.

'The painting belonged to my father-in-law,' she went on to explain frostily, '. . . I know nothing about it at all except that it's not the sort of thing I'd hang on *my* walls.'

Anna tried to feel sorry for her lack of taste, and promised herself that she wouldn't mention the value that Mr Whittaker had hinted at. Nor, either, would she try to argue that in its own unusual way the painting was very beautiful. She could imagine what Mrs Carstairs was likely to prefer instead – gilt-framed family portraits of ancestors and their assorted dogs.

It was a sharp disappointment that the trail back to Steven Curtis had petered out so completely, but she could scarcely blame an unfriendly stranger for that.

'I was hoping you could tell me about the painting because I've inherited one very like it,' she gently explained. 'But I sympathize if you've got the job of clearing out your father-in-law's home; I'm sorry if I am troubling you at a bad time.'

'You needn't be sorry – he isn't dead.' Mrs Carstairs sounded more aggrieved than glad, and Anna saw in her mind's eye the frail, elderly man who'd been bundled out of his home by this unfeeling dragon of a woman. Unexpectedly Mrs Carstairs spoke again.

'My father-in-law is fragile and forgetful but he makes sense most of the time. If you don't mind listening to the muddled reminiscences of his youth there's no reason why you shouldn't ask him about the painting yourself; he *might* remember how he came by it.' There was a brief pause while she found what she was looking for, the name of a residential home and its telephone number. 'You'll have to go there – he hates the telephone – but ring them before you do; he has good days and bad. I hope you won't blame *me* if it's a wasted visit.'

Anna thanked Mrs Carstairs for her help and rang off, thinking that if her father-in-law's carers were even half-way kind he was probably better off where he was. It seemed the forlornest of hopes, to rely on an old man's faltering memory, but she couldn't give up this final chance without a try.

Her telephone call the following morning was answered by a pleasant-sounding woman who decided that he was well enough to receive a brief visit from someone he didn't know. Anna arranged to set out at once, only stopping long enough to take a digital photograph of her own painting. It didn't do justice to what Nikos Kladis had created but it might just remind Mr Carstairs of what he had owned himself.

She hadn't far to drive from Oxford and found the house easily enough, overlooking the river at Wallingford. With the Thames in sullen winter mood the outlook was depressing, and she found herself hoping that the inmates at least lived long enough to see how lovely it would be in the spring.

She was led through the hall and several corridors into a small, comfortably furnished sitting-room that its occupant appeared to have to himself. Her guide introduced her and left, and Anna was faced with a problem that she'd given too little thought to – how to begin so complicated a story for the old man who sat huddled in an armchair watching her. His stare was unnervingly intent, not the vague unfocused gaze she'd been expecting. She suddenly felt ten years old again, required to confess something to her grandmother; but the reminder made her taut face relax into a smile and she could begin to explain why she was there.

Mr Carstairs said nothing at all, even when she produced the photograph she'd brought and offered it to him. 'This was my grandmother's painting, but it's very like the one you owned. I know the name of the painter – a man called Nikos Kladis – and I know that he was my grandfather's close friend; but that's all I know. When I saw your picture in the gallery window it occurred to me that you might have known the painter too.' Still the old man didn't speak, and she felt certain that she had no right to be there. 'I'm sorry,' she said gently. 'I shouldn't be bothering you . . . It was all a long time ago, and you probably just bought the painting because it appealed to you. It was silly of me to assume that you might have known my grandfather, Steven Curtis.'

Suddenly Mr Carstairs spoke, in the slightly querulous voice of old age. 'Of course I knew him . . . Why didn't you mention his name? You talked before about someone I don't remember.' Anna looked at him, suddenly hopeful again, but he was no longer watching her; instead his faded blue eyes seemed to be revisiting something she couldn't see. He was an old man trying to reassemble whatever fragments of the past his memory still held.

Almost afraid to interrupt, she risked a quiet question. 'Did you know Steven Curtis at Oxford, Mr Carstairs?'

The parchment-coloured face in front of her creased into a quiet smile. 'He taught us all to love Greece – spent the vacations taking us there. The "Prof" we called him, although he wasn't much older than us.'

'He died there during the war,' Anna prompted gently. 'Perhaps you knew that.' But Mr Carstairs wasn't listening.

'What places we saw . . . the Parthenon, Olympia, Mycenae, Epidaurus, and Delphi of course . . . Delphi above all; is it still the haunt of eagles, do you know?'

She shook her head. 'I haven't got there yet.' It wasn't the moment to explain that while Lavinia Curtis was alive she'd made no attempt to visit a forbidden country. She was aware, too, that her host was tiring; any moment now he'd forget she was there, and drop into the sudden brief sleep of the very old. With so many questions still unasked, she phrased a final query.

'Was Nikos Kladis with . . . the Prof as well at Delphi? Is that how you came to have one of his paintings?'

She'd made a mistake. His old face looked angry now. 'Of course not, that was somewhere else . . . that was . . .' but where it was he clearly couldn't remember and the failure frustrated and hurt him.

Anna touched his trembling hands with her own warm ones and smiled at him. 'It doesn't matter where it was. Thank you for talking to me – I'm so glad to have met someone who knew and loved my grandfather. But now I must let you rest.'

She stood up to leave, but on a sudden impulse stooped to kiss his cheek before she walked away. Then, at the door, his voice sounded again, making her turn round.

'On the island . . . that's where it was; Prospero's Island . . . *that*'s what Steven called it.'

Then with a contented little smile he fell asleep.

Anna was invited to dinner a few nights later by Victor Melksham, who allowed most of the meal to go by in general conversation before he touched on what was really occupying his mind. 'How are you getting on, by the way, with your journey into the past?'

Anna described what had happened so far, culminating in her visit to Wallingford and Mr Carstairs's parting shot. 'What's your guess?' she finished up. 'I think I know what mine is.'

He lifted his hands in a little gesture of protest. 'My dear girl, I'm a lawyer, not a betting man. Take your pick of the Cyclades, the Sporades, the Dodecanese, and throw in the Ionian Islands too while you're about it – Greece can lay claim to more than two thousand islands!' He saw her wave the total aside, and shook his head. 'Don't tell me Shakespeare identified Prospero's enchanted island for you in *The Tempest*? Well, it's not the sort of evidence that would ever stand up in a court of law.'

'I know that,' Anna conceded, smiling at him. 'But don't you remember what Laurence Durrell's learned friend pointed out? Sycorax, Caliban's hag of a mother, who owned the island before Prospero arrived, must be an obvious anagram for Corcyra. There are other clues as well that I won't bore you with, but the best argument is Nikos Kladis's paintings. The houses *look* Venetian, and we know that Corfu escaped the Turks and was governed by Venice for four hundred years.'

The lawyer's rare smile accepted that now she was on firmer ground. 'So do I take it that you're hell-bent on going to Corcyra – or Corfu, as we have to call it now?'

'Well yes,' said Anna, 'but not straightaway. I've work to finish first, and then I want to spend a little time in Rome with my mother. I can go down to Brindisi from there and take a ferry. It's the right way to approach an island, don't you think . . . by sea?'

Mr Melksham, who refused to approach anywhere by aeroplane, thoughtfully agreed, but went on to say something else. 'Anna, go there by all means – you need a holiday and a change from North Oxford – but don't set your heart on finding any trace of your grandfather. I'm afraid the trail will have gone cold.'

Anna's dark eyes held his with a directness that reminded

him of Lavinia Curtis. 'Do you think I'm wrong to try? My mother's view is that we should leave the past undisturbed – perhaps in case we might find something we don't like. But I *can't* leave things as they are. If I were being fanciful, I'd say that I'm trying to lay to rest my grandfather's ghost – it's not at peace yet.'

'Then go and look,' Melksham said gently. 'Spend Easter in Greece – Steven Curtis would surely have approved of that.'

With the idea planted in her mind, as at least one precise object to aim at, the rest of the journey fell into place easily enough. She would fly to Rome at the beginning of March, where spring would already be on its way, spend Easter on Corfu, and end up on the Greek mainland, visiting the classical sites that Mr Carstairs had remembered the "Prof" taking his students to. Everyone said it was the time to go – while the countryside was awash with wild flowers and the hordes of tourists hadn't yet arrived.

The day before she was due to leave she telephoned Rupert Whittaker at the art gallery.

'You've changed your mind about letting me sell your painting,' he suggested hopefully.

'I'm afraid not, but I promise to let you know if I ever do. I'm really ringing to thank you for putting me in touch with Mr Carstairs,' Anna explained. 'He's an old man with a memory that only works in fits and starts, but it did produce the one essential clue I needed. He remembered that the place we're looking for is an island, not the Greek mainland, and all the books I've consulted since that illustrate the architecture of Corfu Town show houses just like the ones in the Kladis paintings.'

'Of *course*,' Mr Whittaker agreed slowly, '. . . that would explain why so little was heard of him. In the years before the war Corfu was like most other Greek islands, primitive and unvisited, and Kladis was a self-taught natural painter that the art-world knew nothing about. It's splendid to have discovered that much, but incredibly frustrating not to know more!'

Anna admitted that she was still on the trail of Nikos Kladis, and promised to ring again when she got back from Greece. Happy now, Rupert Whittaker wished her a safe and successful journey, and then thought of something else.

'Do you remember Pierre Bouchard, the man who bought the Carstairs painting? He said that *he* would keep in touch as well – perhaps I'm suspected of knowing where there are other Kladis canvases! If he does ring, may I mention Corfu? I shan't of course say that you own one of the very paintings he wants.'

Anna considered the question, wondering why she wanted to say no. There was no excuse to do so, and even if Bouchard had been making guesses of his own, he was only likely to investigate them from the comfort of some exquisite Parisian gallery. She smiled at the idea, aware that it was unreasonable to dislike a man she'd never even met.

'Tell him by all means,' she finally agreed. 'If I'm right about Corfu there may be people there – grandchildren perhaps – who could benefit from his interest in a local painter.'

Her new friend agreed that this was so, and nobly rang off without allowing himself to ask her to snap up anything of interest before Pierre Bouchard got to it himself.

By the following evening she was standing on the terrace of her mother's apartment, watching St Peter's dome silhouetted against a sunset sky. Darkness came more suddenly here than it did at home but while Rome's *tramonto* lasted it was a many-splendoured thing. As the pageant of crimson, purple and gold finally faded into nightfall Anna walked back into the room and slid the heavy glass doors into place. Nicola Rasini looked relieved, although she smiled at her daughter.

'Forget your English upbringing – all good Romans know that it's too early in the year for al fresco star-gazing!'

'And of course they're right,' Anna cheerfully agreed. 'But it's such a stupendous view out there, and a dozen different church-bells seem to be ringing. I hope you're glad you moved into this apartment.' In her own private opinion it was too grand; she preferred the shabby comfort of her own sitting-room. But this matched its elegant owner, and she accepted that her sophisticated mother had outgrown the William Morris furniture and faded chintzes to be found in most Oxford academics' homes.

'I brought you something,' she suddenly remembered, and took out of her pocket the photograph Victor Melksham had given her. 'Granny's lawyer found it in his uncle's commonplace book and was kind enough to realize that we would like it.'

Nicola looked at the pictured face of Steven Curtis for a moment without saying anything. For once her own expression was hard to read, and it was Anna who said the obvious thing.

'You're very like him, but I expect you realize that.'

Nicola smiled suddenly. 'Imagine that fair handsome Englishman surrounded by a pack of swarthy Greeks – it wouldn't be surprising if he knocked all the young women over like ninepins!'

'I think he'd also have been kind and courteous to them,' Anna insisted. '*That* might have made a welcome change, too, sixty years ago.'

Nicola nodded, picking up the photograph to look at it again. 'It's strange to be seeing my father for the first time at the age of sixty-two! There must have been other pictures, but my guess is that Lavinia destroyed them all, once he was dead.'

There was silence for a moment, suddenly broken by the ringing of the telephone. Nicola got up to answer it, then poured wine for them both before she sat down again.

'That was a nice friend you'll meet tomorrow,' she said. 'No guests tonight though; I thought you'd like to get acclimatized. They can all struggle with English, but they'll be happier if you talk to them in Italian.'

'I can manage that,' Anna agreed, 'but I've been wishing

that we were taught Greek at school, as well as Latin. So far all I've got the hang of is the weird alphabet and a few stock phrases.' Her mother looked a question, and she nodded in reply. 'I know you said forget the past, but I think it's time I saw Greece.'

'See it by all means but don't be disappointed if what you find is monotonous food, dreadful wine, and the most talkative, argumentative race on earth. When Enrico insisted that we visit Athens once years ago even he had to admit that one ruined temple looks remarkably like another!' She saw Anna smile but then grow serious again. 'It's not just a holiday, is it? You're going there for a reason. You've got some notion in your stubborn head of finding connections with your grandfather. Darling, do be sensible – he died much too long ago. In any case you've got no idea where to start looking.'

'I have *some* idea,' Anna insisted gently. 'If I'm wrong and it wasn't Corfu where his friends lived, then I'll just give up and go and inspect the Parthenon instead.'

Her mother considered this in silence for a moment, then she gave her usual little shrug, and took a consoling sip of wine. But a moment later she handed Anna back the photograph of Steven Curtis.

'I'd like this back when you go home, but you'd better take it with you. God knows he doesn't look anything like a Greek; so it might just jog someone's memory.'

She didn't refer to her father again for the fortnight that Anna spent with her; they were mother and daughter unexpectedly enjoying one another's company in a city that looked beautiful in the early spring days. The flower-sellers were out already on the Spanish Steps, the fountains glittered in the sunlight, and the small exclusive boutiques along the Via Condotti were too tempting to ignore.

When the morning came for Anna to leave, Nicola Rasini got up early for once to have breakfast with her. She nibbled Melba toast and sipped herbal tea, looking wistfully at her daughter's buttered croissant and jug of coffee.

'Have some,' Anna said, smiling at her. 'Why live miserably?'

'Because I'll get fat if I don't and I promised Enrico I never would.' Nicola looked across the table at her daughter and suddenly said what was in her mind. 'I'll miss you – I wish you weren't going, and most of all I wish you weren't going alone. You *need* someone . . . a man, I mean.'

'And *you*'re a disgrace to our liberated sex! We're supposed to manage our own lives now, and by and large we can.'

But Nicola wasn't to be put off. She'd decided for once to face the truth, however unpleasant it might look. 'Between us Lavinia and I have ruined your life. You grew up feeling that you had to stay with her instead of escaping like I did, and you don't believe that happy, long-lasting marriages exist.'

'I know they do exist,' Anna answered, serious herself now. 'Some of my friends have them. But if there's a man around that I could match with, I haven't met him yet. You didn't ruin anything – I became what I was probably meant to be . . . a watcher of other people; that's what writers are!'

'At thirty-one you should be in the human race, not watching it,' Nicola pointed out. 'You can write about it later.' She took another sip of tea, then returned to where she'd begun. 'I still don't like you travelling alone – Greek men are very predatory, and women travelling on their own are considered fair game.'

'Maybe, but Greeks are also supposed to take good care of strangers – it's called *filoxenia*!' Anna smiled as she said it, but leaned across to pat her mother's hand. 'Don't worry about me, please. I'm not going to wander into some mountain stronghold where men are men and women are merely their chattels. I've very little hope of finding any trace of my grandfather's friends, but I do want to know why he felt Greece was worth dying for.' Then she glanced at her watch, and stood up. 'Almost time to go; the taxi will be here any moment.'

A quarter of an hour later Nicola waved her off to the

station, and then went back inside an apartment that suddenly seemed too large and empty. She was aware of feeling guilty, even though that also felt unfair. As usual when comfort was needed, she looked at Enrico smiling at her from his silver frame. No, he seemed to say; nothing could have been different. God had given her a talent that she'd been bound to use. The person they could all blame was Steven Curtis; he should have stayed quietly in Oxford all those years ago.

Three

Anna's journey down to Brindisi was shared, as it turned out, with an American couple who introduced themselves almost as soon the train pulled out of Rome station. George and Irene Lambert seemed happy to find themselves with a girl they could understand, and Mrs Lambert explained why – they'd been travelling slowly through Italy, and the strain of finding people they could talk to was beginning to tell.

'We've seen just the most wonderful things,' she insisted hastily, 'but there were times – weren't there, George – when we did wish we really knew what was going on.'

'I can manage here,' Anna admitted, 'but I'm on my way to Greece. All I'll be able to do there is make out which street I'm in, if I'm lucky.'

Irene Lambert's face glowed with sudden pleasure. 'You mean *you*'re taking the ferry from Brindisi too? George,' she enquired of her husband when Anna nodded, 'do you hear that?'

It seemed to be a question he was used to because, instead of answering, he looked across at Anna.

'You're all alone? Isn't that kind of . . . lonely?'

She guessed that he'd been going to say something else and tactfully changed his mind in case he worried her.

'Not really, and not risky either, if that's what you're thinking! I'm used to travelling on my own.' Not inclined to go on talking about herself, Anna turned the conversation back to them.

'Is Corfu your last port of call before you go home?'

George smiled at her with a hint of pride. 'It *is* home in a way. That's where my grandfather set out from seventy years ago. His name was Lamberkis then . . . Yannis Lamberkis; but he reckoned on becoming an American citizen so he changed it to John Lambert. He lost touch with his family during the war, but I promised I'd come back and look for them as soon as I retired.'

Anna supposed she should admit that she was on an ancestor trail as well – 'George, do you hear *that*?' she could imagine Irene saying – but instead she merely wished them good luck in their search. 'It's a very ancient tradition for Greeks to emigrate and become successful, but always want to rediscover the country they sprang from. If you *can* trace any relatives, I'm sure they'll welcome you with open arms.'

She was aware of being examined by Irene Lambert, so the question that came next wasn't unexpected. 'Anna Rasini, I think you said your name was, it sounds Italian but you're surely English as can be with that fair hair and lovely accent!'

'Italian father, mostly unknown!' Anna admitted, unable to resent a question that, even if it was personal, she knew was only intended to show interest in a fellow-traveller. 'My mother still prefers to live alone in Italy, but I was brought up in England by my grandmother.'

Irene thought about this for a moment, looking regretful – she had been happily married for forty years, and hated to hear of sad, disrupted families who couldn't live together in harmony. Guessing that his wife's next question would delve into the Rasinis' broken marriage, George hastily spread out a map on the table between them and offered to show Anna where they intended to go. His ancestors had been fishermen on the west coast of the island, he said proudly – brave, skilled sailors whose scarcely seaworthy boats had taken them all round the eastern Mediterranean. But they'd had to work themselves to an early death – no wonder men like his grandfather had arrived in New York with the determination to make a better life for themselves.

Yannis Lamberkis had succeeded, Anna reckoned, judging

by George's air of obvious prosperity, and she regretted not being there to see what happened if he did manage to find any of his family. But Irene Lambert, more curious about a chance-met stranger than her husband's probably now non-existent relatives, asked Anna why *she* was going to Corfu when it wasn't quite the time of the year for lying on a beach and getting suntanned.

Her persistence was irritating and Anna was tempted to invent a rich Greek lover whose yacht was moored in a secluded cove. But she remembered that the gods who might still inhabit Olympus could easily be tempted to make mischief. Corfu was a small island, and she might find herself bumping into the Lamberts again.

It seemed safer to invent a white lie, and she took a paper-back copy of *The Odyssey* out of her shoulder-bag.

'I'm having a break from work and doing a little detection of my own. Everything seems to suggest that it was Corfu Ulysses was washed up on when he was ship-wrecked, but scholars still argue about it. I thought I'd follow Homer's clues and see for myself where he was rescued by Nausicaa, the king's daughter.'

There was silence for a moment, then Irene Lambert rallied. 'Well . . . fancy,' she said bravely, '. . . do you hear that, George?' But he couldn't help her, and she suddenly smiled with a rueful sweetness Anna found shaming. 'I'm not that sure who Nausicaa was, but she sounds like a real nice girl.'

It was time to make amends, and Anna did so by asking about the Lamberts' home and family in America. The subject took them safely the rest of the way to Brindisi – Irene talked, Anna listened and George, who didn't need to listen, read *Time* magazine from cover to cover.

With the ferry not due to sail until an hour before midnight, there was plenty of time to have dinner ashore, but George explained apologetically that they couldn't invite Anna to join them at some nice restaurant. Irene was a bad sailor who only survived sea voyages lying down, preferably on an empty stomach. She would go straight to bed when they got aboard, and he would make do with sandwiches in their cabin. All he could do to help would be to see to Anna's luggage.

She thanked him for his kindness and parted warmly from them both in case she missed them in the morning. Then, while they climbed the gangplank, she set off for a harbour-side taverna and settled for the Brindisi seafood speciality of *cozze alla marinara*. Later, walking back along the quay, she reckoned that Irene was quite safe; there was no breath of wind to ruffle the sea, and a serenely starlit sky surely betokened calm weather. She was too keyed up herself to want to sleep: the country that still lay out of sight over the horizon had been Steven Curtis's Shangri-La, but for her it was an unknown quantity. All she knew for the moment was that it wasn't somewhere to be merely indifferent to. Greece would have to be accepted whole-heartedly or rejected altogether and she had no idea which it would be.

She slept badly in her tiny cabin and then woke later than she meant to. Scrambling into her clothes, she went up on deck to find the ferry already swinging round the top of the island they were approaching. On the mainland side of the channel they were entering, Albania's dark mountains reared up, harshly bare of greenery and still crested with snow. The northern face of Corfu itself wasn't much more hospitable, with its cliffs and rocky caves but she knew that there was lushness to come. Already, also, she knew that she was in another place, not in familiar Italy. The Ionian sea was different from the Adriatic, and the golden Greek light – *to-phos* – lay over everything like a benediction.

The ferry nosed its way into Neó Limáni – the new port, she laboriously worked out – and she said goodbye again to the Lamberts, found among the crowd waiting to disembark. Then she stepped on to Greek soil, to be immediately claimed by a youth whose cap-band bore the name of the Astron Hotel. He explained in basic English that it was near enough to walk to, shouldered her luggage, and instructed her kindly to set off.

Anna commented on the crowded streets and was reminded by the boy of something she'd overlooked in the confusion of arriving. She was just in time for the great parade that took place on Easter Saturday; after that would come the firework display, and the midnight mass that marked the culmination of Holy Week. He recommended the English kyria not to miss any of it – Corfu was famous for its Easter celebrations, he said proudly.

Later in the day she had to admit that he was right. Hemmed in by the throng of people lining the Esplanade, she remembered the tragic gloom of *Semana Santa* in Seville and compared it with the Corfiots' intention to combine orthodox observance with an atmosphere of fairground revelry. Religious novices led the procession, followed by men carrying banners or huge candles; then came the town bands, not always playing the same music, and then the military; finally, among a flock of priests, the archbishop walked beside the canopied sedan-chair that carried the mummified body of St Spiridhon himself in its silver casket. It was one of four appearances he made each year, Anna's neighbour kindly explained, seeing that she was a stranger. He was their much-loved patron saint, the island's sure protector, known to be a very present help in every time of trouble. The same helpful lady recommended her not to miss mass that night in the saint's own church, Áyios Spiridhon, and she was also proved right. Anna knew she would never forget the moment when, in the darkened church, the priest lit the candle of the worshipper nearest to him, who in turn lit his neighbour's, and so on throughout the church until all the candles were lit, and the great shout went up – '*Christos anesti! Alithos anesti!*' – 'Christ is risen!, He is risen indeed!'

By Monday morning the town was returning to normal; it was time, Anna thought, to start her search. She went first to the Palace of SS Michael and George where, her guide-book promised, the Municipal Art Gallery was housed. She spent a little time looking round, saw nothing that resembled her own painting, and finally approached the young woman who sat at the reception desk, behind a small notice that said that English was spoken.

'Good morning,' Anna began. 'I've enjoyed the paintings, but I'm looking for one local artist in particular – a man called Nikos Kladis.'

'Kladis . . . ? I don't know the name; we certainly keep none of his work. Perhaps you've made a mistake.' The girl was polite, but not interested enough to pursue the matter, and Anna was provoked into asking to see whoever was in charge. The receptionist spoke into the intercom, and in her brief conversation the name of Nikos Kladis was mentioned. Then Anna was pointed in the direction of a small office off the main gallery.

A woman of about her own age got up as she went in – elegantly dressed, but just as unsmiling as the receptionist had been. It was early in the season, Anna couldn't help thinking, for *filoxenia* to be wearing thin, but she once again explained why she was there. 'The name is correct – Nikos Kladis,' she finished up, 'but the two paintings I've seen were merely signed with the initials N.K. He was living on Corfu in the nineteen thirties.'

'Then you're in the wrong place, I'm afraid,' the curator pointed out coolly. 'He would be dead by now, and here we exhibit only contemporary artists.'

'Isn't that rather limiting?' Anna ventured. 'He was a fine local painter who is even known about abroad. It seems odd that Corfu isn't proud on him!' She said it with a smile, hoping not to sound too critical, but got an indifferent shrug from a woman who clearly wanted her to go away.

'There's no record of a Kladis painting ever being in the gallery,' the curator commented, 'but we aren't aware of missing anything of great value.' That, she seemed to say, was that and now perhaps a troublesome visitor would go away.

Anna couldn't persist any longer but in a voice now crisp with anger said that she would try the privately owned galleries instead; perhaps the curator could provide her with a list of those?

Apparently not; all that could be suggested was a call at the Tourist Information Office, marked on any city guide. Feeling depressed now as well as angry, Anna thanked her sweetly for being so helpful and marched out. Was it imagination working overtime, or was she right to suspect that the curator *had* known the name of Nikos Kladis, and had been deliberately obstructive? But at least she was right about the Tourist Office; it was easily found, and a pleasantly helpful man there, having no printed list to give her, was prepared to write down the names of art shops and galleries he could call to mind.

'I did that for someone else yesterday,' he said as he handed over his list. 'It took me longer the first time to think of them!'

'For another visitor?' she asked tentatively. '. . . Another foreign visitor perhaps?'

But he smiled and shook his head. 'No, the man spoke in Greek – I'd say he was a rich business man from Athens. Naturally they prefer to come here before the tourists arrive.' Then as he remembered who he was talking to he adroitly saved himself. 'One charming English lady alone is a valued visitor, of course, not a tourist!'

'And not all tourists are ill-mannered louts, I hope,' she suggested, acknowledging what he hadn't quite said. It was tempting to try out the name of Nikos Kladis on him, but while she hesitated someone else came in, so she smiled and left the office.

By lunch-time she'd called at three of the galleries on her list, and met with complete blankness at the first two. At the third she could have sworn she saw a flicker of recognition in the face of its elderly proprietor, but even he seemed not to know whether any member of the Kladis family still lived on the island.

'We had to survive the Italians, then the Germans, and finally a bitter civil war,' he explained sharply, as if she shouldn't need telling these things. 'Whole families disappeared, and some who were still alive chose to escape

Greece's tragedies by emigrating. We didn't even know what happened to our friends, much less anybody else.'

Her visit had achieved nothing except to remind him of an unhappy past. She apologized for troubling him and walked out into the golden sunshine half-inclined to think that her mother had been right. What she was trying to do was not only pointless but probably hurtful as well; better to admit that it had been a stupid idea and catch the next ferry back to the mainland.

But for the moment it was lunch-time and she was tired enough to want to sit down. She stopped at the first taverna she came to and ordered what she knew was called *xoriatiki*, the delicious Greek salad of tomatoes, cucumber, olives and feta cheese. While she waited for it to arrive she thought about her mixed impressions of the morning's conversations; with very little concrete evidence to go on, her conviction was hardening that she had been deliberately steered away from what she'd come to find. She was frowning over that thought when a shadow fell across the table, and she looked up to see a stranger with his hand on the chair facing her own.

'May I?' he enquired, scarcely waiting for her to answer before he sat down.

'There are other, empty tables,' she pointed out coolly, '. . . why not take one of those?'

'Because I'm anxious to talk to you.' He smiled and shook his head. 'This isn't a clumsy way of picking up a companion – I was in the gallery just now and heard you ask about Nikos Kladis. I think I'm speaking to Anna Rasini, am I not?'

The man's English was almost flawless, except for a give-away faint stress on the last syllable of certain words, but she thought she could identify him; her Oxford friend had talked too freely. She struggled to sound calm as she answered. 'And you, I take it, are the "rich Athenian business man" who just happens to speak English with a very faint French accent – Monsieur Bouchard, in fact.'

He shook his head. 'Unfair, mam'selle – my English is perfect; I only gave myself away by using your name. It wasn't difficult to spot someone who looks nothing like a Greek, and asks questions about a man no one else but myself seems at all interested in. In any case, Rupert Whittaker described you very accurately!'

She stared at him for a moment, aware that Pierre Bouchard rated as one of the most self-possessed men she'd ever met. Attractively greying dark hair framed a face that was probably always suntanned – which meant, probably, Cap d'Antibes in summer and winter skiing trips to Klosters or Chamonix to keep it that way. Casual clothes didn't mean carelessness in his case; he was – she admitted to herself – a pleasure to look at; but she registered as well the concentration in his glance and his probably ruthless self-interest.

She stifled a natural longing to know how she'd been described by Rupert Whittaker, and fastened on something else Pierre Bouchard had just said.

'So I didn't imagine it,' she commented, 'there *was* some deliberate attempt to suggest that Nikos Kladis, if he existed at all, was long since dead and best forgotten. The reason might be just simple embarrassment . . . that no one here recognized what was being allowed to slip through their fingers. Can it be that straightforward?'

'It's anything but straightforward,' Bouchard confirmed with a certainty she found irritating. He ordered food from a hovering waiter, and cocked a dark eyebrow at the water in her glass. 'You're in Greece and you don't drink retsina?'

'No – it tastes like turpentine to me,' she said frankly, 'and I pass on ouzo, too. Greek water, on the other hand, is delicious.'

He sipped his own wine without answering and waited, like a good bridge-player, for her to show her hand; but it was a game two could play, and she concentrated on her salad as if she'd forgotten he was there. At last he was forced to speak again.

'You know something about me – I'm a Parisian art-dealer interested in finding more Kladis paintings and probably buying them if I can. But I don't know anything about *you*. Whittaker seemed to think you only wanted information, but I'd like to be sure he was right.'

She could invent the sort of lie she'd offered Irene Lambert on the train, but felt sure he'd see through it. 'I'm not in competition, if that's what is worrying you,' she said finally, 'just here for a holiday and a little private search of my own. There are some gaps in our family history, and Nikos Kladis was a friend of my grandfather's, that's all.' But then she thought of a question of her own. 'How do you come to know about the paintings anyway?'

He waited for the food he'd ordered to be put in front of him, and when he'd spoken to the man in Greek, the waiter returned again with a small glass flagon. 'It's Samian wine, not resined,' Bouchard said, pouring some for her. 'Drink it – apart from being very good, it might make you less suspicious. To answer your question, my father went to Athens as a young man, soon after the war. It was badly damaged, and life for the Greeks was grim. He saw someone trying to scratch a living by selling paintings in a bombed shop. Most of them weren't worth buying but half-a-dozen paintings by one artist stood out as different, quite exceptional. My father bought them all and took them back to Paris. If we had them to sell now they'd fetch a hundred times what he asked then!'

'The man he bought from obviously wasn't the artist himself,' Anna murmured. 'Did he say how the paintings came to be in Athens?'

'No; all he knew about them was that the initials stood for Nikos Kladis. To our subsequent knowledge, no more pictures ever surfaced or changed hands after that until I saw the one in Whittaker's window. It was the merest chance that I should be in Oxford at all, for a meeting at the Ashmolean – when I'm not running the gallery in Paris I arrange for paintings to be borrowed for international exhibitions. Is the wine good?'

Immersed in his story, she'd sipped it absent-mindedly,

and now had the grace to admit that it was very good indeed. He smiled briefly, but then fired his next suggestion.

'We both seem to have come to a dead end. I'm sure there are paintings here that I can't for the moment trace, and you can't find whatever it is that *you*'re looking for. I have the benefit of speaking Greek, your advantage is to be an attractive woman; perhaps we should join forces!'

Anna didn't hesitate about refusing. Notwithstanding his Samian wine, she didn't like Pierre Bouchard as a man, and as a fellow-detective she thought he would be a liability. From the morning's experiences it seemed that the Kladis paintings themselves were what the people there shied away from. But they didn't concern her; her only interest was in the man who'd been her grandfather's dear friend.

'I'd rather continue looking on my own,' she said firmly, 'that is, if I continue at all. When you came and sat down I'd almost decided to catch the ferry to Patras. I'll visit the classical sites on the mainland, and then go home.' She got up as she spoke, holding out her hand. 'I'd wish you success in your hunt, but there probably aren't any more paintings to find. *Au revoir*, Monsieur Bouchard.'

She clasped his fingers briefly and then walked away, unaware that he watched her until she was out of sight – a slender figure in a coral-coloured jacket and skirt, taller than the Greek women around her, and walking with a free, graceful stride they didn't have. Her dark eyes didn't match her fair hair, and there were other surprises about her too – among them the fact that, although her glance seemed direct, he didn't for a moment believe that she was about to abandon Corfu. Anna Rasini knew more than she'd admitted to and – like all the attractive women he was acquainted with – she couldn't be relied upon to tell the truth. He accepted that philosophically, poured himself some more wine, and considered what he should do next.

Four

The afternoon stretching ahead looked empty and – something Anna had denied to George Lamber – lonely as well. The lunch-time encounter with a man as uncongenial as Pierre Bouchard, even *that*, had been enough to remind her of what she missed by being solitary in a country whose language she didn't know. From someone else she might have accepted the offer to pool their efforts, but his air of confident self-assurance was hard to take. And anyway she disliked on sight a man who wore his hair too long and obviously studied his appearance with such care. But there was something even more off-putting as well: he was greedy, wanting the Kladis paintings, if they existed, simply for the high prices they would fetch. She'd been right to stalk away from him. She queried the word in her mind but had to accept that it was right – yes, no two ways about it; she'd stalked.

There remained the problem of what to do next. She could visit the last art shop on her list but she'd lost hope of it producing anything helpful. What she'd said to Pierre Bouchard was true – she was more and more inclined to believe that she was on a fool's errand. Her fine words to Victor Melksham about laying her grandfather's ghost to rest sounded hollow here; better to become a simple tourist after all, follow the well-worn trail to Delphi and Mycenae, and then go home knowing as little about Steven Curtis as when she'd started out.

With the decision firm in her mind, she noticed a bus getting ready to leave, with a sign-board showing the Achilleion as its destination. The name was familiar, because her guidebook rather severely insisted that the palace built originally for the Empress Elizabeth of Austria was 'an alarming mishmash of styles'. Well, she'd go and see it anyway.

Her book turned out to be right, but at least the terraced gardens were lovely, and convenient benches offered splendid views of Corfu Town and the seascape beyond. She sat admiring them for a while, and then on an impulse took out of her bag the photograph that Victor Melksham had given her. Its pictured face half-smiled at her, but she saw sadness in the smile. Steven Curtis had been a brilliant academic with his feet firmly on the ladder of success, but he hadn't been happy. She tucked the photograph back in her bag face-down and, in doing so, looked accidentally at the back of it – the first time that had happened, it must have been, because a word and a date were written there that she'd never noticed before: Mondhiki, '38. Was it a Greek word, or the name of someone . . . even a place name? It seemed almost worse to have a fragment of information she couldn't use than to have nothing at all, but she suddenly remembered who might help her. The bus waited outside the gardens for the return journey and she climbed on board, willing it to leave; the Tourist Office wouldn't stay open late this early in the season.

The blind on the door was being pulled down as she hurried towards it, but the man she'd seen on her first visit recognized her and smilingly let her in.

'You're closing, I can see,' she said breathlessly. 'I must come back tomorrow.'

'Why, when I am here now?' he asked reasonably. 'You found what you were looking for, kyria?'

'I found the galleries, but no one seemed able to help me.' She hesitated over what to say next, aware that her story took too much time to tell. 'I'm trying to trace a family that lived here before the war,' she said as briefly as possible. 'One member of the family – the man who was my grandfather's special friend – was a painter called Nikos Kladis. But no one seems to have heard of him. My only clue is a word on the back of a photograph – Mondhiki. Does it mean anything in Greek?'

Her new friend shook his head. 'It means nothing, and if it's the name of a place I've never heard of it.' But already he was delving behind the counter for a gazetteer and beginning to thumb through it. 'No . . . it doesn't exist . . . there's no such place listed. I'm sorry, kyria.'

She tried to smile at him, but couldn't hide the disappointment in her face. 'Thank you very much for trying at least – now I must go and let you shut up shop.'

'What will you do now?' he wanted to know, scenting a mystery that appealed to his Greek mind. The questions that tourists normally asked were far less interesting than this, and the tourists themselves rarely treated him with this girl's charming courtesy.

'I shall admit defeat and catch tomorrow's ferry,' Anna said ruefully. 'I'm tired of banging my head against a brick wall, if you know that English expression!'

He didn't know it, but he readily understood its meaning when she acted it for him. 'No . . . we are not . . . not at the rope-end yet. Isn't that something else you say?' He beamed with pleasure when she nodded, but then grew serious again. 'Don't catch tomorrow's ferry, kyria; come back here instead. I shall visit my father this evening and ask *him* about Mondhiki. He's an old man but his memory is very good, and he knows more about this island than anyone else you'll ever meet.'

Anna held out her hand. 'Thank you, you've been so kind. Of course I'll come back tomorrow.'

They left the office together, and he only consented to go off in the opposite direction when she assured him that she knew the way back to the hotel. It seemed unlikely that his father would be able to help, but his kindness itself had been enough to make a difference. She'd felt deprived of something until then – the warmth and interest that Greece was said to offer its visitors. Now, walking back through the Campiello, the oldest part of the town where the streets were lined with houses just like the one in her painting at home – gracefully shuttered and painted in a mixture of softly faded colours – she saw for the first time the beauty of where she'd come to.

Later that evening she left her room to go down to the hotel dining-room. Someone who'd been leafing through brochures at a table in the hall turned round and spoke in Greek one of the few phrases she understood.

'*Kali spera, kyria Rasini*,' but it was a Frenchman who spoke the words, and stood waiting for her to answer.

She answered with a nod and a brief 'Good evening,' assuming that he was there to meet someone else. But he stood in front of her, barring her way.

'I hate dining alone. I thought we might eat together – but preferably not here; the local tavernas are much more interesting.'

She smiled sweetly at him. 'Having already walked miles today, the dining-room is as far as I plan to go. Don't let me stop you, though, from sampling a restaurant that oozes local colour.'

He still didn't move, shocked, she supposed by the rare experience of being refused. But then a rueful, rather pleasant smile touched his mouth, disconcerting her.

'You've made your point – it *was* a poorly-phrased invitation! If I apologize nicely will you let me take you to dinner – here if you prefer?'

She nodded again, aware that even Pierre Bouchard's company might be better than eating a lonely meal by herself.

Settled in the dining-room a few minutes later, she confessed that deciphering Greek menus sometimes took longer than the food itself was worth; now at least she could rely on him to order for her something that wasn't octopus or squid.

He studied the list, spoke to the waiter, and then considered her across the table. 'No squid, no retsina . . . you're a very unadventurous traveller; and you're also, I'm afraid, anti-French, like a lot of your compatriots.' It was an opening shot that she hadn't been expecting, and she hesitated too long in answering because he went on himself. 'You think we behaved badly during the last war . . . caved in and collaborated with the Germans . . . and since then, to make up for that humiliation, we've thrown our weight about too much and been altogether far more French than you can bear!'

'*That* bit's true,' Anna agreed calmly. 'About the war, I think we have no right to judge. Twenty blessed miles of sea and some very brave airmen and sailors kept *us* from being invaded. We've no way of knowing how we'd have behaved if that hadn't been the case.' She spoke with a quiet belief in her opinion that he found unusual in the opposite sex; more commonly, they either had no views at all worth listening to or hoisted their intellect like a flag before going into battle.

'Well, at least you're fair,' he commented. 'But it means that the hostility I sense in you has to do with me personally – a blow to my vanity, of course, but I'm also curious as well! Why, if we're *not* competing for the Kladis paintings, are you so wary of a little sensible collaboration?'

Again his directness caught her on the wrong foot because it was unexpected in a Frenchman who, if legend didn't lie, should have been full of Gallic finesse instead. Anna sipped the wine that had been poured for her and considered how to answer.

'I'm not sure that collaboration would be sensible,' she said at last, with equal frankness. 'It seemed to me this morning that what made people shy away from me was mention of the paintings, but they were only my starting point; I'm not looking for *them*, only for my grandfather's connection with the Kladis family.'

Not doubting the Frenchman's intelligence, she waited for the question that would inevitably come next, and come it did a moment later.

'But when you saw the painting in Whittaker's gallery it obviously matched something you were already familiar with – is that not so?'

'Yes, it is so,' she agreed reluctantly. 'I have one very like it at home. It belonged to my grandmother, but before you ask it's not for sale.'

'Then my opinion of Rupert Whittaker goes up – he was very discreet!'

Bouchard halted while the waiter brought their first course – artichokes so small and tender that they could be eaten whole – and then explained that what he'd ordered next was *barbounia*, the delicious red mullet found in Ionian waters. Like the Frenchman he was, he believed their attention should be given to the food, and spoke only of general things while they were eating. It wasn't until coffee was in front of them that he returned to where the conversation had begun.

'What brought your grandfather to Corfu?'

'He was a Classics don at Oxford. Every year he shepherded his students around Greece, determined that they should love it as he did – the man whose painting you bought was one of them; but my grandfather must have brought the students here as well to meet his Kladis friends, because Mr Carstairs knew about the island. That's almost all I can tell.'

'You mean your grandfather didn't even say where to find this family?'

'I never knew him. He was dropped into Greece during the war and died there. My grandmother, who brought me up, never forgave him – a cruelly unnecessary death she thought it, when she had a brilliant academic career mapped out for him.'

There was a long pause before Bouchard spoke again. 'Thank you . . . now I begin to understand. But you think there's more of the story that you don't know?'

'Yes, but I may be wrong, just as *you* may be to expect to find any more paintings.'

'They're here to be found – I'm sure of that. But *how*, when we have nothing to go on?' He was frowning at his coffee as he spoke and Anna had a moment in which to get her expression under control.

'What are you going to do?' he asked suddenly, almost catching her out. 'Admit defeat and leave Corfu?'

'I may just look around a little more,' she said as casually as she could. 'It's a lovely island, and I shall probably never come back.' But the conversation was becoming difficult, and she needed to bring it to an end. 'It's been an interesting day,' she managed to say without blushing, 'but energetic as well! I went out to the Achilleion this afternoon and "did" the gardens thoroughly.'

'And all the trash inside the palace, I suppose; not to mention the hideous statues outside. Henry Miller was right – it's a madhouse of a place.'

'You're as stuffy about it as my guidebook,' Anna said, smiling naturally at him for the first time. 'But I *am* tired, so now I'll thank you for dinner and go to bed.'

He got up to walk with her as far as the stairs, but stood there grasping the hand she held out to him. 'I know what really troubles you about me,' he suddenly remarked. 'You think I'm simply on the trail of profit. Would you believe me if I said that I value Kladis's paintings for themselves – for what, like all fine things, they reveal that we're too blind to see for ourselves?'

He sounded sincere, but even if she could bring herself to trust him, it was too late now to suddenly confess that, after all, she had a clue – Mondniki – worth following up.

'What I think really doesn't matter,' she finally pointed out. 'You know what your own motives are. Thank you again for dinner; now I'll say goodbye.' And with that she began to climb the stairs.

The following morning she set out once again for the Tourist Office, no longer sure whether she wanted an old person's recollections to have yielded anything or not. But the thought reminded her of Mr Carstairs, still able to call up the memory of the Prof with gladness; of course she must still look for information if there was any to be found. Her grandfather surely deserved that.

Already there were other people at the Tourist Office with their lists of questions, but at last it was her turn, and her helpful friend sadly shook his head.

'The gazetteer is right, kyria – my father knows the island very well; he's certain that no town or village by the name you gave me exists.' He let a moment or two go past in order to enjoy the full drama of the occasion. Then he suddenly beamed. 'However, there *is* a house called Mondhiki!'

'A house . . . Where?' Anna almost shouted.

He held up his hands in a little warning gesture. 'There *was* a house, I should have said. My father was remembering it from many years ago, you understand, and much has happened since then. Corfu was heavily bombed during the war . . . whole families disappeared then, or emigrated afterwards.'

'I realize that,' she said quietly now. 'If your father can remember where the house was, I'll certainly look for it, but I won't go expecting too much.'

Then a map was spread out on the counter and his finger slowly traced a line across the island to its western coast. 'Here, kyria, is Paleokastritsa, where all the tourists go to visit the monastery and the old castle of Angelókastro. It was once very beautiful; now, in my view, it's a little spoiled. Further down, the coast is still comparatively undeveloped; there are secluded bays and coves, like this one here, marked Myrtiótissa, and just below *that* is where Mondhiki was, according to my father. It was a farm . . . a small estate . . . growing mostly olives and vines.'

'Did he . . .' Anna cleared the huskiness from her throat and tried again, '. . . did your father remember the name of the family there?'

The man in front of her looked pleased. 'It took a little while, but he thought of it in the end . . . a man called Kladis lived there . . . Yorgos Kladis; there was a wife, and children too, but my father couldn't remember them.'

'Thank him for me, please . . . thank him very much.' Her taut face relaxed into a smile. 'Now all I have to do is find it . . . by bus or hired car?'

'By car, I think, if you don't mind driving on our roads. Buses go from Corfu Town only to the other resorts, not to places in between.' He scribbled a name on a card and gave it to her. 'This is my friend; he will hire you a good car.'

Anna held out her hand to say goodbye. 'You've been so kind . . . I can't thank you enough.' She turned away to leave, then swung round to face him again. 'I'll let you know what I find.'

'Very good . . . *kalo taxeidi, kyria*!'

Assuming that she'd just been wished the equivalent of *bon voyage*, she smiled her thanks again and left the office. An hour later she was ready to set out, car-hire arranged, the route kindly marked for her on her map by the friend of her helpful friend, bottled water on the seat beside her, and a picnic lunch of bread and cheese and grapes. It was almost more than she could believe, but she was finally on her way to find Steven Curtis's Greek family.

Five

Getting out of town unscathed needed all Anna's powers of concentration, and a sizeable chunk of divine blessing as well. The unfamiliar car with its left-hand drive and Corfu's different rules of the road made it hard to spare time for looking at signs as well; and the shaming moment came when she found herself nose to nose with another car in what was clearly a one-way street. There was no doubt who was in the wrong – a volley of comments from helpful passers-by told her so. She smiled gratefully at them and backed her way out, but now the worst was over, and once clear of Corfu Town itself, she even began to enjoy the drive.

Her route lay west, across the narrow central stretch of the island, and then south. She'd been told to head for Pendati, a place of secluded coves where local fishermen still beached their boats undisturbed by tourism and the march of progress. But first she had to skirt Ayios Gordhis, a monstrous development of swimming pools, bars and sports facilities gouged out of the lovely landscape, just one of the holiday centres that were steadily encroaching on traditional ways of life. She thought sadly of Andreas Kalamos at the Tourist Office – she knew his name because it was printed on the card he'd given her – who understood well enough the benefits of mass tourism, but must surely hate the destruction that came with it.

Once clear of the resort, she was in a hilly, wooded land-scape still starred with wild flowers for as long as spring-time didn't give way to the blistering heat of summer. Everywhere she saw, too, the olive trees that Corfu owed to the Venetians. As the breeze moved them they turned from pale-green to silver, clouds of softly changing colour floating between the dark exclamation-marks of pine and cypress trees. Then, to complete the enchantment of the view, occasional small dips in the hills would offer glimpses of the Ionian Sea, blue as indigo against a sapphire sky.

It was lunch-time now but she stopped only long enough to drink some water. If her friend in Corfu Town was right, she surely had to be in the vicinity of Mondhiki, but no sign-posts obligingly led to it, and she couldn't even be sure that it was approachable by car – maybe she had to finish the journey on foot. At last, desperate for some help, she pulled up in a hamlet that consisted of a dozen dwellings and a tiny chapel. Small as it was, the inevitable cluster of old men sat outside the *kafeneio*, with thimblefuls of coffee and tall glasses of water in front of them. Like all Greeks every-where they were deep in conversation but the arrival of a strange car in the little tree-shaded square was an event. As Anna got out and walked towards them, they stopped talking and stared at her instead. Something different to interrupt the usual slow routine of the day was very welcome.

Unnerved by such keen attention, she wished them '*Kali mera*', forgetting that it was past noon and the morning was over. There was no response while they registered the sad fact that here was no proper Greek speaker; and their interest lay in her ability to talk to them – how else were they to find out about a stranger?

She sensed their disappointment and understood the reason for it. 'Please, does anyone speak English – *anglika*?' she asked with a rueful smile.

Only the last word registered, and one of them – the spokesman – shook his head. Then she pulled out her map, pointed to it and said, 'Mondhiki?' Their regretful silence suddenly became something more hostile. She could have sworn that the word meant something to them that they would make no attempt to share with her. At last, too frus-trated to care what might happen next, she almost shouted out the name of Nikos Kladis. There was a moment of frozen stillness, and then they all turned away from her, and the gesture said more than any words could have done that she wasn't welcome there.

She stood in the sunlit square thinking that never in her life before had she felt quite so lonely. Then, because there was nothing else to do – she couldn't even apologize for disturbing them – she walked slowly back to where she'd left the car.

It was now uncomfortably hot inside it, and she wound down the window to let in more air. Her hands, she noticed, were trembling, and when she stared at herself in the mirror above the windscreen, a strained chalk-white face looked back at her. Then, as she finally turned the ignition key, the composition of the group of huddled men changed and one of them walked towards her.

He said nothing even now, but simply pointed back the way she had come. She muttered '*efharisto*' to thank him for troubling to do that much, but realized as she turned the car that he might only have been telling her to leave, not indicating that she'd overshot the place she was looking for.

She drove until she was safely out of sight, then stopped again while her heartbeat slowed down to normal and she could blink away the tears that threatened to blind her. There'd been something deeply disturbing about those few moments in the square – not because she'd felt personally threatened; the old men would have done her no harm; but it was as if she'd awoken in them some memory they preferred to forget.

More or less calm again, she had to decide what to do. It seemed certain that Mondhiki wasn't far away, because the men *had* known of it, but in this secretively wooded landscape she'd need the help of all Olympus's nine gods to stumble on it by chance. Her instinct was that it now lay on her left, because wasn't it likely that Steven Curtis would have brought his students to the coast to relax after their work on the mainland? Her map showed one lane leading off the road down to the sea . . . Beyond that nothing until the outskirts of Ayios Górdhis would be all round her again. She decided to follow it as far as she could; if it led only to some tiny godforsaken beach, she'd admit defeat and return to Corfu Town just long enough to settle her hotel bill and collect her luggage.

The lane soon became a mere track, firm enough to drive on now, but surely unusable even by tractor in times of bad weather. If Mondhiki did by any remote chance lie at the end of it, its inmates must lead a lonely, isolated life in winter. Minute by minute, though, the feeling was growing that she *was* heading towards some kind of settlement. On each side of the track now the olive trees had given way to vines that had been carefully tended . . . she was trespassing on somebody's estate.

She stopped the car at a place where she'd be able to turn it, and started to walk from there. Everything about this strange journey would be lodged in her memory, she thought – the mid-afternoon heat, the silence, the golden dust that her shoes kicked up off the track, and the empty landscape around her. Just the sight of one other human-being would have been a comfort, even if she couldn't communicate with him.

What she eventually stumbled on was a girl, leading a donkey along a track that joined the one she was on herself.

'*Kali spera*,' – she got it right this time – 'please, do you speak English?'

The girl nodded her dark head. 'Some,' she said, '. . . not much.'

Anna's sudden smile was brilliant with relief. 'Even "some" sounds wonderful. Tell me if I shouldn't be here – I'm looking for a place called Mondhiki. It belonged ages ago to the Kladis family.'

There was a pause before the girl answered. 'It still does,' she said slowly. 'Where you are now is Mondhiki. You are English . . . Why are you here?'

It was a reasonable enough question, but underlying it Anna sensed the wariness if not actual hostility that she'd found all along, beginning with the woman at the Municipal Art Gallery.

'The story is long, and I'm interrupting your afternoon,' Anna said apologetically. 'But my grandfather knew the Kladis family long ago – he used to come here, to visit his friend Nikos. I wanted to see if any memory of him remained.'

They stared at each other for a moment. The Greek girl was a little younger than herself, Anna guessed, but dressed in the old way in a long, heavy skirt, dark blouse, and a scarf thrown round her hair – to keep off the sun, or as a concealment from strangers? She wasn't pretty, but her deep-set eyes were beautiful under their dark brows. In her turn the girl examined the stranger in front of her – thinly dressed as foreign women always seemed to be, short fair hair that shone like gold in the sun, and a smile that matched her gentle voice.

How much longer, Anna wondered, were they to stand measuring each other? But the donkey tugged at his rope, wanting to find some greenery to nibble, and the girl half-turned to follow him.

'I am Eleni Kostalis,' she said abruptly. 'My mother is cousin to Stefanos Kladis, the son of Nikos. Mondhiki is his now.' Those were facts she could be certain of; then she sounded less sure. 'I think you shouldn't come to the house – strangers are not usually welcome, only old friends.'

'Then things have changed,' Anna pointed out gently. 'I thought *filoxenia* was a proud Greek tradition.' She smiled at the girl watching her. 'May I not come for a glass of water at least? I'll leave after that if you want me to.'

After a moment the girl's nod agreed reluctantly, but when Anna fell into step beside her she asked a sudden question. 'You are tired? You want to ride the donkey?'

As if he knew what had been said, the animal turned his long grey head to stare at the stranger, and it seemed to Anna that he all but laughed. She thanked her companion for a kind offer but said that she preferred to walk. The girl's face relaxed into a shy smile, as if some kind of understanding had been reached, but they went on in silence until a long, rambling building emerged into view from a surrounding thicket of trees. White-washed, with faded blue shutters at its uncurtained windows, and old roses swarming up its walls, it seemed to have grown there as surely as the greenness all round it. Anna marvelled at the roses, then realized that they grew there protected from the sea-winds that must blow against the other side of the house.

Everything she could see – the house itself, the stone-flagged terrace, where a large table spoke of outdoor meals, and the haphazard scattering of terracotta pots brimming with flowering herbs – had a completely uncontrived kind of beauty. The people who lived here were too busy to think about the nice placing of this or that; things were simply where they were found to be useful.

Looking round she was aware of several certainties at once: her grandfather had loved Mondhiki all the more because of its antithesis to his conventional, Victorian house in Oxford; and Nikos Kladis had surely painted it at different times of day and different seasons of the year. Pierre Bouchard was right – there must have been more paintings than the ones he knew about.

'Sit there,' Eleni said, pointing to the table. 'I shall find someone.' She led the donkey round the side of the house, where the farm buildings presumably were, while Anna did as she was told and pulled out a chair at the table. She was content to stay there, scarcely caring whether Eleni found anyone or not. It was enough to have found her grandfather's Shangri-La; she could go home happy now, leaving undisturbed whatever it was in the past that had caused so much anguish.

But she wasn't alone for long – a middle-aged woman, a servant of some kind judging by her white apron, came out of the house carrying a small tray.

'*Kali spera, dhespinis*,' she said, identifying the guest correctly as an unmarried woman. Anna thanked her as she went away, but stared at what was on the tray – the usual tall glass of ice-cold Greek water and a small dish containing a spoonful of raisin jam . . . Prospero's 'water with berries in it'? It was something to mention to Victor Melksham at home, but more useful to think about now that she was aware of growing very nervous. Mondhiki seemed to be wrapped in an unnatural stillness even if it was the time of day when Greeks habitually retreated indoors from the worst of the heat. It was a working farm . . . surely something ought to be going on?

She made herself eat the jam, and was sipping the water when Eleni finally reappeared. Behind her came a somewhat older man, black-haired, and with the weathered face of a farmer whose life was spent mostly out of doors.

'My cousin, Petros Kladis,' the girl said in a low voice. 'He will speak to you.' And with that she ran back into the house, apparently too uninterested to stay for the rest of the conversation.

While the man seemed prepared for the moment to do nothing but stare at her, Anna knew that she must at least introduce herself. She remembered how the Greeks liked to do it.

'I am Anna Rasini,' she said quietly, 'granddaughter of Steven Curtis, who was the friend of Nikos Kladis.'

'Who was *my* grandfather,' he observed, thereby identifying himself as the son of the man to whom Mondhiki now belonged. 'My father understands English but he doesn't like to speak it – that's why I'm here instead. We don't know why you've come – my grandfather is long dead, yours probably also. Why not leave them where they belong – in the past?'

His dark eyes . . . bright, intelligent Greek eyes . . . still examined her slowly, as if to say that she didn't resemble the women he was accustomed to. It wasn't a friendly inspection, Anna thought, and she saw no reason not to acknowledge that she realized it.

'Eleni said I might not be welcome,' she pointed out. 'If no one will talk about the past I must assume that it's because it's upsetting. And if your father wants me to leave, of course

I'll go away. But I don't think I've done anything wrong in coming here, and I *would* like to know why Steven Curtis's granddaughter isn't welcome.'

Her persistence seemed to irritate him; perhaps women even now in this isolated corner of the world weren't allowed to argue with their menfolk. Perhaps Eleni had been instructed to go away, in case she noticed a difference in the way less downtrodden females behaved. But now Petros Kladis had decided what he wanted to say and she had to concentrate because, although his English was fluent, his accent made the words sound unfamiliar.

'Your lack of welcome has nothing to do with Steven Curtis, although my father remembers his name. The truth is simple – the English are not liked here, that's all.'

'Because of a brief and fairly benign occupation a hundred and fifty years ago, or because our ill-mannered holiday-makers come in their hordes now and spoil once-lovely places?' Anna asked.

'We resent *them*, certainly, but our bitter memories go back fifty years. We blame you for the civil war that tore Greece in half even after we'd done fighting the Italians and the Germans; but of course you're too young to know anything about that.'

'I know *something*,' she admitted, stung by the hostility in his voice. 'We tried to reinstate a king the Greeks despised instead of allowing the Communists who'd fought the war to take over. Yes, blame us for that, but remember what was happening in the rest of Europe – with the Russians in turn enslaving all the people who'd just been freed.'

Petros Kladis nodded briefly. 'Argument enough for what happened here in 1945 in your view perhaps, but not in ours.'

That seemed to be that; she was disliked because she was English. He waited for her to go, but she made one last attempt to talk about the family she'd been deliberately steered away from.

'Before I go, will you at least tell me if your father remembers Steven Curtis? Was he old enough in the years just before the war to remember the Englishman who came here with the students he was teaching to love Greece?'

'My father was a babe in arms in 1939 – what would he remember?'

'Nothing, of course,' Anna mumbled, but, staring at the face of the man in front of her, she sensed that this interview was an ordeal for him as well. He had the Greek's mobile features that normally revealed whatever he was feeling – curiosity, intelligence, and a quick sharp wit – but Petros Kladis was trying hard to express only cold hostility. If they had not been hung about with baggage from the past, she thought they might have liked one another, but there was nothing she could do about it now.

She stood up to go, smiling ruefully at him. 'I can't say I'm sorry to have found Mondhiki. Will you tell your father, please, that I think it's very beautiful?'

'Yes, I'll tell him,' he agreed. 'You came in a car, I suppose?'

'I left it along the track . . . but you don't have to march me off the premises!'

Even that small attempt at humour fell on stony ground; he merely gave a little bow and said that he would see her to the car. She walked past him, halted to pick a sprig of rosemary from one of the pots, and tucked it through the buttonhole of her shirt. 'The better to remember you all by,' she said with a faint smile, but his expression didn't change, and they went along the track in silence. Back at the car, she held out her hand, wondering whether he would ignore it, but his brown fingers touched hers and in them she thought she felt some kind of apology.

'Now to find my way back to the Astron Hotel,' she said. 'By a miracle I didn't actually hit anything on the drive here.'

'The gods are looking after you then – Greek motorists aren't always kind to strangers.'

He opened the car door for her to get in, and she sat for a moment looking at him; but he'd said all he was going to say, and she put the car in gear and drove away.

It had been a very stressful day in ways she didn't dare

examine for the moment; there'd be time enough later on to think quietly about the little Petros Kladis *had* said. She'd eaten nothing except Eleni's offering of jam, but her stomach revolted against the thought of dried-up bread and cheese. She offered both to a different donkey, seen being urged along by a small girl, whose smile said that, for now at least, *she* held no grudge against the English.

With the car in motion again, Anna instructed herself to concentrate on getting safely back to Corfu Town. There, she'd have to face the fact that she'd been turned away from people who should have been her friends. Then, she might be able to decide whether she believed the reason Nikos Kladis's grandson had given her or not.

Six

Eleni Kostalis was waiting when her cousin – second cousin, he was in fact – went back inside the house.

'You sent the Englishwoman away, I suppose,' she suggested, stripping the shells off a heap of broad beans in front of her on the kitchen table.

'It's what I was told to do,' Petros answered calmly. 'Does it matter? She's nothing to do with us.' His eyes met his cousin's dark glance and he gave a little shrug. 'All right, it does matter – we behaved unkindly to a stranger; not the Greek way, only *our* Mondhiki way!'

'But she wasn't quite a stranger, was she; otherwise she wouldn't have come. Why did Cousin Stefanos refuse to speak to her?'

'You must ask him, not me, but I don't think he'll tell you.' Petros looked at her thin brown fingers splitting open the pods as if her life depended on it. As always the sight of her made him feel guilty and sad, and he spoke more gently than usual.

'Forget the English girl, Eleni; she's gone and that's the end of it. Think of yourself instead. You should leave here – make a life for yourself somewhere else.'

Somewhere where she wasn't treated like a servant, he might have said. But even as he spoke the words it didn't need her little smile to tell him how futile they were. She was a glorified housekeeper and tender of the domestic animals, but as such they couldn't do without her; and how, in any case, would she ever fit in with the girls he saw strolling about Corfu Town, in jeans or miniskirts, a mobile phone at their ear, and all today's extraordinary technology at their fingertips?

'Shall I tackle my father again?' he asked gently. 'Say that you should go and train for something, meet people of your own age . . .'

But he didn't go on because she was already shaking her head. 'Don't speak to him, please. Mondhiki is where I belong – I wouldn't be needed anywhere else.' She was silent for a moment, then suddenly reverted to where they'd begun. 'I liked the English girl . . . I wish she could have stayed. I didn't even ask her name.'

'It's Anna – not so very English, and her surname didn't sound English at all.' His hands sketched an impatient gesture. 'Forget her – it's ancient history. She only came because her grandfather and mine were friends a long time ago.'

He smiled at his cousin to end the conversation and walked out of the kitchen. A plantation of new vines needed inspecting, and he certainly looked at them as he went up and down the rows; but his mind was on what he'd said to Eleni. It wasn't ancient history, of course; they still lived with the events of fifty years ago, and would go on doing so at least until Stefanos Kladis died.

Later that night the women of the house – Eleni and Petros's ancient great-aunt – retired early as usual. It left only him and his father in the big room that served all their daytime purposes; the ancient oak table at which they still sat simply divided the kitchen from the armchairs at the other end, grouped round a massive stone fireplace.

Stefanos Kladis looked up from the cigarette-paper he was carefully stuffing with Albanian tobacco brought illegally across the Corfu channel. 'That girl was a fool to come,' he said defiantly, as if he expected his son to contradict him. 'What did she expect – to be welcomed with open arms?'

Petros laid down the newspaper he was reading. 'She knew enough about Greece, according to Eleni, to expect a welcome of some kind. We could at least have given her that before she was asked to leave.' He studied his father's face for a moment – an older version of his own, weather-beaten skin drawn tightly over prominent bones. Greek faces rarely ran to flesh – life was too hard for that. Stefanos was sixty-two now, but he looked older.

'It was a mistake to send her away,' Petros said suddenly. 'It will only have made her more curious. Still, it probably doesn't matter; she won't come back.'

'You don't know that,' his father decided to argue. 'They're stubborn people, the English. There was a time when we were glad of that . . . before we got to hating them.'

He lit his finished cigarette and the fragrant scent of the tobacco drifted across the table. 'What did she look like?' he suddenly asked.

Petros closed his eyes as if trying to call the visitor to mind. 'She looked intelligent . . . dressed differently from our women, of course . . . and seemed rather tired!' But the irritation in his father's face made him answer the question that had really been asked. 'She looked like your father's painting of the Englishman – same fair hair, same features, same half-smile. Why not? She *is* his granddaughter.'

'It doesn't follow,' Stefanos said sharply. 'She has parents – why can't she look like them?' His son didn't answer, and he was forced to go on talking to himself. 'You think I'm wrong, I suppose – just set on remembering the evil that men do, not the good.'

Petros gave a little shrug. 'We're an unforgiving people with long memories. Nursing a grievance might not be what O Christos taught, but then you aren't the Son of God.' He stared at his father's preoccupied face, wondering what it was that really troubled him. 'The English girl claimed that the man called Steven Curtis was your father's friend. She said that he made a habit of bringing his students here, before the war. You were too young to have known him, of course, but didn't you hear about him afterwards?'

Stefanos gave a little shrug. 'I heard about the visits from my uncle, that's all. It was past history even by then.'

Petros nodded and made to leave the room. Then, at the

door, he stopped and turned round. 'We should have given *her* the painting, you know. That's what we should have done.'

Instead of answering, Stefanos seemed to be intent on watching the smoke from his cigarette curl up and fade away. Then he asked another abrupt question. 'What did you say her name was?'

'I didn't say, but she's called Anna.' Then Petros went out and closed the door, leaving his father to go over in his mind once more what he knew of the events of more than half a century before.

Whether watched over by gods who'd chosen to be merciful for once or not, Anna managed to hand back the hired car unscratched. Now, with only the short walk back to the hotel to accomplish, she could reckon the long day over. It seemed safe to assume that she'd seen the last of Pierre Bouchard; she need simply shower away the dust and disappointment of the journey, eat some much-needed food, and go to bed.

But when she asked for her room key the receptionist handed her a note as well. It had been delivered an hour ago, he said helpfully, from the Corfu Palace Hotel. The handwriting on the envelope wasn't familiar, but the style of the message inside was. She could almost hear Irene Lambert's voice urging her to dine with them . . . there was so much to talk about and she did so badly want – George as well of course – to see Anna again.

It was tempting to refuse; she felt hot and tired and troubled, in no mood to socialize with people she scarcely knew. But something about the message made her change her mind; Irene Lambert sounded strangely needful in some way. And in any case eating out was at least better than sitting alone in the Astron's dining-room under the pitying gaze of waiters who reckoned the woman hadn't yet been born who could really prefer not to be escorted by a man.

She telephoned the Corfu Palace, persuaded George Lambert that she could find her own way there, and then set about making herself presentable enough for one of Corfu's grander hostelries. The Lamberts were waiting for her in the lobby when she arrived – Irene obviously fresh from the hands of the hotel's hairdresser and expensively gowned, but nice enough to say without envy of her guest that natural chic was something a girl was born with. George, appealed to, obligingly agreed and Anna found herself glad to be there after all; they were just the antidote she needed to remove the sourness of her visit to Mondhiki. But there was something different about *them* all the same . . . some keyed-up excitement . . . worry . . . dread . . . that perhaps they hadn't even made up their minds whether or not to talk about.

Settled in the splendid dining-room, and with food ordered, Irene asked how her guest's detective work had gone. With a mind still full of the Kladis family, Anna promptly gave herself away.

'I found the place I was looking for but, sadly, I wasn't welcome.'

Confused by this – hadn't the nice Nausicaa girl been there a very long time ago? – Irene was about to ask how she could be sure of the lack of welcome when Anna remembered what she was supposed to have been searching for.

'I'm sorry,' she said ruefully. 'Odysseus's landing-place *was* one objective, but I had another one as well – a family connection to trace, a bit like yours. I wanted to find a family my grandfather knew before the war.'

'You found them?' Irene persisted, glad of the chance to cling to something more tangible than Homer's story. 'But they didn't like *you*? Now isn't that just incredible . . . Wouldn't you say so, George?'

But before he could answer Anna waved the subject aside. 'They weren't expecting a visit – I shouldn't have gone. Tell me about your search instead.'

The Lamberts looked at each other – perhaps to agree which of them should begin, but Anna sensed more indecision than that; they were agitated about something and, for once, not entirely in agreement with each other. Then Irene made a gesture that offered the initiative to George.

He took a little sip of wine without grimacing – retsina was a taste he was determined to acquire – and then began his tale.

'We knew where to look for the Lamberkis family – I think we mentioned that before – and the place wasn't hard to find . . . Linia, it's called, just on the edge of Korission Lagoon. *That* was a find in itself – wasn't it, Irene? It's been made into a wild-life sanctuary . . . turtles, lizards, tortoises, and more kinds of bird than you've ever seen.' He sipped his wine again, and then went on. 'It was great, but we were no nearer finding my family until we ran into the local priest, the *Pappas*, who spoke enough English to hold a conversation with. He said there was something we should see first, so a village lad was told to take us while he waited at the *kafeneio* for us to come back.'

George paused, to heighten the suspense, but Irene couldn't wait and rushed in herself. 'Anna, the boy took us to a *ruin* . . . boarded-up windows, holes in the roof . . . the saddest wreck of a place you ever saw.'

'Irene's right,' her husband agreed. 'No one could have lived there for years . . . we'd come much too late.'

'How sad,' Anna said gently. 'Did you go back and talk to the *Pappas*?'

'Yes, he was still there, and he knew what had happened to the family – my grandfather's elder brother and *his* descendants, who emigrated to Australia at the end of the war. The only one left, because he refused to go, died here two years ago,'

'So that's the end of the story,' Anna commented. 'It's another small part of the tragic history of Greece; but I hope you're still glad you came to find out.'

It was Irene's turn again. In a voice that wavered between terrified excitement and despair she contradicted what Anna had just said. 'It *isn't* the end of the story . . . George wants to buy that ruin and have us go and live there!' She tried to smile at her husband but she was suddenly close to tears, and he covered her trembling fingers with his own for a moment.

'You mean you'd . . . you'd leave America . . . make your home there?' Anna asked, aware that she was expected to say *something*, even if it wasn't what one or other of them wanted to hear. She had little idea of the life they led in America; but what could it possibly have in common with a remote corner of this small island in the Ionian Sea? It was more than likely that George Lambert have never even rowed a boat in the whole of his life, and they were both gregarious, sociable people.

'Corfu looks like paradise now,' she ventured slowly, 'but it's green and beautiful because it gets a lot of rain. You'd be welcome because of your forbears, but you won't get to know your neighbours until you can speak Greek.' Then she smiled apologetically. 'Sorry – you're aware of all these things yourselves.'

George patted her hand as well as keeping hold of his wife's. 'Nothing's fixed, Anna. I don't even know if we can buy that ruined house; there may be legal complications. We'll think about it some more; but I'd *like* to rebuild it, extend it maybe . . . There's quite a lot of land that goes with it. The site's beautiful, facing on to a wonderful sheltered beach, and the lagoon's right next door. I can't think of a nicer place to spend the summers – we could start with that and see what happened.'

His calm voice seemed to console Irene, and now she was able to smile at Anna. 'George has been in real-estate all his working life – he knows about houses,' she said proudly.

'And he wants to complete the Lamberkis story, I think,' Anna suggested, '. . . bring the family back to where it started from.' It was exactly what *had* brought him there, she now realized.

The food so far had been eaten almost unnoticed but they were enjoying the *baklavas* – a delicious concoction of pastry, honey and nuts – recommended by a friendly waiter, when an interruption occurred.

'*Ma chère* Anna . . . what a lovely surprise!' It was the familiar voice of Pierre Bouchard, and when she turned round he was smiling at her as if, instead of expecting her to be at the ends of the earth, he'd suddenly stumbled across a dear friend on Corfu. She was forced, because he waited there, to introduce him to her hosts, and George, obedient to a glance from Irene, invited him to share their coffee and Greek brandy.

Predictably, he charmed Madame Lambert – a name that Irene happily remarked sounded so much nicer pronounced the French way. At ease with him at once, she explained that they'd been delving into the past, and found the very house where George's family had once lived. Then, well-launched by now, she smiled at their other guest across the table. 'Poor Anna found the place *she* was looking for too, but the people there were very unfriendly. I do think that's so sad, don't you, Mr Bouchard?'

It seemed for a moment that he wasn't going to reply, but at last he answered. 'Sad, as you say, *madame*; but perhaps they've found that strangers aren't always trustworthy.' He smiled at Anna as he spoke, to make sure that the barb had gone home.

'It turned out to be nothing personal,' she said with an effort at lightness. 'They simply don't like the English, which of course they're free to do. Some of *us* even dislike the French!'

Sweetly she managed to return Pierre Bouchard's smile and hoped that honours were even. Then she looked at her hosts. 'It's been lovely to meet you again, but now forgive me if I say thank you and good night – it's been a long day! But I'd like very much to know what happens about the house.' She fumbled in her bag and drew out a card. 'Here's my address in Oxford; I'll be back there in another week or two.'

Irene took charge of the card, and George said that he'd escort Anna to a taxi at the hotel door, but Pierre Bouchard explained that since his own route lay in the same direction as hers *he* would provide the escort.

Anna held her tongue until they'd parted from the Lamberts in the hall and got outside the door. 'Before you speak another word, I don't need an escort, and I'm too exhausted to go on arguing about it. So I'll just say good-night.'

The lamplight fell on her face, showing him the tiredness and strain the day had left there. Much to her surprise, he simply touched her cheek with gentle fingers.

'All right – no more words tonight. But we do need to talk. Will you promise not to run away before I come to the Astron tomorrow . . . please, Anna?'

She nodded her head and he knew that the reluctant promise had been given. He flagged a waiting taxi, paid the cabbie in advance, and stood watching while she was driven away. Ten minutes later she fell into bed, too tired to be kept awake even by the events of a day that had been the most stressful she could remember.

Seven

With the dazzling light of an April morning filling her room, she woke with the certainty that, in some subconscious process while she slept, decisions had been taken – it was time to give up on the Kladis family, time to leave Corfu. She'd take away with her simply the memory of an old white house perched close to the sea and that would have to be enough.

A telephone call to her mother in Rome reported the visit to Mondhiki in the briefest terms; Nicola Rasini rightly guessed that there was more to tell, but agreed to wait patiently for the rest of the story. She wished her daughter joy of the ruined temples she was now about to inspect on the mainland, and recommended comfortable shoes, the best available sun-glasses, and due care in dealing with would-be Greek guides.

Anna rang off smiling at a typical conversation, and then picked up the telephone again to speak to her friend at the Tourist Information Office.

Andreas Kalamos sounded genuinely pleased to hear that she'd found Mondhiki but brushed her thanks aside. He was there to help, he pointed out, but admitted to getting more pleasure from helping some visitors than others; now, though, he feared that his English kyria would be leaving Corfu. Anna agreed, but unblushingly asked for yet more help. He listened to her questions, promised to ring her back with the answers, and did so even before she was called downstairs to find Pierre Bouchard waiting in the lobby.

He inspected her face with impersonal thoroughness and

announced that she looked better than she'd done the night before. It seemed a tepid compliment but she thanked him politely and waited for what he'd say next.

'It's a lovely morning – shall we go out?' he suggested. 'If you haven't climbed to the top of the Old Fort it's worth the effort just for the view.'

Anna declined the walk on the grounds that she was short of time and, without argument, was led instead in the direction of the Listón – the elegant, arcaded street bordering the Esplanade, which a French architect had designed in the hope of making it resemble the Rue de Rivoli in Paris.

With a café selected and coffee ordered, Anna waited for the interrogation to begin.

'*You* can start,' Bouchard suggested unsmilingly. 'Tell me first of all how you came to know where to find the Kladis family.'

'I *didn't* know until the afternoon before last,' she insisted. 'I'd brought with me a photograph I was given before I left Oxford; there was a word written on the back of it that I'd never even noticed – Mondhiki. A very helpful man at the Tourist Office eventually traced it as the name of a farm; and I drove there yesterday.'

She drank some of the coffee that had arrived, but Pierre Bouchard shook his head. 'Don't stop yet; I want to know what happened.'

Anna gave a little shrug. 'You heard last night – I didn't even get inside the house. First I met a girl who reluctantly led me as far as the terrace, because I asked for a glass of water. Then the son of the present owner appeared to escort me off the premises. All in all, a fruitless visit, except that I now know how beautiful Mondhiki is – I can see why my grandfather loved it.'

'No reason given for the lack of welcome?'

'Only that they blame the English for their terrible civil war. Petros Kladis insisted that his father, Stefanos, never even knew my grandfather – they all just dislike us on principle.' She sounded apologetic for what came next. 'I didn't ask about paintings, I'm afraid – the atmosphere wasn't quite friendly enough for that.'

A real smile touched Bouchard's face for a moment, making it suddenly attractive. '*N'importe!* I've had a little success myself. I put an advertisement in the town newspaper, and netted a man with two Kladis paintings to sell. I'd just met him when I saw you in the hotel dining-room last night.'

'And you're going to buy them?'

'Of course – they're beautiful. One's simplicity itself – a dazzling white chapel on a hilltop against a background of cobalt-coloured sea; the other's quite different but just as wonderful: small, laughing children grouped around a donkey in a sunlit olive grove. Both of them are the essence of this place.' Pierre Bouchard drank his coffee, then pushed the cup away so that he could lean more easily on the table and look at Anna. 'That isn't quite all. I went to the municipal archives to try to track down Nikos. Some of the records were destroyed during the war, but I did find an entry for his marriage to Katerina Pappas in 1938, and their subsequent registration of two children – Stefanos, the man you didn't get to meet, and a daughter called Dassia. Strangely, neither Nikos nor his wife were recorded as having died here although they must certainly both be dead by now.'

'It's just one more mystery,' Anna said slowly. 'Not surprising, though; the whole thing is wrapped in secrecy and sadness; just like Mondhiki itself, lovely though it is.'

'Why not come with me this afternoon to collect the paintings?' Bouchard suddenly suggested. 'They're worth seeing, and Mr Kostalis won't mind.'

'*Kostalis*!' The name echoed in her mind, conjuring up the image of a girl's sad, withdrawn face. 'It was Eleni Kostalis that I met first yesterday – she said her mother was Stefanos Kladis's cousin.'

'Don't be surprised; this is a small island. But the family connection explains how Kostalis comes to have the paintings. All the more reason for you to come with me?'

But Anna shook her head. 'I've finished delving into my

grandfather's life; perhaps my mother was right and I should never have begun. I'll let the dead keep their secrets. I've got a flight booked to Athens this afternoon.'

Bouchard made a slight gesture of regret but on the whole, Anna thought, he probably preferred her not to be there, spoiling any contact he might make with the Kladis family. 'Try to see the Parthenon for the first time at sunset,' he merely suggested. 'It's a sight you'll never forget. I suppose you've somewhere to stay?'

'A room at the Phoenix Hotel, booked for me by my friend Andreas Kalamos – he says it's central, clean, and cheap.' She stood up to leave, and held out her hand as he got to his feet as well. 'I'll say goodbye now – I've got some shopping to do. You were right to suspect that I disliked your hunt for Kladis paintings, but I accept now that you could just be buying them for yourself because you love them. I'm glad that at least you found two.'

He smiled at her warmly for the second time. 'Handsomely said, Anna, especially when your own search was so disappointing. Shall we agree that French and English aren't obliged to disapprove of each other?'

'If you like, although it seems a pity when we all enjoy doing it so much!'

Her fingers felt cool and delicate against his own, then she released herself and walked away – watched with interest, he noticed, by several passing Greeks. Her slender height and fairness made her different from their own women, of course. But he saw her leave without regret, he decided, as he sat down again and ordered more coffee. No doubt Anna Rasini appealed to the men here, but he'd always fought shy of cool blondes who made no effort to meet him half-way. They wouldn't ever meet again; now he could forget their brief acquaintance and think about the Kladis family instead.

It was maddeningly frustrating not to know what had happened to Nikos Kladis, but obvious at least that he'd died much too young. He was tempted to ask Anna's friend at the Tourist Office to direct *him* to Mondhiki as well, but there *had*, surely, been tragedy of some kind, and, whichever way he looked at it, for a stranger to pursue the family there would be too much of an intrusion. He'd just be grateful for what he'd got from Kostalis and leave for Paris in the morning.

That was the plan firmly settled on in his mind. It survived until he walked back to his hotel at lunch-time and found a stranger waiting for him in the lobby. Dear God – another possible painting perhaps? – the man certainly had a package under one arm. But his thin brown face looked too unfriendly; he hadn't come to sell, or even bargain.

'Pierre Bouchard? My name is Kladis,' he said abruptly. 'Petros Kladis. I speak English, but very little French.'

'English will do, *monsieur*,' Pierre agreed with equal curtness.

'I saw your advertisement, but I'm not here to offer you any of my grandfather's paintings. Someone else – an Englishwoman – has been asking about my family at the same time. She is called Anna Rasini.' His dark eyes were fastened on Pierre's face. 'I see that at least you know the name. I thought that she might have a connection with you. If not, do you know where she is? At the Astron they told me she'd left.'

'She is on her way to Athens.' Pierre stared at the visitor's package and then heard himself say words that he hadn't known were on his lips. 'I'm going there tomorrow morning. If that package is for her, I could deliver it.'

Petros Kladis, in turn, examined a Frenchman whom instinctively he didn't like – Pierre Bouchard was too urbanely sure of himself, too sophisticated, too used to being in control of events. It put a Greek where he most hated to be – at a disadvantage.

'I'm not sure that would do,' he began. 'The package is not of value to anyone but her; still, even so . . .'

'. . . even so, you're not sure that you can trust me.' Pierre finished the sentence for him with a spark of anger in his eyes. 'With *that* I can't help you; you must decide for yourself. But I'm not in the habit of stealing what belongs to someone else.'

Petros Kladis stared at him a moment longer, then answered by holding out the package. 'Anna Rasini should have been given this when she came to Mondhiki. It took a little while for my father to decided to hand it over. It's a long story . . . not of interest to you in any case.' Then at last his face relaxed into a faint smile. 'If you like my grandfather's paintings, I hope you found some.'

'I've found two, and both of them I shall take back to Paris.' Pierre hesitated for a moment over what to say next. 'If there are any others at Mondhiki I should like to see *them* even if they're not for sale.'

Petros shook his head. 'When the Germans were here during the war a lot of work got destroyed.'

'Then that's a tragedy,' Pierre said quietly. 'Nikos Kladis was a fine painter – one of the very best. He died much too young, I'm afraid.'

But the implied invitation to explain what had happened to him wasn't taken up, and that in itself made a direct question impossible. The Greek would have refused to answer, Pierre felt sure, on the same grounds as before – the story would interest no one else. Instead, he took a card out of his pocket. 'Here's my address in Paris in case you ever decided to get in touch with me. I'll ask Anna to confirm to you that she's received your package safely.'

'There's no need,' the visitor said with a return to his earlier stiffness.

'I think there is,' he was told gently. 'I don't know whether Greeks trust each other; they certainly aren't inclined to trust the rest of us – but perhaps history has taught them not to.' Then Pierre Bouchard held out his hand to say goodbye. '*Au revoir, monsieur*; I'm very glad to have met Nikos Kladis's grandson.'

Petros only nodded in reply. He now found himself wanting to say a lot of things . . . to explain why Greeks were as they were . . . why his disconnected family was the way it was. But they were things that couldn't be said, at least not to this smooth, experienced Frenchman.

Instead, he gripped the hand being held out to him, muttered a farewell in Greek, and made for the door. Then he turned and walked back, because there *was* something left undone.

'When you see Anna tell her . . . tell her, please, that Eleni was sorry not to say goodbye. We were not kind the day she came . . . but there were things she didn't understand.'

'Perhaps if she were told what they were she *would* understand,' Pierre suggested. But Petros Kladis shook his dark head.

'Not possible now, and since eventually they won't matter anyway, for the moment we leave them as they are.' Then with a sadly haunting smile, he finally left the hotel.

Pierre climbed the stairs to his room, clutching the package and considering the Greek's cryptic last remark. At a guess it meant that his father, Stefanos, was the one who wouldn't allow whatever skeleton was in the family cupboard to see the light of day. As a point of view it seemed absurdly out-of-date, but this was Greece still and its people had their own ways of doing things. Anna Rasini had never had the faintest chance of being allowed inside the family's castle walls.

Now there was the package to consider as well, surely another painting that Petros had talked his father into giving up. The temptation to inspect it was almost overwhelming, but he resisted it; the painting had to be delivered as he'd received it, because it was part of the story that Stefanos had refused to tell. Pierre stared at it, cursing himself for the fool he hadn't suspected that he was. Ten minutes ago his nice neat plan had been to fly to Athens in the morning and catch the connecting flight to Paris. Now he was committed to breaking his journey there and combing Greek temple ruins for Anna Rasini. If he failed to find her he'd have to make another visit to Oxford as well. And worst of all, at the end of so much time and effort, he still wouldn't know, any more than he did now, what had happened to Nikos Kladis and a woman called Katerina who had simply disappeared into oblivion.

Eight

The Phoenix Hotel was what Andreas had said it would be, spartan after the comfort of the Astron in Corfu, but clean, adequate, and central. Anna checked in, but went out again at once into the rush and noise of the city's early-evening traffic. She would be just in time to follow the advice she'd been given . . . if not to wander slowly about the Acropolis, at least to watch the golden columns of the Parthenon itself change as the light changed – first rose, then mauve, then purple. From where she stood in front of the great entrance gate – the Propylaea – she could also look out over the city clustered below and see the mountains that ringed it – Parnes, Aegaleos, Hymettus, home of the best of all honey, and Pentelicon, whose rock had produced the golden marble from which the Parthenon was built.

She stayed there until evening faded into dusk, aware that Pierre Bouchard had been quite right: she'd glimpsed something magical, at a time of day when most visitors had already left. In such things at least his advice was to be entirely trusted.

The walk back to the hotel wasn't far, but she now felt conspicuous alone and pretended not to hear the invitations of the young men loitering at street café tables. They weren't threatening, but they were tiresome – just as Nicola, experienced in the ways of the world, had said they would be. She was glad to get back to the hotel, to eat a not very exciting supper there rather than venture out again on her own. The fact had to be accepted during a lonely meal that some knowledgeable companion would have been welcome

. . . a Greek-speaker like Pierre Bouchard, for instance. But she brushed the image of him from her mind and doggedly concentrated on her phrase-book again – there must surely be a neat, effective way of saying 'Get lost . . . my brother is a very large policeman.'

The following morning she had a different objective – not ruined temples but the archives of a much more recent past – and, thanks to Andreas Kalamos, she knew exactly where to go and whom to ask for. The girl at the desk she was directed to smiled a welcome . . . yes, the kyria's visit had been expected, and there'd been time to search the records for the name of Steven Curtis. It was more than Anna thought she had any right to expect, and her smile glowed with gratitude.

'You mean you actually found something . . . ?' she almost stuttered in her eagerness to frame the question.

The girl nodded. 'Things were difficult at the end of the war, chaotic in fact; but gradually information was pieced together and recorded. It was our duty,' she added with a touch of pride. 'We were preserving this country's history, and men like your grandfather played a part in it.' She stared at Anna for a moment, then put into words the question in her mind. 'Any information we collected would have been sent to England eventually. Wasn't it kept by your own family?'

'It should have been, but wasn't,' Anna had to admit. 'That's why I'm here, bothering you. Was my grandfather in Athens during the war?'

'No, his group of partisans fought over some of the most sacred ground of all – up above Delphi, on Mount Parnassus itself. That is where he died.'

It was, Anna thought, where he might have chosen to die if he had to die at all. But the girl was delving among her papers again and fished out what she'd been looking for.

'Some of the group survived – a few only; but one of them who was just a young boy then is still alive and living in Athens. I have a number I could ring for you.'

She smiled at the expression on Anna's face, picked up the telephone and had an animated conversation in Greek. 'Michaelis Sarannis speaks English – he became a teacher after the war. He is old now, of course, but a daughter takes care of him. She said that you'd be welcome to call on them.'

Five minutes later, with an address written down to show the taxi-driver, Anna was on her way to the suburbs, where modern apartment blocks now ringed the ancient heart of the city. The cabbie saw no reason not to wait – he was happy to be paid, he said, while he studied the morning's newspaper. It was, she realized, a combination dear to a Greek's heart – profit and politics being pursued together.

Inside the building, unsure what to expect, she found herself confronting a middle-aged woman who smiled pleasantly but couldn't get far beyond a simple greeting in English. The man she'd come to see, white-haired and frail, sat by the window of the apartment's sitting-room, and she was reminded sharply of her visit to Wallingford at the beginning of this odyssey she'd embarked on. But Michaelis Sarannis hoisted himself to his feet when she walked in and with courtly grace invited her to sit down.

Anna began by taking out the photograph of Steven Curtis. 'My grandfather,' she said quietly. 'I believe you knew him during the war – you were on Mount Parnassus together.'

The old man stared at the pictured face, then in an unexpected gesture touched it with a gentle finger. 'Stefanos, we called him, kyria. *We* weren't much more than boys, so he took charge because he was older and more wise. He was a lovely man . . . We were lucky to have him.' He fell silent for a moment, lost in the memory of a time that had been terrible and wonderful in roughly equal parts. Then he looked at the girl who'd come so surprisingly to remind him of it – yes, fair she was, as Stefanos had been; fair and gentle. But now that she was there, he knew there was something else he had to say.

'He shouldn't have died . . . wouldn't have done if we

could have got help after he was shot. But the Germans were waiting for us to make a move, and Stefanos refused to let anyone leave the cave. I think we *should* have saved him . . . I'm sorry, kyria.'

Close to tears, Anna shook her head. 'He knew better – you would all have been killed.'

The old man nodded, perhaps glad to accept what Stefanos's granddaughter had said. Then he made a sign to his daughter and, as if expecting it, she brought them a small, carefully wrapped parcel.

'*You* must have this now,' he said to Anna. 'I've kept it all these years, but it properly belongs to you.'

Inside were two dog-eared battered paperbacks – *The Odyssey* and *The Iliad* – with Steven Curtis's name written on each fly-leaf in his minuscule hand; his inevitable choice of what to take with him to war.

Anna tried to insist that the books should remain where they were, but her host grew agitated. Stefanos, he said, would have wanted her to have them. There could be no more argument after that. She put them in her shoulder-bag, and then accepted the coffee and glasses of water that his daughter brought next. At last, afraid of tiring him too much, Anna kissed them both goodbye, and went out into the bright morning sunlight to find her taxi-driver.

A return visit to thank the girl who'd sent her to Michaelis Sarannis was necessary, so that it was well into the Athenian lunch-break by the time she got back to the Phoenix. She'd discovered by now the pleasantest part of the hotel, a roof-garden, properly green and shaded, where drinks and snacks were served. She was sitting there hesitating over what to order when a remembered voice spoke behind her . . . history repeating itself.

'May I join you, Anna?'

Again as before, Pierre Bouchard didn't wait for permission; he simply sat down. She said nothing for a moment, struggling with a mixture of emotions that there wasn't time to sort out. At last, sure that her voice, at least, was now under control, she managed to speak calmly.

'You keep popping up like the demon-king in pantomime. I'm quite pleased to see you . . . but are *you* as cross as you look?'

'I'm thirsty, hungry, and marooned in a fifth-rate Athenian hotel when I ought to be walking into my comfortable apartment in Paris right now – so yes, I'd say I'm cross.'

She smiled at him, wondering why she didn't mind . . . Was she *that* pleased to see him? Surely not; they'd barely got as far as agreeing not to disapprove of one another.

'Here's the waiter coming,' she pointed out. 'The food isn't wonderful, but you'll feel better when you've eaten something. You might even feel strong enough to tell me why you're here – I thought you *were* going straight back to Paris.'

He spoke to the waiter, ordered food for them both, and then answered her. 'I *was*, until Petros Kladis paid me a visit. My advertisement told him where to find me, and he had some extraordinary idea that you and I might be working together!' He let the irony of that sink in, and then went blandly on. 'So when the Astron people said you'd left he decided to try me.'

'But *why?*' Anna wanted to know. 'He couldn't get rid of me fast enough when I went to Mondhiki.'

'Repentance, let's say – he knew they'd behaved badly . . . I was to mention by the way that Eleni Kostalis was especially sorry not to bid you a proper goodbye.' Pierre halted for a moment, then placed on the table the package he'd been holding. 'I was also to give you this – it's really why I went to the trouble of finding you in Athens.'

Anna undid the wrapping and found herself staring at the face of a fair-haired man, half-smiling as if at some small private joke. It was a sketch rather than a finished portrait, but anything added to it would have spoiled it, she thought; even in the dashed-off likeness Nikos had somehow caught the essence of his friend.

'I'm to *keep* this?' Anna scarcely dared to ask.

'Yes – I think that Petros had talked his father into admitting it was something you ought to have.'

'It's been a very emotional day,' she commented unsteadily, 'and it's also the second time that I've been given something I "ought to have".' In as few words as possible she explained how the morning had been spent, then took out of her bag the books Michaelis Saranniss had insisted she keep.

Pierre Bouchard handled them with care, she noticed; almost with a kind of reverence. 'Homer in the original, of course – your grandfather wouldn't have needed anyone else's translation.'

Anna hesitated, then made up her mind what to say next. 'There was a letter still folded inside one of the books – used as a bookmark, probably – but it's in Greek. Would you translate it for me, please?' She handed him a sheet of yellowed paper. 'The ink is very faded, but I think it's still legible.'

He studied the message for a while, then slowly read out its meaning. 'It's dated March 1943, and addressed to "My dear Stefanos . . . Another spring, and still no end to this dreadful war; in fact things get worse now . . . The Germans are more efficient occupiers than the Italians were, and we know of people who are being deported. But we manage here well enough so far, and your namesake – nearly four! – is thriving. Athina remains in the town with her brute of a husband, but I shall have to do something about that; she's too unhappy, even with a beautiful little daughter, for the marriage to go on. I'll try to write again when I know a caique is leaving for Patras. Take care of yourself, best of friends. God knows when we shall see each other again."'

Pierre cleared the huskiness from his voice. 'It's just signed "N.K.", like the paintings – I suppose names and places couldn't be given away in those dreadful days.'

He saw the tears glistening on Anna's cheeks and shook his head. 'Don't cry, please; here comes the waiter with our no doubt inedible omelettes – he'll think *I*'m upsetting you.'

She smeared away her tears and managed to smile at the waiter. She even picked up a fork in a pretence of eating, then put it down again.

'The letter just deepens the mystery,' she said slowly. 'Whatever went wrong it wasn't between Nikos and my grandfather . . . couldn't have been for him to write in those terms.'

'And Steven Curtis was obviously godfather to Nikos's son – his *koumbaros* in Greek. It's a very important relationship here – almost as sacred as natural father and son.'

Anna abandoned her omelette altogether and sipped the wine that had been poured for her instead. 'I feel like a terrier at a rabbit-hole,' she said with sudden distaste, 'ferreting for what I've no right to know. Being given the portrait and the books is already more than I could possibly have hoped for. I was going to see Delphi anyway, and I want to go all the more now, just to pay my tribute to Mount Parnassus; but then I shall go home.'

Comforted by that decision, she smiled at Pierre Bouchard. 'We've only talked about my affairs. Did you get the paintings from Mr Kostalis?'

'Of course, and I doubt if I shall ever be able to part with them.' Then he spoke without his usual self-assurance. 'I know what you said just now, and I understand how you feel about not intruding on the past. But Kostalis did add another small piece to the puzzle. Eleni is his niece. Her mother must have been the little girl mentioned in Nikos Kladis's letter . . . and *her* mother would have been Nikos's sister, Athina – the girl with the "brute of a husband"!'

'So is Eleni's mother still at Mondhiki as well . . . Did he know about that?'

'She is here in Athens,' Pierre said. 'When her husband died she simply gave up a normal life and entered a closed order of Catholic nuns. Kostalis didn't say why – perhaps he didn't even know.'

Anna thought of the girl she'd met on the track leading to Mondhiki . . . isolated, lonely and orphaned to all intents and purposes, but even so with kindness enough to have offered an unwelcome stranger a lift on her donkey. 'Poor Eleni,' she murmured, finding nothing else to say. Then her thin hands sketched a gesture, pushing away the picture in her mind.

'I haven't thanked you for bringing me the painting . . . I *can't* thank you adequately, except to say that I shall treasure it. Now, you want to get home, of course, and make up for lost time.'

Pierre's shoulders lifted in a little shrug. 'Since I'm here I'll look up some friends I was going to ignore – wrongly, of course; because they're all people I should keep in touch with.' He watched Anna carefully wrapping up her painting again, and realized how strange it felt to know that he wasn't going to see her again. Not strange . . . wrong! She was irritatingly cool, and disinclined to trust him, and there were differences between them that they might never overcome; but it was the Fates who'd chosen to link them together, and when in Greece no sensible man thumbed his nose at *them*; it was too dangerous.

'How will you get to Delphi – I assume you're going tomorrow?' he asked.

'There's a bus,' Anna said. 'It takes quite a long time, so I might have to find somewhere to stay the night.'

It was becoming a habit, he thought, to hear himself once again say something he hadn't known was in his mind. 'If it isn't a very private pilgrimage you're making, I'd rather like to be in at the end of your search. May I come too?'

She didn't reply at once, and her expression suggested that when she did she was going to refuse.

'Greek buses are bone-shaking things,' he added casually. 'A hired car and chauffeur – even a French one! – now wouldn't that seem more desirable?'

'Well, it might,' she admitted cautiously. 'I've already discovered that my mother was right – a lone foreign female is fair game here; it's probably our own fault for being too oncoming. And the other thing in your favour, of course, is that you speak Greek.'

It wasn't an exciting assessment of his value as a travelling companion, but he tried not to feel piqued by it. 'Don't spare the chauffeur's feelings if you think he won't do! Shall I hire a car or not?'

'I think you're being kind,' she said, trying not to laugh. 'You've probably visited Delphi often enough in the past; but I shan't go on arguing against myself. Please hire the car, and tell me what I ought to see at Delphi.'

He simply nodded and asked a different question. 'Have you been to the Acropolis yet?'

'Yesterday evening – there was just time to look up from the entrance gate. I shall go again this afternoon, but you were quite right – it *was* the perfect moment to be there.'

Pierre hesitated again – really he was behaving very untypically, he thought. 'My friends will certainly invite me to dine with them tonight; shall I ask them to include you, too?'

She shook her head, determined not to be looked after to this extent. 'Thanks, but no; you'll want to speak Greek together. I'll eat here and be ready for you in the morning.'

She sounded cheerful about foregoing his company, and he reflected that altogether Anna Rasini was a good but painful corrective to a man's self-esteem. How nice it would be to get back to his friends in Paris who at least knew how to value him properly.

'Then I'll call for you at eight o'clock,' he said, 'and if you've been poisoned by then from eating the food in this repellent lodging-house it will be your own fault. *A bientôt*, Anna.' And with that he walked away, angry again it seemed. Anna thought he was a man of very uncertain temper – spoiled, perhaps, by too many adoring women friends.

She put the thought aside but stayed sitting where she was, considering the discoveries of the morning. Most puzzling of all had been Petros's journey to Corfu Town to find her. Was the gift of the portrait a way of saying that it was to be the end of any contact with the Kladis family? It seemed the most likely explanation; but just suppose he and perhaps Eleni too, had been trying to suggest that she shouldn't give up? Suppose they *wanted* her to go back to Mondhiki. Now her firm decision was going awry again. Taken all in all, Greece was a damnably unsettling country. But at least she knew how she was going to spend the rest of the afternoon – she'd explore every inch of the Acropolis, come back to sleep the sleep of the just, and leave it to the ancient Sibyl of Delphi to tell her what to do after that.

Nine

Anna was ready in good time the following morning, looking neat but not gaudy, she hoped, in jacket and slacks of pale-green linen. Following Nicola's advice, her shoes were comfortable and her sun-glasses expensive, but she wasn't sure that she'd chosen the day's guide with the same amount of care. There was too much she didn't know about Pierre Bouchard; only now was too late to realize it because he was already walking into the lobby.

His glance swept over her, but she had no idea whether she measured up to a sophisticated Parisian's standards or not; probably not, because all he said was, 'That's an unusual colour for a blonde to wear.'

'You're right,' Anna agreed calmly. 'Being blue-eyed, they mostly wear blue instead.' She pointed to the bag slung over her shoulder. 'I've brought overnight things, so I can come back on the bus tomorrow if you want to return sooner than that.'

'I also have my toothbrush with me,' he pointed out. 'Even this early in the season Delphi will be crowded; I thought we'd stay in Arachova instead. Let's get going, shall we?'

The guide clearly *had* been ill-chosen, and the expedition already seemed doomed. She was on the point of saying that he could still change his mind, but he was half-way to the door and there seemed nothing to be done but follow him.

Settled in the car, she finally found something to say. 'Which do you prefer: a passenger who holds her tongue while you drive, or one who provides light-hearted badinage to keep you awake?'

'It's eight in the morning and I'm not in imminent danger of dropping off at the wheel. You're allowed to speak occasionally, but not to chatter non-stop.'

With that agreed between them, she gave up on small-talk and stared out of the window instead. And there was more than enough to think about, seeing that they were driving along what had been the sacred way to Eleusis. The sea bordering one side of the road was the very Bay of Salamis where Themistocles had smashed the Persian fleet. On the other side there should have been the Goddess Demeter's sacred lake, and already they were approaching the place where her most secret and mysterious Eleusian rites were carried out. So much ancient history . . . so many legends echoing down the millennia. But what they were actually driving through was a smoke-enshrouded industrial wasteland of cement factories and smelting-works! And further on, Thebes – the very place where Antigone had led the blinded Oedipus out into exile – was just as heart-breakingly disappointing. Dear God, was *this* the glory that was Greece?

'You *are* allowed to speak, you know,' Pierre's amused voice broke in on her thoughts. 'Say *something,* please.'

She vaguely registered the fact that whatever ill-humour he'd started out in had somehow faded away, but now she had a problem of her own to deal with. 'I'm trying to come to terms with this country,' she said seriously.

'By which I suppose you mean there's too big a gap between ancient and modern Greece. You can't, for instance, reconcile the Parthenon – serenely beautiful as it is even in its ruined state – with the crowded, noisy, polluted city sprawling at its feet?' He turned to glance at her for a moment, and she saw not only amusement but also understanding in his face. 'There are only two ways of approaching Greece,' he suggested. 'Either you should come knowing so much of the past – as your grandfather probably did – that the present goes unnoticed; or you must come knowing nothing at all, in which case the smog and the traffic and the modern ugliness won't bother you. Take comfort from the fact that most of Greece *can't* be spoilt – its natural geography takes care of that.'

She could see that it was true; because already ugliness was being left behind, and the road was climbing through a landscape that mercifully *hadn't* changed – olive- or vine-clad hills, white-washed hamlets, old ladies leading donkeys, and always range upon range of mountains silhouetted against the ineffable Greek sky.

'You're right, of course,' Anna admitted, 'and thank you for not reminding me that a country can't live on its past. These people were desperately poor for so long – how could they *not* have wanted to move into today's world even with all its attendant nastiness?'

Another silence fell, but this time it felt comfortable; chauffeur and passenger seemed to be at ease with one another now, whether they talked or not. She watched his brown hands on the steering-wheel, holding it lightly instead of wrestling with it as so many drivers found it necessary to do. Probably this was how he handled the whole of his life – with no undue haste, no unnecessary exertion; everything managed with ease and skill. It made him a restful companion, but she could see that he'd be hard to live up to.

By mid-morning the journey was nearly over; and, with Delphi only ten kilometres away according to the signpost they'd just passed, they were climbing into Arachova. Perched high on a ridge, it was almost self-consciously picturesque with its cluster of white-washed houses clinging to the hillside. Flowers and greenery spilled over every wall, and skeins of wool dyed all the colours of the rainbow were hanging out to dry for the rugs that, Pierre explained, were made there.

'You can explore here tomorrow morning,' he said. 'We'll keep straight on now.'

But he pulled up short of the sanctuary at a vantage spot where they could safely get out and look towards it. The road they were on cut horizontally through the site, with a mass of tumbled masonry lying below it. Above the road were the remains of treasury buildings, the theatre, the stadium, and – most heart-catching of all – the apricot-coloured columns of Apollo's temple. Behind *them* rose up a perpendicular wall of cliffs – the Shining Ones, Pierre said they were called.

'The German Schliemann discovered Troy,' he added quietly. 'The English unearthed the Minoan civilization at Knossos, but the French can take credit for Delphi – little more than a hundred years ago it was all still entirely built over; hard to imagine that now.'

Anna scarcely paid heed to what had been a heroic piece of excavation; she was thinking of the men who'd first been inspired to build just *there* a temple to the great God of Light. They'd chosen an incomparable site carved out of the side of the mountain; above it, Parnassus shouldered its way into the sky; and, 1800 feet below, the River Pleistos wandered to the sea through a silver-green valley of olive trees, whose colour shifted with the slightest movement of the breeze.

Almost bereft of words, Anna pointed down towards the valley below them. 'Is it still eagle-haunted? Someone told me once that it was.'

'They're not as common as they were, but you can still find yourself looking down on a eagle in flight,' Pierre answered. 'Now, shall we go on? There will be busloads of other visitors, I'm afraid – another bit of modern Greece for you to dislike – but don't let them spoil it for you. It's still one of the wonders of the world.'

In the car-park proper, Anna looked at her guide. 'Would it seem very churlish of me to ask if I can wander about by myself now? It's no reflection on my very kind chauffeur . . . the truth is that I'm more accustomed to being on my own.'

But Pierre saw her glance at the great sweep of the mountain, riven by fissures and rock-falls and the weathering of unnumbered winters.

'Somewhere up there,' he said quietly, 'your grandfather

lived and fought and ultimately died. Why should you want company while you come to terms with that tremendous fact?'

He was, it seemed the perfect guide after all, and her smile thanked him more than words could have done. 'I'm sorry if it's a wasted day for you,' she suggested, but he shook his head.

'Not at all – I shall call on friends at the museum, and make a nuisance of myself by visiting the French archaeologists who still work here. *You* mustn't miss the museum, by the way. I'll be waiting there for you at closing-time.' He escorted her as far as the sanctuary entrance, and then disappeared – leaving her to realize that the day seemed suddenly lonely without him.

But with the official leaflet in her hand, she drank the obligatory sip of water from the Castalian spring, and then began slowly to climb from level to level. There *were* many other visitors, but they were noticeably quiet as if awed by the mysterious serenity of the place. And there would always have been pilgrims in any case, she reflected – winding their way up from the little port of Itea, with their eyes fixed on the Shining Ones guarding Apollo's temple.

Late in the afternoon she came to rest in the stadium at the highest point of the sanctuary. Now laid out with grass and trees, it was a blessed relief from the glare of sunlight on marble, and she stayed there, content to let her thoughts wander from past to future. But the shadows creeping up the hillside were a reminder that it was time to leave, and reluctantly she made her way down to the museum.

Pierre was waiting for her at the entrance. 'You've cut it fine,' he said, 'but there's just time for you to see one thing. Close your eyes.' She was taken by the hand, and led into a gallery, and told that she could now look. 'Meet my friend, *The Charioteer*,' he murmured beside her.

She was staring at the figure of a youth a little taller than herself, wearing a stone tunic magically carved into folds as fluid as silk. His arms were held out as if still holding the horse's reins, and a gentle smile of happiness touched his mouth because of the victor's fillet round his head.

'He's only just this minute won,' Anna said quietly at last, '. . . what's a millennium or two, time here doesn't mean anything at all.'

'Then you *are* learning about Greece,' Pierre commented with a faint smile. 'Now, they're waiting for us to leave, and you've got to meet another friend of mine – it's her house we're going to stay in.'

They drove in silence back to Arachova, to a charming white house tucked into the hillside. It looked to Anna's eye as if it might easily slide straight down to the bottom of the valley, but the view across to the distant mountains was worth a slight feeling of anxiety. Its owner, Evgenia Vassilikos, was a white-haired, elegant woman who greeted both her guests with eagerness and one of them with great affection. Her late husband and she had been close friends of Pierre's father in Paris, she explained to Anna. If she thought it odd to be confronted with a strange Englishwoman, she was too courteous to say so, but simply made her welcome in the English she seemed to speak as fluently as French.

Anna was shown to a small guest-room almost austere in its furnishings, but the adjoining bathroom offered abundant hot water and an efficient lavatory – blessings not to be taken for granted outside Athens. The only gesture Anna could make towards dressing for dinner was to exchange her jacket for a delicate cashmere sweater, and with the evening temperature dropping fast she was glad to have brought it in her bag. Tired but refreshed, she went downstairs, aware of feeling strangely content. The truth seemed to be that she was happy to be where she was, in a white house on a Greek hilltop, with its gracious owner and Pierre Bouchard for company.

A smiling, middle-aged maid called Thekli served dinner: tiny fish fried in batter, meatballs in a herb-scented tomato sauce, with courgettes dressed in fragrant olive oil and lemon, and finally goat's cheese and small green pears that looked hard but tasted as sweet as honey.

Finally, when coffee and Greek brandy were brought to the table, Evgenia stood up, smiling at them. 'This is where I leave you to linger as long as you like. Sadly, caffeine and alcohol don't agree with old ladies, and if we are sensible we know when to retire! I shall see you in the morning.'

Pierre escorted Evgenia to the door and then came back again, apparently quite content to linger. Tired after the long day, Anna was content just to watch the star-filled sky that hung round the sheltered verandah they sat in, unaware that she was being observed herself. As companions went, he thought, she had less compunction than most. He understood why she'd left him to his own devices the moment they arrived in Delphi; but now, instead of paying some vestigial amount of attention to him, she was studying the night sky as if her life depended on it. And the worst thing of all was that the less interest she took in him, the more – much more – he wanted to take in her. Throughout the day he'd been tempted to leave his friends and go looking for her; now they *were* together, but she was still eluding him . . . still lost in some thought process of her own.

At last his voice interrupted her. 'I know almost nothing about you. Why, for instance, are you in the habit of doing your wandering alone? No husband, lover, family, or at the very least friends?'

She turned her head slightly to smile at him. 'Friends, yes, but not much family – simply my mother living in Rome and an unknown father who absconded before I was born; husband or lover not at all. Now it's your turn – what does your own family amount to?'

'My father died ten years ago – much missed; he was nice man. My mother is frail, but still alive. She hated Paris, and when she became a widow moved back to the Haute Savoie region her family belongs to – she missed the mountains! Her brother is a landowner there, and I've cousins and nieces and nephews galore. I visit them when time allows.' Pierre then turned the conversation back on Anna herself. 'From Rupert Whittaker I know you live in Oxford. What do you do there?'

'I write,' she said, driven into a corner. 'I write quite well according to some literary critics, which might explain why I'm not hugely successful!' She smiled at what she'd just said. 'Put another way, I like to explore relationships; life with my grandmother on Oxford's academic fringe didn't equip me to drag in sex and sadomasochism on every page. I suppose I write rather small-scale books – old-fashioned, you'd probably think them.'

It was his turn to smile, but he still went on. 'Your father disappeared; why didn't you live with your mother?'

She didn't resent the questioning, only felt surprised that her life should be of any interest to him. 'I think I told you that when Steven didn't come home from a war my grandmother thought he should never have joined she became an unhappy, embittered woman, with the result that Nicola, my mother, disliked *her* and hated Oxford. She escaped to London to study music, fell in love with and married an Italian tenor, and had me – by which time he'd already left. She was rescued by another Italian – an impresario who looked after her until he died – and she became a rather famous opera star. But there was no room in such a peripatetic life for a small child, so I was left in Oxford with Lavinia Curtis.'

'Did you hate *your* mother for that?' Pierre asked. 'I think you had reason to.'

Anna considered the question for a moment, then shook her head. 'No . . . I just loved it when she came; she was very beautiful – still is – and fun to be with, which she still is; but I think I always understood that it was useless to apply to her the rules *we* lived by. She doesn't sing in public any more, and her dear Enrico is dead. But she and I have become good friends.'

'And what about Lavinia Curtis – how did her story end?'

'She died at the beginning of this year at the age of eighty-six. She'd been a widow for forty-six years, so perhaps it was understandable that she never talked about my grandfather. But when I cleared out her room after she died there was no trace that he'd ever been a part of her life. She was an unforgiving woman, but courageous in her own way, and in the end I grew fond of her.' Anna smiled across the table at her companion. 'There . . . that's surely enough about me.'

'Not quite, we've still scarcely talked about *you*. No sex in your books, you said; does that mean none in your life as well? Most of the time you're as remote as the "*princesse lointaine*" herself, but your parentage gives the lie to that, as do your dark eyes!'

She withdrew a little into her chair, suddenly feeling nervous; even the airy verandah had become too enclosed and intimate, and she was troublingly aware of the man who watched her with something more than amusement in his face. He was too complex – arrogant but perceptive; careless but kind – and, if she was honest with herself, physically too attractive as well. Even Evgenia, old and retired from the world, clearly recognized that. Prudence suggested that she should follow her hostess's example and go to bed, but Pierre sat between her and the door, and her strong intuition was that she wouldn't be allowed to leave until his interrogation was complete.

His question still hung unanswered in the air and at last she dealt with it as lightly as she could. 'Yes, I tried sex – who hasn't at the age of thirty-one?'

'And . . . ?'

'I just found myself wondering what all the fuss was about.'

At least his shout of laughter was a relief; it lessened the charge of electricity in the air, even at the cost of making her feel slightly ridiculous. But as if sensing that it had, he grew serious again himself.

'Dear Anna, either your heart wasn't in it or you chose a very poor partner, I'm afraid.'

'A bit of both perhaps, but the failure was mostly mine. You smiled when I talked about my low-key books, but the truth is that I had a low-key upbringing – no lack of care, but a great lack of affection translated into what a child needs: hugs, kisses, the certainty of being loved. I grew up knowing very little about the pleasures of actual contact between human-beings.'

And that, she thought, brought them to a hideous fresh difficulty – suppose she'd seemed to be offering a challenge he had to accept? She'd refuse of course, but it would be . . . embarrassing was the ridiculous word that came to mind; but perhaps that was what she was in such matters thanks to Lavinia – shamefully inadequate and ridiculous.

'Before you tie yourself into knots of anxiety about saying no,' Pierre's still amused voice broke in on her chaotic thoughts, 'I've no intention of asking to make love to you – although I'd like to, Anna, very much, because I think the "*princesse lointaine*" disguise is simply that.' He leaned across the table and traced the outline of her mouth with a gentle finger. 'Yes, it's just a disguise.' Unable to say anything at all even if she was required to, she waited for him to go on, and he did so in a voice that now sounded unexpectedly sad. 'Unfortunately, there are rules about these things, you see. One is that I don't ask to share your bed while we're guests in Evgenia's house. Another is that I don't conceal the fact that in Paris I have a wife and ten-year-old daughter.'

Anna went back to staring at the star-scattered sky, wondering why moments of revelation gave no warning to the people they were approaching. During the hours she'd spent alone at Delphi the knowledge that she'd soon be meeting him again had lain warmly at the back of her mind, but there'd been no need, then, to work out why that was so; but now, between one moment and the next, she *knew*, beyond the slightest doubt, that what she couldn't have was exactly what was essential for happiness. At last, she managed to find something to say. 'I think I expected an elegant, Parisian wife; the small daughter is more of a surprise. You must want to be at home with them, not looking after me.'

She shook her head when Pierre offered her more brandy, and he poured some into his own glass instead.

'My wife doesn't need looking after,' he said quietly. 'She's something of a household name in France – a political commentator who interviews ministers on television and routinely humiliates them; it's a game that our generous-minded public enjoys.' He smiled at the expression on Anna's face. 'It's a cut-throat world, didn't you know?'

'It's your wife's job, I suppose,' she had to suggest, 'her *métier*, as you say. It doesn't stop her loving you and your daughter.'

'How true, but in fact the loving ended a long time ago. We share my house in the Rue Jacob – the very model of an enlightened, intellectual Left-Bank family – but I inhabit the ground floor while Madeleine and Amélie live upstairs. We preserve the appearance of a successful family because my wife prefers it that way – it's good for her professionally – and because I don't want to lose my daughter.'

His voice stopped suddenly, as if there was nothing more to say. Anna heard the echo of it in her mind, but thought about the image he presented to the world. She knew she was long past believing that appearances were always, or even ever, what they seemed, but still what he'd just said was shocking.

'It's a . . . convenient arrangement,' she commented at last, 'if not exactly an ideal marriage.' Then she made the mistake of looking at him and saw the sadness in his face. 'I'm so sorry,' she said in a low voice. 'Thank you for telling me, though.' But he didn't answer and she had to go on herself. 'I usually take pride in assessing other people . . . it's part of what a writer's supposed to do, after all; but I've been much more wrong than right about you. I hope it will be a lesson to me in future.'

She was talking too much, chattering non-stop, he'd call it, but something, some words however pointless, had to fill the moments until she could get up and say good night. What she couldn't do was stay there pretending that they could go back to where they'd begun; she knew too much about him, and she must leave before he understood about her.

But Pierre himself brought the extraordinary evening to an end. He lifted his glass in a little gesture of salute, and then smiled at her. 'Dear Anna, go to bed – it's been a strenuous day, one way and another. You can safely leave me here to finish my brandy – I long ago gave up trying to drink my cares away!'

He stood up as she pushed back her chair, and waited for her to leave.

'Thank you for bringing me here,' she said gravely, 'not only to Delphi but here to meet Evgenia as well. I shan't forget any of it.'

'And nor shall I; but now go, Anna, before I get as far as suggesting that rules are only rules, made to be broken occasionally!'

She did as she was told, and climbed the stairs to her little white room, aware that if he *had* got that far, she would have had to agree with him.

Ten

With too much to think about Anna slept badly, then woke too late to watch the dawn flood into the valley outside her window, as she'd meant to. She dressed hurriedly but her mind wrestled with two related problems: the discovery about herself must somehow be hidden, most of all from Pierre himself, until it was safe to think how she could deal with it; but there remained the journey back to Athens with a man who almost certainly now regretted his conversation of the night before. Unless her estimate of Pierre Bouchard was still hopelessly wide of the mark, he didn't make a habit of sharing his failures with other people – and the sort of marriage he'd described had to be reckoned a failure.

Her problem hadn't been solved by the time she went downstairs and found the verandah – obviously Evgenia's dining-room – empty except for Thekli quietly laying the breakfast-table. A beaming smile answered Anna's '*Kali mera*', and then she pointed to the open front door.

Outside, illuminated by the golden morning light, Pierre was on a ladder, snipping at the rose that swarmed over the street side of the house. Evgenia, also there, directed the operation from ground level, but stopped to smile at her guest.

'You'll think us mad pruning this now, but it's a Rosa Banksiae and it blooms so early here that already it's almost over. If it isn't trimmed now we soon shan't see out of the windows.'

'And you also have someone available to climb the ladder!' Anna suggested.

Her hostess happily agreed, but then there came a shout from above.

'*Chère Evgenia*, I'm a very willing handyman but I need instruction – what, please, am I to chop next?'

'The branch just by your left hand, my darling; then you can descend to breakfast. The boy will clear up all the mess you've made.'

Back on terra firma, he greeted Anna pleasantly enough but she sensed at once that the drive back to Athens could be managed after all, because they *were* back where they'd begun . . . acquaintances whom chance had brought together. Last night's confession, if it had happened at all, could be forgotten now; a self-assured, successful man was entirely himself again. *This* Pierre Bouchard wasn't the one who'd hurried her to see *The Charioteer*. Yesterday had been a different day, and now his smiling glance was saying that it wouldn't be repeated. It was even safe to relax a little herself; there was no likelihood of giving anything away to this rediscovered stranger

Back indoors, they sat down to freshly-squeezed orange juice, warm rolls and honey of course, from Hymettus. Evgenia ate little, but she enjoyed watching her guests, and talked herself, she said, so that they could concentrate on eating.

'I hope you won't mind,' she suggested with a smile at Anna, 'Pierre told me a little about your grandfather. I'm sorry I never met him – I was in Athens during the war, not here – but we owed men like him such a great deal. It's very strange, shaming also, that you weren't made welcome by his friend's family; Greeks usually have long memories for bravery and comradeship.'

'We let Greece down, they said,' Anna explained, 'by giving them back a king they didn't want and thereby causing a dreadful civil war. I'm sure there's some truth in that, even if we thought we had good reason at the time, but I don't believe I was sent away because of a political decision taken more than fifty years ago; there's more involved than that.'

Evgenia stared at her across the table. 'Well, my dear, you tried to make contact with people who should have been your friends; it will be something for them to remember uncomfortably at least. Now what do you intend to do – go on visiting our past glories, or forget Greece altogether and return to England?'

Anna set down her coffee cup and carefully didn't look at Pierre. 'I'll go home eventually, of course, but I promised myself a three-month break from work, so I've time in hand still. You'll think I can't take a very decided "no" for an answer, but I'm going back to Corfu. My grandfather used to take his students to stay with the Kladis family at Mondhiki. If there was space for them, surely they can fit me in for a week or two as some kind of lodger. And if Stefanos Kladis still refuses to have me there he'll have to tell me why.'

Evgenia clapped her hands. 'Quite right, Anna! It's exactly what you must do.'

But there was no approval from the other side of the table. Instead, Pierre directed a fierce glance at his friend. 'Don't encourage her, Evgenia; she can be foolish enough all on her own.' Then he frowned at Anna. 'My dear girl, think, please. You aren't Queen Boudicca lambasting an unruly barbarian tribe; you're not even Lady Thatcher knocking hell out of some unfortunate French president. You've been refused admittance to a man's private home, that's all – strange, even churlish perhaps; but it *is* for Stephanos Kladis to make that choice. Why let yourself be hurt and turned away a second time?'

'That might happen . . . in which case I shall give up and go home. But Petros *did* bring the painting, and I can't help thinking that he did it for a reason. If I don't make one more try now I can't ever go back again, and I shall always regret not doing so.'

Evgenia smiled at the expression on Pierre's face. 'Darling, she can't help it . . . the English are very stubborn, didn't you know?'

'She *can* help it – she's half Italian,' he said wrathfully.

But he stared at her for a moment knowing that he could offer no good reason for a swamping wave of concern that simply made him sound irritable. Whatever happened at Mondhiki was nothing to do with him. He would drive her back to Athens and board the next flight to Paris, where he was already overdue. In no time at all she'd be the fading memory of a cool and tiresome Englishwoman using a fixation with her dead grandfather to escape from living in the real world.

'I shall say no more,' he announced with a dignity only slightly spoiled by the fact that Evgenia's mouth was twitching. 'Anna must hear the siren voice of Petros Kladis calling her back to Mondhiki if she wants to. I shall have returned to Paris.'

This was greeted by a moment's respectful silence. Then he stood up and further announced that he would take a short stroll while his passenger got herself ready for the journey.

'*Very* put out,' Evgenia observed with interest when he'd closed the front door behind him. 'I wonder why?'

Anna did her best with a question that wasn't as innocent as it seemed. 'Perhaps he dislikes people who keep changing their minds. I *did* say that I'd leave the story of my grandfather's friendship with the Kladis family alone; the people most concerned are dead now in any case.' But Anna's dark eyes were fixed on her companion, asking her to understand behaviour that was far from typical of herself and not easy to explain. 'I'm not usually so presumptuous, but I just have this feeling of something left undone . . . something that needs doing. There's a young girl at Mondhiki who doesn't know how to smile . . . Why? When her father died her mother left her and entered a closed order of nuns . . . Why? And why did her cousin drive all the way to Corfu Town with a portrait of my grandfather that I didn't even know existed?'

'Of course you must go back,' Evgenia said at once, 'but you need an excuse – a cover-story, don't they call it? Now, what shall it be?'

Anna pointed to a row of Shakespeare plays on one of the bookshelves. 'There it is – I'll be investigating the theory that Corfu was the setting for *The Tempest* – Prospero's island.' It reminded her of something else and she smiled ruefully at her hostess. 'I'm becoming an accomplished liar – I've already pretended to be looking for the place where Odysseus came ashore and met Nausicaa, much to the mystification of the nice American woman I tried it out on!'

Evgenia dealt firmly with this. 'There is lying and there's charming invention, Anna; you mustn't confuse the two! But I hope you realize that you must keep me informed from now on. We're friends, are we not, and friends share things.'

Agreement reached on this point, Anna was tempted for a moment to ask Evgenia to share what she knew of Pierre's life in Paris – was he content with his sham marriage, or deeply upset by it? But it wasn't a permissible question, and instead she laboured to explain the chance that had led his path to cross with her own. 'We were looking for different things, but in the same place at the same time, as it happened,' she finished up lamely, aware that it scarcely accounted for the fact that they now seemed to be touring the mainland together.

Evgenia seemed not to notice this, being hesitant herself for once about what to say next. It was perfectly clear that her guests had resisted the temptation to sleep together, but she was equally aware of the condition they were in, and her heart ached for them both. Pierre wouldn't leave Madeleine since it would effectively mean leaving his daughter as well; Anna could hope for nothing except snatched moments that she would probably come to hate.

Looking at her now, Evgenia suddenly said what was in her mind. 'Pierre was cross a moment ago because he doesn't want you to be hurt. I don't want you to be hurt either, my dear girl, but I'm afraid you will be.'

'Because he'll stay with his wife, you mean,' Anna managed to say after a little silence. 'I expect it *will* hurt, but after a while I might be able to remember that I didn't even like him to begin with! Then it will hurt less, I expect.' Then she smiled at her hostess. 'I'm rather glad you know.'

'You've promised to stay in touch,' Evgenia reminded her, '. . . I shall require a regular letter from you, Anna, and I shall write one back.'

And there the conversation ended because Pierre returned to point out that it was time they left.

Affectionate goodbyes were said, and very soon they were on the road back to Athens.

'I feel privileged to have met Evgenia,' Anna said at once. 'She's a lovely person.'

'Lovely and brave – a wartime heroine decorated by your king as well as by the Greeks; but she's funny and wise as well.' Pierre glanced briefly at his passenger and then returned his attention to the road again. 'I suppose you had a sudden inspiration over the breakfast rolls to go back to Corfu – otherwise you might have mentioned it last night.'

It seemed that he was still put out, but it was hard to understand why when his own interest in Corfu seemed to be over. 'It wasn't as sudden as all that,' she explained calmly. 'I think I knew when you brought me the portrait; but I spent a long time up in the stadium yesterday afternoon – it was cool and quiet up there and I could hear myself think. Then I knew for certain that I'd have to go back and try to find out why they all seem to be so unhappy.'

Pierre let several miles go by while he concentrated on a particularly steep and twisting piece of road. Then, when she'd given up waiting for him to answer, he suddenly did.

'The chances are that you *won't* find out because they won't allow you to. But if by some miracle of persuasion you do get inside the Kladis citadel, I can predict what will happen next. Petros Kladis will fall in love with you – Greek men find fair women irresistible – and then be deeply hurt when you don't stay at Mondhiki . . . which I assume you won't want to do. Eleni will have her poor little nose put even more out of joint by a beautiful visitor; and God knows what Stefanos Kladis will do since he already sounds half-insane. Are you prepared to admit that any of that is likely?'

'No, I'm not,' Anna said slowly. 'And I'm not even going to go on discussing it because nothing I can say will make you understand. The only thing you're right about is that I probably shan't get any nearer to them than I did the first time; which means that at least I shan't be able to do them any harm.'

With that said, she stared out of the window to indicate that his job was to drive while she thought thoughts that only concerned herself. But there wasn't enough space in a not very large car, not nearly enough distance between them to pretend that they were travelling alone. They were too aware of each other and gradually the air filled with such an electric charge of tension that she found it almost a relief when he finally acknowledged the fact by turning off the road into a track that led up into the hillside.

'I can't drive and talk to you at the same time,' he said quietly, 'and before we reach Athens I need to apologize. I made a fool of myself at breakfast, and Evgenia only just managed not to tell me so. She usually says exactly what she thinks, but kindness tied her tongue this morning; she knew why I didn't want you to go back to Corfu.'

'I thought you'd decided to accept that I'm not competing with you to find more Nikos Kladis paintings.'

'It has nothing to do with paintings; I'm afraid my problem is simply you!'

She looked at him expecting to see in his face the mocking amusement she often seemed to have caused, but it was disconcerting to find him looking serious and sad.

'I'm *not* your problem,' she managed to insist. 'I'm free, and long past twenty-one – responsible for myself in other words. If Mondhiki still doesn't want me I shall go sedately home, not throw myself off the nearest cliff in deep despair.'

Pierre shook his head regretfully, like a teacher whose pupil had come up with the wrong answer. 'You haven't even identified my problem – Evgenia did, of course, but I should have expected that.' He lifted his hands in a little gesture that said that whatever it was was put aside. 'May I just beg you to remember where you are? This is Greece, not rural England; memories are long here and violence has never been far below the surface even when blood wasn't actually flowing down the gutters.' He put a gentle finger over her mouth to stop her interrupting. 'I don't mean that the Kladis family would do you any harm; but tragic things have happened – I'd stake my life on that – and they are still living with them as best they can; you might upset whatever equilibrium they *have* managed to achieve.'

She heard the gravity of what he said, and had to acknowledge it, but then went on gravely herself. 'I'm not going out of curiosity or pique or because I can't think of anything else to do. Up on Parnassus yesterday I had the certainty that my grandfather was involved in whatever happened . . . and to some extent, therefore, I'm involved myself. Maybe whatever equilibrium they've achieved at Mondhiki is wrong and *should* be disturbed. I have to try to find out, that's all.'

Pierre was silent for a moment, then, switching on the ignition, he found something to say. 'You aren't nearly Italian enough – they're usually much more persuadable.'

'I know,' Anna agreed apologetically, 'but I did say my father abandoned us very early on.'

Only a little further along the road they had to stop again because the bus in front of them suddenly pulled up almost nose to nose with a large lorry coming the other way. Spectators appeared on the scene as if by magic . . . the stage was set and their amusement for the day was now assured. Pierre wound down his window to hear what was being said and, with his attention fixed on the dialogue outside, it seemed to Anna that it was safe to look at him. She might not remember for long the curve of brow and cheek-bone, or the way his schooled mouth changed when he smiled; but she *would* see in her mind's eye his brown hands lying loosely on the steering-wheel. Hands fixed themselves in her memory, and his were beautiful.

'You like this country . . . these people, don't you?' she suggested suddenly, and he turned to smile at her.

'Very much – they can even make a philosophical debate out of a traffic jam! I've been in places where a local war would have broken out by now.'

Popular opinion was settling the dispute: both bus and lorry would retreat a little at the same time – no dishonour in that – and realign themselves differently; thus a collision could be avoided and the traffic start to flow again.

On the move once more, it was Pierre's turn to ask a question. 'What are you going to do – fly back to Corfu?'

'No, take the ferry tomorrow, I think. I'll stay at the Phoenix tonight.'

'Would you like to consider another idea?' he suggested quietly. 'Shall we pretend just for today that the world's our oyster . . . that we can forget all the rules and duties and worries that tie us up in knots?'

She didn't answer for a moment or two. 'I thought you decided last night that it wasn't possible,' she finally pointed out.

'I did, but perhaps the gods will allow us just one day stolen out of time. Will you come to another place I want you to see? You must make up your mind soon because we'd have to turn off right at Eleusis, not left.'

'Then let's turn right,' she said slowly . . . and so they did, and came at last to Epidaurus, sanctuary of Asclepius, god of healing, and also the site of the loveliest theatre in all Greece.

Throughout the long leisurely afternoon they wandered about, content to be together in a place that, like Delphi, had its own unmistakable, unforgettable spirit of serenity and grace. Finally Anna climbed to the top-most tier of stone seats, while Pierre, as she had asked him to, stood in the centre of the orchestra far down below and spoke some lines of verse. She'd left the choice to him, but what she listened to – clear, beautiful, and inevitable, it seemed – was Prospero speaking . . .

These our actors
As I foretold you, were all spirits and
Are melted into air, into thin air:
. . . We are such stuff
As dreams are made of, and our little life
Is rounded with a sleep.

Then, because she didn't trust herself to descend straightaway, he climbed up to where she sat, and took her hand to guide her down.

'It's a longish drive back to Athens,' he said when they finally got back to the car again. 'May we stop somewhere on the way and make an early start in the morning?'

Anna nodded, aware by now of how their stolen day was bound to end . . . it couldn't end in any other way. As dusk fell they stopped at a roadside taverna offering accommodation as well as food, and because nothing could go wrong with this day stolen out of time it was as clean as a new pin, and a smiling proprietress offered them freshly-caught fish if they would only be content to drink a little wine while she cooked it for them. They sat on a verandah rather like Evgenia's at Arachova, and watched the stars come out in the darkening sky.

'Tomorrow, Anna . . . what shall we do tomorrow?' Pierre asked, watching her as she watched night fall – head tilted back revealing the delicate line of jaw-bone and throat. His question seemed to suggest that they had all the time in the world in front of them but she gravely shook her head.

'*We* don't have tomorrow; we'll drive to Athens, where you will catch a flight to Paris, and I shall take the ferry to Corfu. I've made you late already . . . Amélie will want to see you back.'

'My daughter may not even have noticed that I've been away,' he said truthfully, then smiled with sad wryness at the expression on Anna's face. 'She leads a very busy life, you see! It's true that school hours are long in France, and other things have to be squeezed in as well – piano lessons, dancing, riding . . . but she's already dangerously aware of the world her mother inhabits so successfully and begins to think of it as the real world. That's why I stay, Anna – to prevent her being spoiled if I can.' Anna didn't answer, but simply put out her hand and felt him cover it with his own. 'There's one other thing to say before the lady of the house brings our dinner,' he went on. 'You don't have to let me sleep with you tonight – she has two rooms.'

Anna took time to think about this. 'Why give her so much bother?' she suggested after a moment, and watched him smile.

If the day had been perfect, so was the night that followed . . . their coming-together full of mutual delight, passion offered and taken, tenderness and even laughter shared afterwards.

'I hope you now know what "all the fuss was about",' Pierre quoted gently, when she lay in his arms. His fingers traced the outline of her mouth. 'I was right . . . the *princesse lointaine* was a disguise.'

'And I know something I didn't know before,' she said when she had kissed his fingers, each one in turn. 'Shared need is wonderful, but not what matters most – it's the knowledge that, even if it's only for a little while, you've become part of someone else; I was afraid that would never happen to me . . . now it has.' She turned her head away to look out of the window. 'It's dawn already . . . another day, but this one doesn't belong to us.' She tried to smile at him but her lips trembled.

His only answer was to bury his face against her hair and hold her close until the morning light filled the room.

The return journey didn't take very long, and there was nothing that needed to be said until Pierre stopped the car at the entrance to the hotel.

'After Corfu, what then . . . back to Oxford?'

'I'm not sure,' Anna said. 'The tenants who share my

house would like to buy it. I must think about that and decide what to do – perhaps this is the moment to sell it and move to Rome. My mother would like that. She's lonely now without Enrico.'

'This is all wrong,' Pierre suddenly burst out. 'Yesterday was *meant* to last – for the rest of our lives.'

She leaned forward to leave a brief, sweet kiss on his mouth. 'No it wasn't. We knew what we were being given . . . just a day and a night we might never forget. You still have a small daughter who needs you.'

He framed her face in his hands. 'My love, I want you to know this. Amélie wasn't the careless result of lust – she was wanted then, and still is. But what happened last night I shan't find again . . . I shan't ever look for it again.' Then he released her and fumbled in his wallet for a card which he tucked into the pocket of her jacket with unsteady fingers. 'My whereabouts in Paris – if you ever need me I'll come . . . Promise to remember that at least.'

She nodded, but didn't answer, knowing that whatever difficulties she got into in future must be for her to solve. Her hand found the door-handle and she opened the door. 'Don't get out, please – just drive away.'

A moment later she was gone, and he lost sight of her inside the hotel.

At the airport half an hour later Pierre was offered a seat on a flight already waiting on the tarmac. Being hustled through the formalities of checking in, explaining the Kladis paintings which he'd taken out of their frames and carried in a large folder, these things kept his mind occupied. It was only when he found his seat on the plane and there was nothing more to do that loneliness more desolate than he'd ever known washed over him. This was how life would be from now on – meaningless. Were the gods above howling with laughter? Another self-sufficient human tripped and sent headlong, just when he least expected it to happen? And was Anna as unhappy as he was himself? That thought hurt more than anything else. Beside him a fellow-passenger introduced herself and spent the first ten minutes of the flight trying to get him to take an interest her – after all she *was* an American journalist on an important European assignment. But he barely heard what she said, and she spent the rest of the time composing an article that would do justice to her dislike of the men who seemed to litter the civilized world; they were supercilious and arrogant . . . and so very often French!

Eleven

Anna's room at the Phoenix Hotel looked even less appealing than it had before – and with the window closed it was airless, with it open the noise of the traffic deafened her. She told herself that it was the comparison with Evgenia's charming house at Arachova that made this seem so unbearable. Then she made the mistake of staring at herself in the dressing-table mirror. The glass was flawed – it was that kind of hotel – and the face that stared back at her looked tragic enough for a Greek heroine. She tried to make it smile, but felt much more like weeping instead. The truth was simple enough, but she must reduce it to something manageable; she was no better than a child with a borrowed toy who'd been made to return it where it properly belonged, but it hurt . . . dear heaven, how it hurt.

At last a glimmer of comfort penetrated the fog of misery she was in; at least there was no need to stay where she was, in a crowded, noisy city that she didn't like. A call to the shipping office produced the offer of an armchair in the saloon on the night ferry to Corfu, although the cabins had all been taken. She accepted the armchair, rang the Astron Hotel in Corfu Town, and finally booked a taxi to take her to the ferry terminal at Patras that evening. Eased by the knowledge that she wouldn't have to spend another night in Athens, she tried to smile at the mirror again . . . It still wasn't very successful, but she was in control of herself again, not mindlessly going round and round on a treadmill of despair.

She made herself write a thank-you letter to Arachova, and if the version that was sent suggested a single, uninterrupted drive back to Athens, Evgenia herself had suggested that there were lies and lies and some were permissible. Instead of telephoning Rome, she also wrote to her mother to explain that she was going back to Corfu. Conversations were more difficult to edit than letters, and in any case Nicola had never properly understood why she'd gone to Corfu at all.

She ate some supper in the hotel's cheerless dining-room, and then waited for her taxi to arrive – glad to be leaving a city that, except for its incomparable ruins on the Acropolis, she hadn't much enjoyed. Driving away from it, her mind veered to a different capital, but she refused to think of Pierre returning to a house in the Rue Jacob that he shared with a clever, celebrated Parisienne and a precocious child.

The night was windless and the short voyage up through the Ionian Sea smooth and uneventful. They docked early the next morning and she stepped ashore with the feeling of having returned to a place that was familiar and friendly. The old town's pastel colours glowed in the dazzling light and seemed to make her welcome.

She hired two boys to carry her luggage to the hotel, and walked beside them enjoying the inevitable barrage of questions: she was German, of course, being so fair? American then, being so obviously wealthy? And why was the kyria alone, being still quite young and nice to look at? She thanked them for this kindness, invented a mythical fiancé trapped by work in London, and finally persuaded them to accept some money in return for helping her.

With the long morning ahead of her, she could find an Italian-speaking hairdresser to cut her hair, hire the car she would need tomorrow, and return to the Tourist Office to let Andreas know that she was back on Corfu.

Andreas's thin, dark face lit up when she walked in. 'I didn't expect to see you again,' he told her. 'If it means you prefer our island to the mainland then I'm very glad. But I hope your visit to Athens was successful.'

'It was – entirely thanks to you. I was even able to meet

a man who fought with my grandfather during the war – they were up on Parnassus together. He's very old now but he clearly remembered Steven Curtis. The most wonderful thing of all was that he'd kept two books belonging to my grandfather and insisted on giving them to me.'

'Of course he should have done,' Andreas said seriously, '. . . nevertheless, he did well.' Then he smiled at Anna. 'Now, what else can I do for you?'

'Absolutely nothing; I'm just here to thank you and say goodbye. I'm going to visit Mondhiki again; after that I'll leave the way I first arrived, by the Brindisi ferry. I prefer ships to aeroplanes!'

Then, as she was on the point of leaving, the door was pushed open and a thick-set, middle-aged man strode in. His angry flood of Greek broke into their conversation, with no apology to Anna and an ill-tempered thump on the desk for Andreas in case he was missing the finer points of the man's diatribe. Then he turned and marched out, unable to slam the door as he went out because it was fastened back.

'Not a visitor, at least,' Anna ventured after a glance at Andrea's taut face. 'I'm glad about that.'

'No, not a visitor; just someone who thinks he's the only man who matters in Corfu Town. He's not the mayor, nor the chief of police, and certainly not the Archbishop! – just Loukas Pandelios, rich, powerful, and disliked by many people.' Andreas looked down at his hands, saw them still shaking, and thrust them into the pockets of his jacket.

'Why was he so objectionable just now?' Anna asked. 'Or is that how he always behaves?'

'Yes, to minions like me, although he crawls on his nose to the people who have more money than he's got himself. He's a lawyer, like his father before him – another very unpleasant man – but Loukas has got rich by buying land and selling it to the developers who are doing so much to spoil this island.'

'Shouldn't he stay on good terms with you – after all you help the tourists he must want to see here?'

Andreas gave a tired shrug. 'I tried to warn someone against selling to him. Loukas got to hear about that, and wants to get me fired. My boss is a fair man . . . I shall probably be all right as long as I don't upset the great Pandelios again!' He smiled at Anna because she was looking upset. '*Someone* will murder him one of these days, but it won't be me, so don't look so anxious, please.'

'Well at least give me the name of your boss,' she insisted. 'I want to write and tell him how kind you've been – I'll say that this office can't possibly do without you.'

He produced a card, and as she took it, caught hold of her hand and kissed it. Then he walked with her to the door and opened it just as another customer came in. She could only smile goodbye and walk away, still thinking of the unpleasant little scene she'd had to watch a few moments before. On a fair morning in late-spring Corfu looked to be the Shangri-La her grandfather seemed to have found it, but it wasn't Heaven on earth after all – it had its share of men like Loukas Pandelios.

She spent the afternoon doing what all visitors did – looking at the marvellous ikons and frescoes in the Orthodox Cathedral, dipping into ancient Corfu at the Archeological Museum, and finally climbing to the top of the Paleó Froúrio – as Pierre had invited her to – simply to sit down to rest and admire the stunning view. There, at least, it seemed permissible to think about him and to face the truth that without him she was back to being incomplete again, and would be from now on. He'd been a perfect lover, but it was the happiness of the day they'd spent together that seemed most totally unexpected and most irreplaceable. She found herself praying that Amélie *had* noticed he'd been away, and found the time to run and kiss him.

Back at the hotel, facing the prospect of dinner on her own, she suddenly telephoned the Corfu Palace and asked if Mr and Mrs Lambert were still staying there. A moment later Irene cautiously enquired who was calling.

'It's Anna Rasini, Irene, delighted to find you still here. I got back today from Athens, and couldn't help wondering how you're getting on.'

'Oh, my dear, I'm so pleased to hear your lovely accent,' said Irene, with a slight quaver in her own voice. 'To think you're back just *now* when I do so need someone to talk to . . . It's Saint Spiros's doing. I expect. I prayed to him real hard for help this afternoon.'

'Poor girl, what's wrong . . . Is something the matter with George.'

'No, but he's not here; he flew to Athens this morning; and I was dreading a night alone. If you'd just come right over we could have dinner downstairs, and talk . . . Now don't say you can't come.'

Anna promised to arrive in good time, but hung up puzzling over the note almost of panic in Irene Lambert's voice. Irene might not enjoy spending a night on her own in a foreign hotel, but in the Corfu Palace she was scarcely going to be laid open to rape or abduction for the white slave traffic. It seemed most likely that her heart still wasn't in the adventure of acquiring a home in the Ionian Sea, so one of them – she or George – was going to be unhappy. But, settled in the hotel dining-room with her half an hour later, Anna had to acknowledge that her American friend had reason to be anxious. George had got the bit between his teeth and when that happened, said Irene with a mixture of pride and despair, there really was no holding him.

'Why is he in Athens?' Anna asked, wondering where to begin.

'To find the best lawyer he can. He needs the best, he reckons, to outsmart Pandelios.'

Anna stared at her with her own face full of astonishment. 'I know Corfu's a small island, but even so, it's a strange coincidence. I bumped into someone by that name this morning – a thoroughly obnoxious, bullying sort of man.'

'That's Loukas Pandelios,' Irene said with certainty. 'You've got *him* nailed down.'

Anna shook her head. 'I haven't got anything nailed down. Start at the beginning, please, because I'm all at sea.'

Now rather pleased not to be having to share the recital with George, Irene took a deep breath and plunged in. 'It was all going very well to begin with . . . too well from my point of view if I'm honest, because I'm not as set on living here as George is. Never mind that; a lawyer in the town contacted the Lambekis family living in Australia and they were only too pleased to be paid for having a ruin taken off their hands. George was already drawing up plans – a room added here, a courtyard there, proper bathrooms . . . you know the sort of thing. Then out of the blue comes a letter from Pandelios telling George to back off because he's already got *his* eye on it – not the ruin but the land.'

'To "develop" it,' Anna put in, 'that's what he does: develop and ruin as much of Corfu as he can get his hands on.' She saw in her mind's eye the face of Loukas Pandelios, and feared for George's dream, if that was what it was, of recreating the home his family had once lived in. 'Irene, does your husband know what he's up against?' she finally asked. 'Pandelios has the advantage of being a local man, but add to that the fact that he's powerful and not accustomed to being beaten.'

'Just the sort of opponent George likes,' Irene had to admit. 'You know how it is with men, Anna – they think they want something, but it's no big deal. Tell them they can't have it, though, because someone tougher and pushier wants it too, and it becomes the thing they can't live without. That's how it is with George. He really *wants* his family's home.'

'Then I hope a clever Athenian lawyer can help him get it,' Anna said definitely. She looked at her companion across the table. 'What about you, though? Wouldn't you be thankful in your heart of hearts if it didn't work out and you could go back to New York knowing that you needn't give Corfu another thought?'

Irene took time to consider how to reply. 'A week ago I'd have been glad for the lawyer here to say that the family wouldn't sell, even though I knew that George really wants that bit of Greek land and the ruin that sits on it. But the moment he's told by someone else to forget that it's where his family began is the moment that changes things. He'll fight, my dear, and I'll be right behind him.'

'I'm glad,' Anna said, now smiling at her. 'What George needs is for his Australian kith and kin to say that they'll only sell to *him*. Pray to St Spiridhon for that, Irene, because Pandelios will offer them more money, I'm afraid – anything not to lose what he's decided he wants.'

'I'll pray hard, Anna, and I'll warn George to watch his back. Now, that's enough about the Lamberts – what about you? I didn't think you meant to come back once you'd left.'

'I didn't, but something happened in Athens to make me change my mind. It may well be a waste of time, but I'm going to have one more go at getting my foot inside the door at Mondhiki before I finally give up and admit defeat.' She smiled at Irene. 'We have a saying at home – "it's dogged as does it"!'

Irene considered her for a moment, wondering whether the change she thought she saw was imaginary or not. 'What happened to that nice Frenchman, Mr Bouchard? Well, I thought he was just lovely; I'm not sure I can say the same for you; you acted like a cat with its fur rubbed the wrong way!'

Prepared for the question, Anna reckoned she could have produced a pat enough answer. Taken unawares, she struggled to hide a sudden stab of pain that made it hard to speak. 'We got off to a bad start,' she finally managed to say. 'Here, we only seemed to be getting in each other's way. Then when we met again on the mainland we went to Delphi together; and that turned out to be very . . . very enjoyable.' She tried to smile at the hopeful expression on Irene's face. 'But no holiday romance – he's gone home to a wife and daughter in Paris.'

Irene nodded, unsurprised by this news. 'He was bound to belong to someone already; the nice ones always do.' She gave a little sigh that said life was full of such disappointments and Anna seized the chance to lead the conversation back to the Lamberts' own affairs.

'If the lawyers in Athens think that Pandelios can't be stopped, what then – will George give up?'

Irene nodded again, looking sadder still. 'He knows he's at a disadvantage, coming from outside. But he'll never stop regretting it if he loses – it's seemed to him that he was meant to come here and set the place to rights.'

Anna visualized again the flushed, angry face of the man who had pounded Andreas's desk. He was surely the very opposite of the noble Greek ideal of nothing to excess – obviously a glutton for food and wine, but too fond of money as well and the power it could buy. It would be poetic justice if he didn't live much longer to enjoy such pleasures, but Nemesis couldn't always be relied on to deliver punishment where it was deserved. Loukas Pandelios would probably live to a great age to go on browbeating other people and taking what he wanted from them. How long would it be before Corfu was ruined by such men, just as the Mediterranean coasts of France and Spain had already been ruined?

'It's time I took myself back to the Astron,' Anna said at last. 'I'll be setting off early tomorrow before George gets back, but I'll ring you to find out what happened.' She stood up to leave, but then held out her hands to Irene. 'I'm not quite sure what to pray for – because I can't help feeling that *you*'re torn, too, wanting whatever George needs to make him happy, but wishing on your own account that you could just go home!'

Irene smiled wistfully. 'Yes, I'd be happy to forget about Corfu now, although I'll always be glad we came to see it. But George *won't* forget, and much more than anything for myself I want *him* to be happy. If he came back from Athens and said, "Honey, get ready to live here, please," I'd do just *that*; but I'm afraid it's not going to happen.'

Anna smiled at her with sudden affection. 'I shan't feel too sorry for him even if he's disappointed. He has a very nice wife to make up for it!' Then she kissed Irene goodnight and went out into the lobby to ask for a taxi to be called.

Twelve

The drive to Mondhiki the next morning was almost uneventful, not counting a brush with a laden donkey who suddenly took exception to being overtaken, and a misunderstanding with a bus that looked as if it would never move again but decided to roar into life just as she went by. Still, on the whole she felt pleased with herself – she was mastering the art of driving a strange car on a foreign island with considerable aplomb. The omens looked so encouraging that she was even beginning to consider the possibility of being made welcome at the end of her journey.

Aware, now, of what to look out for, she spotted the track that led to Mondhiki and tried to make up her mind as she bumped and rattled along it whether to leave the car as she'd done before or drive up to the courtyard in full view of anyone who might be inside the house. She finally stopped halfway between the two, opened the driver's door, and stepped out – on to a loose lump of stone that slid sideways into a gully running beside the track, taking her with it.

One moment she'd been sitting calmly in the car; the next she was sprawling in the dusty bottom of the gully, with an exquisite pain shooting through the ankle she'd twisted as the stone gave way. The omens had obviously lied, and this ill-timed joke on the part of the gods was a much surer sign that she should never have come after all.

After a moment or two she managed to get on to all fours and then to stand upright, balanced on one leg, leaning against the car. Driving it was out of the question, but if she could only get inside and sit down, perhaps the pain would gradually lessen. Weeping with exasperation at her own stupidity she was considering how to climb out of the ditch when the remembered voice of Petros Kladis spoke behind her.

'I didn't expect to see you again. But if you were coming to the house what are you doing down there?'

'I fell when I got out of the car, and if you didn't leave loose chunks of stone lying around the place I wouldn't now be standing on one leg wondering what to do next.' She sounded merely cross, but he couldn't miss the distress in her face, and the next moment he was in the ditch beside her.

'I'm sorry . . . you're hurt and I didn't realize it.' She was picked up and put over his shoulder while with some effort he hauled them both back on to the track again. Then, when she'd been deposited in the passenger seat, and he'd climbed in beside her, Anna put out a grubby hand to stop him starting the car.

'I came to thank you and your father for the painting – it means a great deal to me to have it because I had only a photograph to tell me what my grandfather looked like. But now all I've done is make a nuisance of myself. I don't think I *can* drive the car for the moment, so you're stuck with me even when you'd much rather I went away.' Her voice wobbled and she was further betrayed by the tears that she had to smear away. But the sight of her face now streaked with dirt at least had the effect of making Petros smile.

'I think you need a wash, a drink, and somewhere to rest your ankle – let's go back to the house.'

She thought of Stefanos Kladis no doubt there as well, but decided that she must leave Petros to deal with him. Her own task was to pray to St Spiridhon that her ankle was only sprained, not broken; otherwise she could see nothing but difficulty and stress ahead.

Petros parked the car as close to the courtyard as he could get, then turned to look at her. 'Wait there while I go and find Eleni – we need *her* help as well, I think.'

He disappeared inside the house and returned a moment or two later with the dark-haired girl she'd met on her first visit. Eleni opened the car door, looking serious but not hostile. 'Petros says you've hurt your ankle. I'll look at it when he's carried you indoors.'

'I can hop,' Anna suggested with a faint hope of making her smile.

'That would be silly,' she was told gravely, 'when you don't have to.' Then Eleni stepped aside and led the way into the house.

There was no one else in the large room they went into and for this at least Anna was grateful; Stephanos Kladis would have to be met before long, but she didn't feel like facing him just yet. Instead, she was lowered on to a sofa and Eleni knelt beside her to remove her sandal. The Greek girl had cool, gentle hands that felt skilful even though it hurt to be made to move her foot this way and that. At last Eleni nodded as if satisfied.

'I'm sure it isn't broken, only wrenched,' she said firmly. 'But you won't be able to walk on it for a day or two. Stay there – I shall be back soon.' With that she went out of the room, and it was Petros's turn to say something.

'You can believe what my cousin decides – she is very good at treating people as well as animals.'

'I'm sure of it,' Anna agreed quickly, 'but is there a taverna nearby where I could stay? Your father won't want me here.' With a perfect excuse to become a guest at Mondhiki, she was irritated with herself to find that the one thing she now wanted was to get away. It was Pierre's fault – she could hear the echo of his voice suggesting that her visit might do nothing but upset this unhappy family.

'What my father might prefer,' Petros answered, 'is not what he will think is proper. He'll say that you must stay until your ankle is mended. Now I'll leave Eleni to look after you because my mother is no longer alive; the only other woman in the house is my great-aunt, Theodora Kladis, but she is very old now.'

He lifted his hand in a little salute and went away just as Eleni returned with a bowl, flannel and a towel for Anna to wash the dirt off her face and hands. Another trip outside produced another bowl – of ice-cold water this time – with which she bathed her patient's ankle, and then it was anointed with something smelling sweetly of herbs and strapped up.

'Thank you, Eleni,' Anna said gratefully. 'It feels so much more comfortable like that.' The Greek girl smiled wholeheartedly for the first time and the change in her usually sombre face was startling.

'I have things I can lend you,' she offered shyly, '. . . not pretty like yours, I expect, but . . .' then she stopped because Anna was shaking her head.

'Thank you, but there's no need. All my luggage is in the car – I was going from here to catch the ferry to Brindisi.' It was true, she told herself, even though it omitted the fact that she'd hoped to stay at Mondhiki first. Eleni looked relieved not to have to share her meagre wardrobe with a girl obviously used to finer things, and now almost cheerfully recommended her to rest until lunch-time came.

'My great-aunt Theodora will join us then,' she added. 'She won't say very much in English, but she understands it quite well.'

Then she walked away, leaving Anna to contemplate the prospect of a meal shared with an ancient, untalkative Greek lady and a host who would only tolerate her as a guest because he felt that he had to. Pierre had been right, she realized; she'd invaded Stefanos Kladis's home much too carelessly.

At the far end of the huge room the servant she'd met on her first visit moved about, quietly preparing food and laying the table on the terrace outside. Her deliberate way of working was soothing to watch, and about them the old house seemed settled in some age-old state of serenity; whatever storms it had witnessed seemed to be over now. Not quite asleep, Anna lay where she'd been told to stay, trying to imagine what it had been like when Steven Curtis had come with his young friends.

A noise close by disturbed her and she opened her eyes to find that she was being stared at by an older version of Petros Kladis. This was the moment to confront his father – a grey-haired, solidly-built man whose craggy face gave away nothing of what was in his mind.

He didn't speak at once and Anna struggled to say something herself. 'I'm sorry that I can't apologize in Greek, Mr Kladis, for being here at all, much less for being such a nuisance. I'll leave as soon as I can.'

'You were not invited, it is true,' he answered with the deliberate care of someone feeling his way in an unfamiliar language. 'But you now must stay while your ankle mends. Eleni will look after you, but she has work to do and no time to waste.'

'I understand,' Anna said, 'and I'll be as little trouble to her as I can.' She stared at his unyielding expression for a moment. 'I came to thank you for the portrait of my grandfather. He died long before I was born, but I know that he loved coming here, and that your father was his dear friend.'

If she hoped for something friendly in reply, she was disappointed. Stefanos's face looked even more shuttered than before. 'I was a small child when Steven Curtis was last here – I have nothing to tell you about him. Like my father, he is long dead, and the past is buried with them.'

Long dead but *not* forgotten, Anna thought; he might school his face, but she could still hear the throb of emotion in his deep voice: what was it – grief, anger, undying resentment because Steven Curtis had been English, as she was herself? But the question couldn't be put into words, and she felt relieved when he gave a little nod to signify that the conversation was over. He'd done his duty as her host, and probably hoped not to have to speak to her again until it was time to say goodbye.

Eleni came back into the room to say that lunch was ready – where did Anna want to eat? Indoors, or with the rest of them on the terrace?

'Tell me where I shall be the least trouble,' Anna suggested.

'A guest is not a trouble,' Eleni said gravely. 'We don't see many visitors; I hope you'll eat with us.'

'Then help me hop outside, please – I'd rather not have to be carried.'

With Eleni steadying her, she made ungainly progress to the terrace and was settled there with her foot propped up on a stool by the time Stefanos reappeared. Then Petros came out, followed by a small lady dressed in black from head to foot – the life-long uniform of a Greek widow. She was introduced to Anna as Petros's great-aunt Theodora.

The old lady stared at their guest with bright, dark eyes set in a lined face that had once been very beautiful. Her lips moved silently as if she was having a conversation with herself, but Anna decided that this was a habit she'd acquired in a household whose other members were mostly too busy to talk to her; she was anything but senile, and she was perfectly well aware of the identity of the stranger at the table.

The food they ate was simple, but beautifully prepared and presented; either Maria, the servant who waited on them, was the artist in the kitchen, or Eleni was. There was little conversation, and what there was she owed to Petros, who took the trouble to ask about her visit to Athens.

'I also went to Delphi,' she said with a defiant look at Stefano Kladis, seated at the head of the table. 'I discovered that Mount Parnassus was where my grandfather was killed with the partisans; I particularly wanted to go there.'

The quality of the silence round the table insisted that she'd told them something they didn't know. Stephanos's deep-set eyes met hers for a moment but, if he was aware of having been offered a challenge, he simply ignored it and took another sip of wine. Anna's glance moved on round the table and she found that she was being stared at in her turn by Theodora Kladis – a woman who, because of the age she was, must surely have known at first-hand things that her nephew could only have learned afterwards. But even without the language problem it seemed unlikely that she would talk.

Greek women of her generation had been conditioned to stay in the background, entirely subservient to the men who ruled their lives.

With the meal over, Eleni went back to her next task, the old lady went indoors to rest, and Stephanos also disappeared. Only Petros lingered to ask Anna where she wanted to spend the afternoon – out on the terrace or indoors.

'Out here, please,' she answered. 'It's beautiful, with so many things blooming at once – different from my rather ordered garden at home.'

Petros still lingered, and finally put into words what had to be said. 'I'm sorry about your grandfather, Anna – we didn't know that he died for Greece; you must have thought it very strange that we didn't welcome you the first time you came.'

She ignored that but hesitated over what to say next. 'I'm sure there's work waiting for you, but could you talk to me for a few minutes?' She sounded so diffident that his face relaxed into the shy smile he shared with Eleni.

'You've probably noticed that we don't talk much at Mondhiki, but I'll do my best!'

'Your father refuses to say anything at all,' she pointed out, 'but I can't help feeling that what I hoped to find out *is* known here. My grandfather came back year after year; he and *your* grandfather, Nikos Kladis, were best friends – Steven Curtis was "*koumbaros*" to your father, another Steven – and they were still in touch during the war through some underground partisan channel. We know what happened to my grandfather at the beginning of 1944, but yours simply seemed to disappear. Even the art experts in Corfu Town didn't know what became of him or his marvellous paintings.'

There was a little silence and she waited for Petros to repeat what he'd said before, that it was ancient history, best forgotten. But, perhaps because he couldn't resist the pleading in her face, he finally began to talk.

'The people in Corfu Town are probably too ashamed to tell you what they know,' he answered slowly. 'I don't know the whole story even now, but I know some of it. Nikos married a girl called Katerina Pappas in the year before the war began. She was the talented and much-loved daughter of a doctor in Corfu Town, and she and Nikos were very happy together. The following summer my father was born and, as you say, Steven Curtis was his godfather. Then war was declared and Nikos and Steven never saw each other again. But my grandfather died before yours did – in a German concentration camp.'

After a moment's shocked silence Anna found something to say. 'There was tragedy in that, but surely no shame,'

'There was *much* shame,' Petros insisted. 'The Pappas family were Corfiot Jews, settled here for many generations. They were betrayed to the Germans by a *Greek* – Dr Pappas and his wife first, and then Katerina. Nikos went to try to free her but was caught himself – he was a partisan, of course; and it was a convenient way of eliminating him. The children, Stefanos and Dassia, were hidden here at Mondhiki, so they survived.'

Anna swallowed the lump in her throat and huskily spoke of someone else. 'What happened to Athina? In Athens I was given the books my grandfather had with him on Parnassus. There was a scribbled note inside from Nikos that mentioned Athina's beautiful little daughter and an unpleasant husband.'

Petros now seemed to be withdrawn into a past that was as real to him as if he'd lived through it. 'Athina left her husband after Nikos and Katerina were seized; she came here with her daughter, and drowned not long afterwards – not in our bay, in another one further down the coast.'

'And the daughter grew up to be Eleni's mother,' Anna said with difficulty, 'but she isn't here either.'

'She was married to a man called Kostalis, much older than herself. When he died she became a nun; she's that still, in a convent in Athens.'

Anna nodded, familiar with that part of the story already, but there was one final question to ask. 'Who betrayed the Pappas family – was that ever discovered?'

'It didn't need discovering,' Petros answered roughly. 'Athina's husband boasted to her afterwards of what he'd done. That was when she walked out. I don't know why, but he'd come to hate her and the Kladis family, so it seemed a neat revenge.'

'Dear God, what wickedness!' Anna buried her face in her hands, thinking how right Pierre had been. There'd been too much tragedy, and all she'd done by coming here was to make these people relieve it again. 'I hope Athina's husband got the punishment he deserved,' she said finally.

'Not at all – Yorgos Pandelios was much too big a man to be punished; unlike everyone else, he was even richer at the end of the war than when it started. He married again, and had a son who still lives in Corfu Town.'

'It seems incredible,' Anna said slowly, 'but I think I met him by chance – an odious man called Loukas Pandelios?' She saw Petros nod, but went on herself. 'The law of co-incidence seems to work overtime here! I even heard about him again from some American friends of mine – he is trying to browbeat them into giving up some family land they're hoping to buy.'

'That sounds just like Loukas,' Petros said grimly. 'I ought to kill him for what his father did, and there are people here who hate him quite as much on his own account, but we live in what are supposed to be law-abiding days. He is rich and powerful, and very happily aware of the fact that his enemies can't touch him now.'

Anna touched Petros's hand where it rested on the table. 'Thank you for telling me all that. Pierre Bouchard, the Frenchman you met in Corfu Town, told me that I should only stir up old grief by coming. I refused to listen to him, but he was right.'

A fleeting smile touched the Greek's mouth. 'I made him angry, I'm afraid – he was right to say that we trust foreigners even less than we trust each other!'

She'd mentioned Pierre simply for the comfort of saying his name, but there was someone else who needed to be talked about. 'I know Eleni's been taken care of here, and she's had the good fortune to live in a place that's beautiful, but I've never seen a girl so in need of warmth and affection. Why does your father treat her like a servant?'

The expression on the dark face frowning at her across the table was a warning that she'd gone too far, and she waited for him to say that now she was interfering in things that didn't concern her. But what he actually said came as a surprise.

'I've offered to speak to my father, again and again. Each time Eleni has begged me not to; she feels useful here and doesn't want to go away. She's content at Mondhiki.'

He was too ready to believe so, Anna thought, of a girl who was given no option except to be useful. 'When did she last speak to someone of her own age apart from you? When did she wear something pretty instead of clothes that look like widow's weeds?' Anna realized that anger would alienate Petros and tried to speak more calmly. 'I'm not suggesting that she shouldn't go on living here . . . working here even; but why can't she be treated as though she's loved?'

As if he understood that real concern underlay the question he didn't get angry with her; instead, he spoke almost sadly. 'There are still things you don't understand about us, Anna. Greece *is* slowly hauling itself into the modern world, but old habits die hard; women here still aren't able to do whatever they want, unless perhaps they lead sophisticated lives in Athens. And there's something else to think about as well: Eleni is Pandelios's granddaughter; I doubt if my father can help remembering that whenever he looks at her. Memories are long in Greece.'

'"And the sins of the fathers shall be visited upon their children and upon their children's children" . . .' Anna quoted slowly. 'Yes, I had forgotten that.'

Petros watched her, unobserved because she was now lost in her own thoughts. He was aware of too many things that confused and troubled him . . . He still remembered her fragrance when he'd carried her into the house and knew that he wanted to touch her again, and stroke the softness of her bright hair. He'd told her more than his father would have wanted her to know; and he wished most of all that she had never come to Mondhiki, because now they wouldn't be able to forget her.

But Eleni chose that moment to come out on to the terrace, bringing a jug of water for Anna. If she wondered what had kept Petros there for so long, talking to their guest, she gave no sign of expecting to be told what the conversation had been about. She simply put down the tray, said that she would bathe Anna's ankle again before the evening meal, and went away again. Reminded that he'd been there too long himself, Petros got up and said that he would carry her indoors when she grew tired of the terrace. Then he walked away, and she was left alone to go over what she now knew of the Kladis family.

Thirteen

Supper was eaten indoors because when the sun went down in the evening in late April it was still too cool outside on the terrace. But it was an easier meal than lunch had been; Stefanos Kladis wasn't at home and in his absence even Eleni shared in the conversation, defending her opinions with a stubbornness that Anna found hopeful. Not all Petros's gentle teasing could shake her conviction that Corfu was the most beautiful of Greek islands, and Mondhiki the best that Corfu itself could offer. Flushed and almost pretty, she suggested that their guest should stay on when her ankle had mended, and learn to love the island as it deserved.

'It's very tempting,' Anna agreed, smiling at her. 'I must return to work, and also take some decisions about the future, but there's no reason why I shouldn't come back one day; Corfu feels like home already!'

An old voice suddenly spoke across the table. 'That's what your grandfather used to say.' Theodora watched the effect of this on Anna. 'I remember him, you know . . . you look like him.' But, as if her nephew had just walked into the room and forbidden her to go on talking, she apparently forgot what else she'd meant to say and insisted instead that she needed to go to bed. It was deeply frustrating not to be able to question her, but she *was* old, Anna reminded herself, and the old did tire suddenly. She would have to find another opportunity to talk to Theodora alone.

A household that rose at dawn retired early as well, and it wasn't long before Petros offered to carry Anna upstairs, but she firmly refused, insisting that she preferred the challenge of getting there under her own steam, despite the undignified business of going up sitting on one stair at a time. The reason for this was that in the course of the evening she felt sure she'd learned why Eleni stayed at Mondhiki. Even servitude was preferable when going away would mean leaving Petros Kladis; all the happiness she knew came from her certainty that at least he needed her there. But Anna knew also that again Pierre had been right, and the lonely, isolated, still-young man that Petros Kladis was could easily be dazzled by someone different from the few women he knew. The less he had to carry her about, the better.

Installed at last in bed in a room next to what seemed to be Mondhiki's only bathroom, Anna decided that her grandfather and his students must have bathed in the sea that lay on the other side of the house. In the morning she'd be able to see from her bedroom window the indescribable blue waters of the Ionian, and the path that led to the sea down a flower-sprinkled and wooded hillside. Eleni was quite right: Mondhiki *was* beautiful.

But there were other things to think about as well – for instance Stefanos's unexpected treatment of his aunt. He was respectful of her age, but there was something more that amounted to real affection – surprising in so harsh a man until Anna remembered that Theodora must have taken the place of his mother once Katerina Kladis had been seized by the Germans. Petros's position was also hard to define: he didn't challenge his father's authority, and yet from her observation during the long afternoon it seemed certain that he mostly ran the estate and supervised the men who worked it for them. And there was still the strange absence of Eleni's mother – why, after marriage and the birth of her child, had she suddenly turned her back on the world and chosen a totally different way of life?

The next morning Eleni brought coffee, bread and honey to her guest in bed, inspected her ankle, and pronounced it to be mending nicely.

'Thanks to you,' Anna said, 'you're a good nurse; in fact a born healer, I would guess. It feels so much better that you must stop waiting on me, please. I can't laze about while you keep working.'

'One more day's rest,' Eleni insisted with the firmness she occasionally showed, '. . . after that you should be able to walk on it.' She sat on the end of the bed, watching Anna spread honey on a piece of bread. 'What is Oxford like? I know your grandfather was a teacher there; Petros told me that.'

'It's ugly in parts, like most of our cities, but in other parts very beautiful . . . with ancient college buildings lost among lovely gardens and trees; everything stays green because we have a lot of rain! It's full of untidy, rumbustious students in term-time, and amazingly peaceful when they go home. I've lived there all my life, but now I'm thinking of leaving, to go and join with my mother in Rome.' She saw the Greek girl's expression change, and immediately apologized for her clumsiness. 'I'm sorry – forgive me, Eleni. You must still miss your own mother.'

'She preferred to be with the good sisters,' Eleni explained quietly. 'No one has ever told me why she was unhappy living a normal life with us . . . but she must have been, I think.'

It was Anna's strong conviction that if either Theodora or Stefanos knew the reason they should certainly have shared it with her, if only to lessen Eleni's painful sense of rejection.

'It couldn't have been that she didn't love you,' she insisted herself, 'there must have been some very strong religious vocation to make her give you up.'

Eleni answered this with a sad nod, then concentrated on her guest again; but suddenly her face changed. 'I know . . . Ernestine can take you down to the bay . . . Wouldn't you like that instead of sitting on the terrace all day?'

If Ernestine was the donkey met on her first visit, Anna thought it was tempting to opt for the terrace; but the pleasure in Eleni's face at the brilliance of her idea made it impossible to refuse.

'I'm not sure how Ernestine will feel about,' she pointed out cautiously, 'but if *she*'s game, so am I.'

It was a new expression for Eleni that, having been explained, set her giggling like the young girl she really was. Still laughing, she ran out of the room, promising to enquire how the donkey felt about an English passenger. Half an hour later Anna descended the stairs in the same way that she'd gone up, and found her steed waiting just below the terrace, happy to nibble at a succulent fennel bush while she had the chance.

On the table were the things that Eleni thought her guest might need – a basket holding grapes and a flask of water, an old rug, and a very large umbrella to be used as a sunshade.

'We have rain too,' she said with a grin, pointing at it.

Even the problem of getting a disabled rider aloft had been thought of: Anna was to hobble to the edge of the terrace; there, she could stand on her good leg while she hoisted the other one over Ernestine's back. It was accomplished rather well, Anna reckoned, given her lack of acquaintance to date with a breed of animal not noted for its co-operative spirit. Eleni then gave Ernestine the rug to carry as well, and they set off together round the side of the house.

The donkey knew the path down to the bay and had no objection to a route she enjoyed. The air was pleasantly resin-scented, and she liked the cushion of pine needles underneath her feet. Enjoying the journey too, Anna knew she wouldn't forget the moment when the deep shade of the woodland path gave way suddenly to dazzling light. They'd come to a small, half-moon bay of shingle and white sand, held by two dark-green, pine-covered spurs of land curving out into the sea like protecting arms. The water was sapphire coloured further out, green as emeralds where it ran in shallowly over the sand. Here, surely, had been her grandfather's enchanted place.

Satisfied that Anna had been made comfortable, Eleni promised to come back for her at lunch-time and then mounted Ernestine herself for the ride home. Anna took a book out of her bag but made no attempt to read; it was enough for the moment to listen to the whisper of the sea against a small outcrop of rocks – the perfect place for a swimmer to launch out into deep water – and to imagine how life had been in this idyllic place before war had come to tear it to pieces. The contrast between then and now seemed more, not less, cruel for the enchantment of the setting. There should have been comfort in so much beauty, but it seemed to make the tragedy worse. Athina Pandelios hadn't drowned here, but probably in a nearby bay that was just as lovely. And Nikos, Katerina, and Steven Curtis had also not only died much too young but, in their dying, had wrecked other lives as well.

Anna came at last to her own heart's grief. She wouldn't die of it; happiness couldn't depend entirely on just one other human being. Gradually, a day at a time, she'd learn not to miss a man she'd scarcely had a chance to get to know. He would forget her, and slowly she would forget him . . . but for now, dear God, how lonely it was without him.

She heard the jingle of Ernestine's harness too late to wipe away the tears that trickled down her face and Petros saw them as he suddenly sat down beside her.

'You were weeping because you were cross last time,' he pointed out, '. . . but you can't be angry now.'

Anna fumbled in her bag for a tissue, mopped her cheeks, and tried to smile at him. 'I was having a little wallow in sadness instead! Contrary to appearances, I don't make habit of bursting into tears; but it's the effect this country is having on me.'

'They're old tragedies, better forgotten. I told you that before,' he said with sudden gentleness, and saw her shake her head.

'But not forgotten yet,' she pointed out. 'Not properly admitted even. I think that's what troubles the people who are still here.'

He stared at her face, shadowed by the umbrella, but

nothing could dim the brightness of her hair. It would feel like silk, he thought, if he allowed himself to touch it.

'Will you go away when your ankle is mended?' he asked in a low voice. 'I'd like you to stay . . . Couldn't you do that, Anna?'

She turned to look at him and saw the entreaty in his face. 'I'd be of no use to Mondhiki,' she had to point out. 'I'm a writer, Petros, leading a different kind of life altogether, I can't do any of the things that Eleni does so beautifully.' In case that wasn't enough to convince him, she held up her hand to stop him speaking. 'There's another problem as well. I was weeping for myself just now, as well as for everything that's happened here. I met someone I thought I didn't like, then fell in love with him instead – no wonder I can't cope with Greece!' She said it lightly, but he understood the effort she'd had to make, and had to make an effort himself to ask his next question.

'Shall I guess, the Frenchman, Anna . . . Is that who it was?'

She nodded and managed to smile. 'It was much too late, though. He has a wife and a daughter in Paris.'

They sat for a moment or two without speaking until Anna thought they could safely talk of something else. 'Petros, tell me if this is one of the subjects your father refuses to have discussed, but why are there none of your grandfather's paintings at Mondhiki?'

He looked surprised that she had asked. 'You haven't seen them, but there *are* some . . . in the room that was called the salon in my great-grandmother's time; now we call it the painting room. She was still alive when I was born, but I don't remember her.' Petros looked ruefully at Anna. 'Pierre Bouchard asked if there were any painting left and I just said that many were destroyed in the war. That was true – my grandfather had a studio in his father-in-law's house in Corfu Town, and what was there *was* destroyed; but I didn't mention the paintings at Mondhiki. I knew my father would refuse to sell them.'

'May I see them at least?' Anna asked.

'Why not? They're hanging on the walls at home.' He glanced at his watch and pulled a face. 'Time to go – Maria will soon be serving lunch.'

He pulled Anna to her feet, lifted her up and settled her on the waiting donkey.

'It's uphill all the way,' she said doubtfully, 'isn't it a bit unfair?'

Petros touched her cheek with a gentle finger. 'Dear Anna, she's a pack animal, used to loads much heavier than you.'

'There you are, you see – donkeys aren't part of normal daily life in Oxford and she knows it! If she wasn't the sweet-natured gentle creature she is, she'd throw me off and trot home by herself.'

With one hand he held the animal still for a moment while he turned Anna's face towards him with the other. 'I understood what you said about not belonging here, and I'm sorry about the Frenchman, but I shall remember you all my life and be glad you came to Mondhiki.'

She touched his hand with her own, as the only answer she could manage; then he released her and Ernestine was told to start for home. They went in silence until the house was in sight, then Anna asked one last question.

'Does Eleni know that it was her grandfather who betrayed the Pappas family?'

'She knows only that he was called Yorgos Pandelios, and that he fathered another family after her grandmother died. There's no need for her to know what she sprang from.'

Anna nodded, and waved to the girl who was waiting for them on the terrace.

When lunch was over Anna asked why her host had still been missing from the table.

'He goes to the north of the island to visit his sister and brother-in-law,' Eleni explained. 'Dassia's husband inherited a hotel from his parents at Kassiopi and they still run it. A famous English writer lived there before the war – Dassia's parents-in-law knew him.'

'Lawrence Durrell,' Anna agreed. 'He wrote a well-known book about it.' She hesitated for a moment, then went on. 'I thought there weren't any of Nikos Kladis's paintings here, but this morning Petros told me they're in a room his great-grandmother liked to use. Will you show them to me?' She didn't say 'before Stefanos comes home' but as if Eleni grasped the point without being told, she answered at once.

'I'll show you now. It's cool in the salon and shaded from the sun, which is good for the paintings, of course.' She led Anna along a corridor and into a formal room that scarcely seemed to belong to the rest of the old house. It was elegantly furnished by comparison with the big, all-purpose kitchen, but Anna did no more than glance around it; her attention was riveted on what hung on the white-washed walls – the cool, perfect background for a dozen or so glowing canvases so full of colour and life that no one could look at them without smiling for sheer pleasure.

There were some paintings of Mondhiki itself, the old white house almost lost in a summer tide of greenery, and several of the bay she'd visited that morning – either caught in moments of enchanted stillness, or lashed by a winter storm; and even an exquisite night-time study of moonlight laying a bar of silver across the dark water.

Anna looked at them for a long time, wondering how she could describe them to Pierre, supposing that they should be described at all. If he was never going to be allowed to see them it might be better that he should never be told they were there. Then she thought of Nikos Kladis dragged away to die in a concentration camp, and knew what Pierre would say: the world *should* know about so fine an artist, and have the chance to see what he'd created.

She turned round at last to find that Eleni had left the room to return to some task or other. It was time to hobble back to the terrace and begin her own work of recording everything she could remember of her visit, to Corfu and to the mainland. Parts of it were unforgettable, but she wanted no details to be lost.

She was interrupted an hour or so later by Theodora Kladis, who pattered out to the terrace after her post-luncheon rest carrying what Anna recognized as a backgammon board.

'You play?' she asked hopefully, with her head on one side like a small, expectant blackbird.

'Not very well, but I think I can remember how it goes,' Anna said, smiling at her.

Theodora certainly understood the gist of this, at least, and looked very pleased. Someone to play with was good, someone she was likely to beat was even better.

Anna put aside her notes, the board was laid out and the game began. At the end of it she was cheerfully acknowledging defeat just as Stefanos Kladis, back from Kassiopi, walked out on to the terrace. His expression was almost amiable as he saw his unwanted guest at least behaving as she ought. Theodora was well cared for, that went without saying, but in a household where everyone else worked long hours, she often had to be left alone; Anna Rasini, unwelcome though she was, could at least be useful in keeping Theodora company.

When Eleni had brought out a drinks tray and gone indoors again, Stefanos poured a small glass of wine for his aunt, and then looked enquiringly at Anna.

'Water, please,' she said, 'it tastes so good here.'

'Your ankle is mending? You are being looked after?'

She could answer these questions easily enough. 'It's mending very well, thank you, and I've been wrapped in kindness.' Then, in case the rare moment of affability might not come again, she risked what she wanted to say next.

'Kyrie Stefanos, I hope you won't mind that I looked at your father's paintings this afternoon. They are so beautiful that I'd like to tell someone I know about them . . . a French art expert. He would understand that they're not for sale, but just to know that the paintings exist would be important to him. May I mention them to him?'

As she feared, her host's pleasant expression had already faded; his usual frown was in place again by the time he'd decided how to answer. 'You're right – the paintings are not for sale, and I see no point in having them talked about. They only concern my family.'

'My friend Pierre Bouchard would disagree with you,' she ventured, aware that Theodora Kladis's interested stare was fastened on each of them in turn. 'Pierre believes that great art – which is what these paintings are – should be shared, and that its creators should be properly honoured.'

'So they should,' Stefanos agreed grimly. 'Instead of that my father's life ended in the obscenity of a death camp. I'm afraid neither your Frenchman nor anyone else is going to share the paintings with us.'

'Very well,' Anna agreed with the calmness of despair. She took a sip of water, then looked at him again. 'Now I'd like to ask you something else, and perhaps you'll refuse this as well. Before I leave Mondhiki I want to give Eleni a present for all her kindness to me. As soon as I'm able to drive the car – tomorrow I hope – I'd like to drive her to Corfu Town so that she can choose something for herself. It would also be a little outing for her . . . don't you think?'

In the silence that followed she wondered what he would say: that Greek women's role in life was to work, without the bribe of presents or outings; that if she, Anna, was capable of driving her car, it was clearly already time for her to leave Mondhiki and not come back? But her dark eyes held his and this time he suspected that she wouldn't give in without a struggle – she was obstinate, despite her gentle manner, obstinate and troublesome, as the English usually were.

'Eleni doesn't need a present for doing what she's required to do,' he said finally, 'but a visit to Corfu Town needn't take all day, I suppose. She may go as long as Maria is given instructions, and the goats and chickens are seen to.'

Anna smiled at him, he thought, as if he'd just given *her* a present. 'Thank you,' she said, '. . . I'll go and tell her.'

Theodora sipped her wine, and shot small enquiring glances

at the man who sat frowning into space across the table. 'I thought I'd forgotten those times long ago,' she said in Greek, as if talking to herself, 'but this girl has made me remember them again. I can see the fair Englishman sitting where she sat, smiling at something Nikos said – they laughed a lot together, those two young men . . . Athina, too, was happy then; she shouldn't have been made to marry Yorgos Pandelios. That was your grandfather's fault, Stefanos.'

'But it's Anna Rasini's fault that we're talking about it now,' he said roughly. 'She shouldn't have come at all.'

Theodora's little nod agreed, but what else she thought would keep, she decided. Stefanos didn't need to be told just yet that more would have to be said before the Englishman's granddaughter left Mondhiki.

Fourteen

Eleni had to be convinced that her day out was agreed to by Stefanos; it was easier to believe that Anna's suggestion would have been turned down. Still, she could at least imagine what it would be like to stroll along the Listón, and window-gaze, and pretend that she was there to buy. At last, Anna took hold of her thin shoulders and gently shook her.

'Eleni, love, you're how old – twenty-four, twenty-five? You don't *need* your cousin's permission to take a day off from constant toil. I only asked him out of courtesy because I'm here as a guest he doesn't want. You must sort out Maria's instructions about feeding the livestock and what to serve for lunch; then we'll leave in the morning as soon as you're ready.'

And so they did, Eleni having got up in the night-watches, Anna suspected, to make sure that they could set off after breakfast. But once on the road, her face changed, and her only concern now was that Anna's ankle might be hurting. Assured that this wasn't the case, Eleni gave a little sigh of pleasure and settled down to enjoy the luxury of being driven through the countryside. They were approaching Corfu Town when a fresh worry occurred to her. She kept staring down at her black blouse and skirt and finally put the problem into words.

'I shan't look right, Anna . . . This isn't how town women dress . . . They'll all be like you.'

'Very true – that's why we're going shopping before we meet someone at lunch-time that I want you to know. She's an American called Irene Lambert, and she's staying at the Corfu Palace Hotel with her husband George.'

Eleni's face was now a mask of despair. 'You'll have to leave me in the car . . . I can't . . . won't . . . go to such a place looking like this; they'll think a peasant has walked in.'

Anna turned to smile at her while they waited for the traffic lights to change. 'You weren't listening – I said shopping *first*, then lunch. You'll like Irene, by the way, she and George are hoping to rebuild his grandfather's old home a little further down the coast from Mondhiki. Unfortunately someone else is trying to buy it as well, but George is determined to win. That's why I particularly want you to meet Irene; she might be a neighbour one day.'

Then the traffic started moving again and required all the driver's concentration as they reached the town. A quarter of an hour later they were outside the boutique Anna had mentally selected – it was full of clothes that were pretty and colourful, but not so fashionably extreme as to frighten Eleni away from even going inside.

It took Eleni a dazed minute or two to register that their shopping was to be for her, as a gift from Anna, but when they eventually emerged again the black uniform was being carried in a bag, and a different Eleni walked along the Listón, trying not to smile at herself in every shop-window they passed. Her flame-red skirt was short enough to show off slender brown legs, and a candy-striped shirt of red and white, and white doeskin sandals completed the outfit. Also in her bag was a multi-coloured patchwork skirt, a white top to go with it, and some pretty underclothes like the ones she now wore.

What the inmates of Mondhiki would make of the transformation, its provider couldn't guess, but Eleni herself no longer seemed to care. It was as if some hidden spirit of freedom and gaiety had been liberated by the simple change of clothes, and Anna reckoned it had been worth coming back to Mondhiki just for that.

Irene was waiting for them in the hotel lobby, looking so sincerely pleased to be making a new acquaintance that her

English friend recognized it as a nice and peculiarly American trait; it was more usual for people at home to be suspicious about strangers being met for the first time. In a telephone conversation the previous evening Irene had been warned not to mention the name of Pandelios so she tactfully skirted round the identity of the man who was causing her husband such problems.

'The lawyer in Athens reckons that George has right on *his* side; there's no reason in law not to go ahead,' she said, trying to sound cheerful

'But . . . ? There *is* a "but", isn't there?' Anna guessed from her tone of voice.

'He also thinks that the man we're up against won't fight fairly. The people we need – builders and such-like – would be frightened off working for us.' Irene's smile was strained but she managed a brave shrug. 'George is ready for a fight, I guess; he's becoming more Greek minute by minute!' Then she waved the subject aside and asked about Anna's unexpected stay at Mondhiki.

'I was stupid enough to sprain my ankle on the way there, so Eleni's cousin had very little option but to put up with me for a few days. I've been beautifully looked after, and I now know why my grandfather loved going to stay with his Kladis friends. I shall hate leaving.'

'Then don't go, Anna,' Eleni put in. 'None of us wants you to – not even Cousin Stefanos, I think.'

That, at least, seemed unlikely, but Anna didn't labour the point. 'I've almost used up the holiday I gave myself,' she said instead. 'It's time to get back to work. But I shall like to think that you two know each other – it isn't far from Mondhiki to Linia.'

Then Irene had to hear about the journey down to the beach by courtesy of Ernestine, and she in turn described George's rebuilding plans. It wasn't until lunch was over and they were getting ready to leave that Irene spoke to Anna alone when Eleni disappeared to the ladies' room.

'I'm not as optimistic as George is, you know. Even the

lawyer he first went to here won't have anything more to do with him . . . he's been warned off, too.'

Without thinking, Anna spoke the words that were suddenly in her mind. 'I know more than I did about the Pandelios family. If things turn really nasty I might be able to do something to help; but it mustn't involve the Kladis family – there's enough bad blood there already. I'll have to think about it and talk to George before I leave the island.'

Then Eleni returned and, goodbyes said, they were in the car again heading for home.

'I shan't forget today,' Eleni said quietly.

Knowing how completely she'd just been thanked, Anna smiled at Eleni but didn't answer. She wanted to beg the girl beside her to remember it by not sinking back into being the rejected slave of her family, but there was a limit to the extent she could interfere in someone else's life and she'd reached it already. It only remained to be seen what happened when they got back to Mondhiki. She half-expected Eleni to ask her to stop on the way, so that she could climb back into her black clothes again. But her passenger said nothing more, and when they arrived Anna watched the moment at which Petros and Stefanos caught sight of her.

The gods were kind for once, and it was Petros who, after a moment of speechless astonishment, found something to say first. 'Very pretty, Eleni . . . lovely, in fact.'

It wouldn't have mattered after that, Anna thought, if Stefanos had ripped the shirt off her back, but he only stared at her, and then growled at the one he knew he should blame.

'You're very late . . . you didn't say you'd take all day just to buy a present.'

'I'm sorry,' she said, smiling at him. 'There was a lot of traffic and we got held up. But it's been a lovely day.' It left him nothing to say, he realized, and Theodora's smile across the table confirmed that for once he'd been not only out-manoeuvered but completely rolled up as well.

* * *

Anna didn't regret the victory but she knew what it meant: Stefanos Kladis saw her as a thorn in his flesh that he needn't put up with any longer. She was now capable of driving herself away, and the sooner she went, the better! There were still questions that she wouldn't find an answer to, and she'd leave still forbidden to let Pierre know about the paintings.

After supper she talked about the Lamberts and asked if she might stay one more day so that she could visit Linia, and the wild-life sanctuary that George had said was established in the lagoon. Stefanos knew about it, of course, and allowed himself the pleasure of saying how much better it was for the island than the cheap, ugly developments rushed up to satisfy holiday tour operators from Britain.

Petros was brave enough to point out that the tourists, though often ill-behaved and a discredit to *whatever* country they came from, had at least raised the standard of living of many Corfiots who'd once been on the poverty line.

'It's not an argument,' Anna said quickly, 'because you're both right. What Corfu needs, what every lovely, desirable place needs, is a manageable number of pleasant visitors who do nothing to destroy the beauty of what they come to see. But in the world as it is, that seems to be asking for the moon.'

Her request to stay another day hadn't been answered, but it hadn't been refused, so she set off alone the following morning, aware that to take Eleni out again would probably provoke a storm she was anxious to avoid. The lagoon was as fascinating as George Lambert had said, and just beyond it she found Linia and the lovely bay that his ruined house overlooked. It wasn't hard to imagine what would become of it if he lost his battle with Loukas Pandelios. She'd offered to help, and to preserve so peaceful a place it would be a pleasure to go to war on George's side.

Back at Mondhiki later that afternoon, she took a final look at the paintings in the salon. They were going to be there, unknown about and unrecorded, certainly for the lifetime of their present owner. And it was all too likely that, when his own turn came, Petros would feel obliged to behave in exactly the same way as his father had done.

She turned to leave the room and found that Theodora Kladis had come in behind her, too quietly to be heard. Something seemed to need saying, and Anna gestured to the paintings. 'They're so beautiful that it hurts to think very few people are ever going to see them.'

The old lady's glance went round the room and there was such sadness in it that Anna thought it permissible at last to refer to the past. 'Does it distress you to remember what life was like here? If not, will you tell me about Nikos, and his English friend?' Theodora didn't answer, and Anna went on herself. 'I have a very small photograph of my grandfather, and the sketch that Nikos made of him. But I wish I knew what the rest of you looked like then.'

'I can show you,' the old lady said unexpectedly. She walked to a nearby shelf and pulled out what looked like a bound book among many others, but it was an album of photographs. Beginning to leaf through it, she made a little noise of disapproval.

'It's too dark in here – we must go outside to look at them.' They settled themselves at the table on the terrace and Theodora smiled at Anna's expectant face. 'Now we can begin!'

The photographs were already fading with age, and not captioned in any way, but this was no problem for Theodora; for what had happened fifty years before her memory was still crystal-clear. The earliest photographs had been taken in the years before the war when Steven Curtis had first come to Corfu – still a student himself then, but immediately recognizable from his fair head and gentle smile. Anna was reminded of Pierre's friend at Delphi – the charioteer – and felt her heart contract with pain. But Theodora was talking again.

'Here is Nikos,' she said, pointing to a dark-haired man whose identity Anna thought she might have guessed – the ugly, bony face full of charm and humour was exactly as she'd pictured it. Then came a group of laughing people – Steven and Nikos again, his younger brother, Yannis, who became Theodora's husband, and the vivid, dark girl who had been their sister, Athina.

'So happy they all were together,' Theodora said sadly, '. . . always laughing then. Look, here is Nikos with Katerina, and Stefanos just a tiny boy. But the war came, and everything changed . . .' Her voice faded into silence as she looked back into the past, and Anna had to prompt her with a question.

'Kyria Theodora, this is Athina, I think, but who is the little girl?' She pointed to a later photograph – Nikos's sister, obviously, holding a child on the back of a donkey.

'That's Miranda – Athina's daughter.'

Anna kept staring at the photograph, aware that her hands were suddenly clammy and her heart was beating too fast. Surely it wasn't possible, the thought that was now in her mind . . . but how else to explain the child's golden hair shining in the sunlight? Back in Wallingford old Mr Carstairs had remembered clearly enough that Prospero's island was what the 'Prof' had called it – was it just a coincidence that Athina had given her child the very name of Prospero's daughter?

She rubbed her hands on her skirt and saw that they were shaking. Then she looked at Theodora and saw in her lined face certain confirmation of what she was thinking. She was still wondering what it would be safe to say when the voice of Stefanos Kladis spoke behind her, full of anger and pain that the years had done nothing to lessen. 'Why do you rummage like a thief in what doesn't concern you? You have no right to touch those photographs.'

Anna turned to look at him, aware that she ought to be afraid, because he was a strong man with emotions barely under control. But whatever happened now, there was no way back; they had to finish what had been started.

'I think I do have a right,' she said unsteadily. 'I think you know that Steven Curtis was the father of Athina's daughter – *that*'s why you hate the English; it had very little to do with what happened after the war. It's also why Yorgos Pandelios loathed the Kladis family; they'd let him marry Athina knowing that she was already pregnant with someone else's child. From that came everything else – his betrayal of your parents and their death at Buchenwald.' Anna wiped a hand across her face, unaware that Petros, fetched by Theodora, had come out of the house in time to hear what she'd said. Behind him, Theodora and Eleni also now stood listening. If Stefanos noticed them, he no longer cared; his only concern was with the white-faced girl who so resembled Steven Curtis.

'Even though I never knew your grandfather I grew up hating him,' he said roughly. 'My father's brother told me what had happened as soon as I was old enough to understand. I didn't tell my own son; I wanted the past to die with me – as it would have done if you hadn't come here.' Anna said nothing, and after a moment he went on himself. 'As soon as Athina's child was born Pandelios knew it wasn't his. But he made her stay with him until he could take his revenge when the Germans came looking for Jews. Then he told her what he'd done. She took the child and brought her here, then committed suicide. Now do you understand why I hate the very name of Steven Curtis – the cause of all that sorrow?'

Unable to speak, she could only nod her head. With heart and mind in turmoil, her only coherent thought was that Pierre had been entirely right to warn her of the damage she might do at Mondhiki. How criminally stupid and cocksure she'd been not to listen.

But now someone else – Petros – was speaking in a voice she scarcely recognized. 'Let me get this right. Have we just been told that Eleni isn't Pandelios's granddaughter . . . that what you've let us believe all these years has been a lie?'

Beneath its weathering, Stefanos's face was now grey, but he looked unflinchingly at his son. 'Yes, it was a lie, but your uncle and I agreed that the truth was better not known.

We wanted to hide the wrong that Athina had done . . . Her memory was still precious to us. But it was the Englishman who really betrayed the family he was supposed to love.'

It seemed so unarguable that Anna made no attempt to defend her grandfather, but suddenly someone else did. Theodora's voice, quiet but firm, interrupted the silence.

'The Englishman wasn't to blame. I was younger than Athina, but we were friends and she needed someone to talk to. She was being married to Yorgos Pandelios against her will, because he was wealthy and powerful. She loved her brother's English friend but Steven knew he couldn't take her away to Oxford – she was a wild thing who belonged where she'd been born – and in any case the marriage with Pandelios had been arranged. Just before he left for England she begged him to love her – just once, so that she could pretend it was him she was with after she was Pandelios's wife; if he refused, she promised to kill herself. If that was betraying the family he *did* love, what choice did he have?'

'Who else knew?' Stefanos asked in a hoarse voice.

'Steven *never* knew Miranda was his child; Nikos wasn't told, and only guessed when the child was born, so Pandelios betrayed him and Katerina and her parents for nothing.'

'Why didn't you tell me before?'

Theodora lifted her hands in a gesture of despair. 'What did it matter after the war? Steven never came back to Mondhiki. I've only told you now because his English granddaughter *is* here instead.'

The mention of herself broke the paralysis that had kept Anna rooted to the spot. She got up and went to put her arms round Eleni, still frozen into complete stillness. 'I'm glad we share a grandfather . . . you be glad too, please; he was good, gentle man.' Then she turned round to face Stefanos again.

'Why did Miranda abandon her daughter? If you know, isn't it time you told Eleni?'

'Yes, I know,' he said heavily. 'When we were children together it didn't seem to matter, but even then she knew that she was different from us . . . that she was the cause of something terrible that had happened. When the time came she married Kostalis, but he died soon after Eleni was born, and she became convinced that people close to her *did* die. She believed that if she went away herself nothing would happen to her daughter.' He looked at Eleni. 'I'm sorry I didn't tell you . . . but it would have meant telling the whole story. Now I'm glad you know.' Then he went to his aunt. 'Let me take you indoors . . . I think you need to rest a little after all this talking.'

With more gentleness than Anna had known he possessed, he lifted Theodora out of her chair and took her into the house. They left a silence behind which Anna was finally the one to break.

'Kyrie Stefanos won't forgive me for coming to Mondhiki, but I hope you both will. I doubt if he will ever think differently of Steven Curtis either, even though my grandfather must have loved Athina very much. He married someone else back in England, but his heart was in Greece, and I doubt if he minded dying here.' Then she tried to smile at them. 'I'll leave early in the morning so I'd better go and pack.'

She walked away but turned to look at them before she went into the house. Eleni was weeping, but Petros had moved to put his arms around her and it was all the comfort she would ever need.

Fifteen

The packing had been an excuse; there was little enough to do. Then Anna had to decide whether to go downstairs again or to stay where she was – out of sight at least, if not out of mind; that was surely what they would prefer. Half an hour later she was standing at her bedroom window, watching the sun set for the last time over a sea that had now darkened to the colour of indigo; then there came a gentle tap at the door. Eleni stood there, still looking serious but no longer weeping.

'Cousin Stefanos sent me to ask why you are not at the supper-table, Anna. We cannot begin until you come, and Petros says he's hungry.' Although not smiling, she had a different air about her now. Happiness wasn't yet certain by any means but she could see its distant gleam, like the first streak of gold that dawn painted along the horizon every morning.

Anna registered the change and felt her own cloud of misery lift a little. *Something* good at least had come out of so much unhappiness. She smiled at Eleni and said untruthfully that she was hungry too.

The others were already seated, and Maria was bringing out the platter of stuffed vine leaves that began the meal. The terrace was now in the evening shadow of the house, and the table was lamp-lit. Anna looked round it, anxious not to forget any detail of the scene, with the soft light falling on their Greek faces, and on the crystal of the water-flagon, and the golden wine bubbles in her glass. She'd be able to superimpose these present pictures on what imagination could paint of the past, and even if she never saw Mondhiki again, she would know how it had been for the men and women who'd been young in Theodora's photographs.

Petros quietly queried a matter concerning the estate and, as if grateful for the reminder that life could become normal again, Stefanos went on himself to talk about the prospects for the grape harvest. Even Eleni found the courage to ask him a question – something not known before, Anna suspected – and gradually it began to seem that the tensions were melting. Just as a thunderstorm cleared the air of its burden of electricity, so had the emotional cloudburst of an hour ago washed away some of the bitterness of the past.

At last Eleni saw her great-aunt indoors to bed, and Petros remembered a small task still to be done. It left Anna alone at the table with Stefanos but there was nothing, she thought, that they could bear to talk about. Then it occurred to her that at least she could say goodbye.

'Kyrie Stefanos, perhaps you'll be out early tomorrow as usual, so I'll thank you now for letting me stay at Mondhiki. I shall remember it always and pray that whatever damage I did by coming can be mended.'

He shook his grey head, brushing the apology aside like an animal ridding itself of an unwanted fly.

'I'm not sorry to have met the granddaughter of Steven Curtis,' he said formally, 'despite the trouble she has been.' Unable to decide how to reply, Anna said nothing at all, and then his voice went on again. 'No doubt you are glad to have seen where he died – bravely, I expect; the men your country sent us did die bravely.'

She nodded, afraid that if she tried to speak now she would burst into tears. Stefanos watched her stand up to leave the table, and held out his hand to keep her there a moment longer.

'My father's paintings won't be sold, by me or by Petros later on. But if the Frenchman you spoke of wishes to come and see them he'll be welcome.'

'Thank you . . . thank you very much,' Anna managed to get out, and then made a dash for the house.

* * *

She left after breakfast the following morning, with a farewell message for Theodora who never rose early, and with Petros and Eleni to see her off.

'What will you do – go straight back to England?' Petros asked.

'Not quite; I've something to do in Corfu Town first, and a call to make in Rome. *Then* I'll go home.' She smiled at Eleni, back in her working rig again but still with an air of contentment about her that the black clothes couldn't destroy. 'Don't forget Irene Lambert, please. If she and George come to Linia she'll be glad of a friend.'

'*You*'ll come back as well, Anna? Promise you will,' Eleni insisted.

'I won't promise, but I'll try.' She kissed them both and got into the car, wound down the window to say, 'Take care of each other,' and then started the engine. It might not happen very soon, but that one day Petros would make Eleni his wife, she now felt sure. Already he was seeing her differently, happy to remember that there was no Pandelios blood in her veins after all. Anna watched them in the driving mirror as they waved her away, and knew that their air of togetherness made her feel lonely.

By the time she reached Corfu Town she had a plan clear in her mind, but first she must talk to the Lamberts. She drove straight to their hotel and found them just leaving the dining-room after lunch. They both looked dejected, she thought.

'Come and drink some more coffee while I eat a sandwich,' she suggested. 'I need to see you, but I'm hungry!'

Settled at a table again, and her food ordered, George opened the conversation. 'If you're about to ask about how we're getting on, Anna, the answer is that we aren't! It goes against the grain, I can tell you, but I can't beat Pandelios at his own game. I can buy what should be ours, but no one will work on it for me; I can bring men from the mainland and make myself even more unpopular – but we can't live here like that.'

'No, of course you can't,' she agreed, 'but nor should this man be allowed to bullock everyone else out of his way. Will you let me see what I can do before you give up? My scheme may not work, but if it doesn't you'll be no worse off than you are now.'

George's expression said that he doubted what she could do, but he was too kind to put doubt into words. 'Are you going to tell us what the scheme is?'

'Not yet at least; it involves a story that isn't really mine to tell. If Pandelios is around I'll beard him in his den this afternoon; if not I must wait until tomorrow. But I'll ring you here as soon as I've seen him.'

Irene was now looking doubtful. 'Should we let Anna do this, George? He's a bad man for her to have dealings with.'

'I shall be in his office in broad daylight; he can't do me any harm . . . won't even try . . . except perhaps to shout at me!' She smiled reassuringly at them both. 'Don't worry – I'm rather looking forward to meeting him.'

She said goodbye, and went to the Tourist Office. Her friend was there; another stroke of luck, because it might have been his day off – the gods were looking after her today – and he was eager to be helpful as usual.

'It's a strange request this time,' she admitted, 'and it will take too long to explain why I'm making it; in any case I'd rather you weren't involved. I just need to know where I can find Loukas Pandelios.'

'I'd rather persuade you not to try,' Andreas said earnestly. 'He's not a good man to know.'

'All the same . . . please? If you can't tell me I must struggle to decipher the telephone directory, but it will take a long time.'

He realized she meant what she said, and reluctantly wrote down an address for her. 'Any taxi-driver will know it – he's a very important citizen. But he may not be here – he's trying hard to get elected to Parliament in Athens; a very ambitious man is Loukas Pandelios.'

'All the better,' Anna said cheerfully. 'Thank you very

much for telling me. But now I've got to hurry away. *Yía sou*, Andreas.'

He echoed her goodbye, hoping that she'd find Pandelios absent from his office, but Anna could have assured Andreas that he would be there – it was the rare sort of day when things fell into place just as they were required to. The first obstacle only came with an unhelpful woman who guarded his door. Mr Pandelios was too busy to be seen without an appointment; the English kyria would do better to go away. The kyria smiled at her and said she would wait, however long it took.

'Then you are wasting your time,' the dragon said, 'but that's up to you.'

'Perhaps not if you'd be so kind as to give him this,' Anna suggested, scribbling her name on the card supplied by her prestigious publishers in London. A quarter of an hour went by, which she used to polish up her story. Then someone came out of Pandelios's room, and his assistant walked in, taking the card with her. She emerged a moment later and simply held the door open. Anna walked into a large office dominated by an imposing desk. Behind it sat the man who'd brayed at Andreas in the Tourist Office. He didn't get up when she walked in and the discourtesy made her feel better. What she was about to do would have been more difficult if he'd behaved like a reasonable human-being.

'My secretary says you insist on seeing me – what about?'

'Some property at Linia that belongs to the Lamberkis family,' Anna answered with equal baldness. 'My friends, the Lamberts, hope to restore it and live there. It's a worthwhile ambition, don't you think?'

'My own ambition is more useful – to pull down a ruin and redevelop the site: more work, more income, for all the people concerned.'

'Including you, Mr Pandelios, not to mention more destruction of this island's natural beauty.'

He flipped her card between his fingers. 'However *you* see it, Miss Rasini, the matter concerns me and the Lamberts. Is that all you came to say?'

Anna smiled at him. 'Not quite, but I'll be as brief as I can. A beautiful painting I inherited brought me to Corfu. By chance I met a German staying at the hotel whose reason for coming here was strangely the same as mine – he also had a painting by Nikos Kladis. There *was* a difference, though. Mine was a gift taken back to England before the war; his was stolen by his father, then a young officer in the German army, in 1943. The artist and his family had been deported to Germany because of their Jewish connections: and his canvasses were all supposedly to be destroyed. But the officer recognized their quality and kept one for himself.'

'Interesting, I'm sure, but what does this ancient history have to do with me? You're wasting my time, Miss Rasini.'

'I'm afraid I have to waste a little more,' Anna said apologetically. 'The officer was haunted by what had been done to a fine artist and never forgot the name of the Greek who had betrayed Nikos Kladis. His son was kind enough to tell me what it was. The last thing to mention is that I'm an author, keen to write about Corfu's wartime history, and I can't help wondering what it would do to your parliamentary ambitions.'

There was silence in the room, but only for as long as it took Loukas Pandelios to recover himself. His voice was still thick with anger when he spoke.

'So that's what brings you here – I believe it's how some authors get rich, by blackmail.'

She went white as his fists banged the desk; life in North Oxford hadn't prepared her for the emotional helter-skelter she'd been on for the past few weeks. But she answered him as calmly as she could.

'It's scarcely blackmail to write factually of some of the two thousand Jewish Corfiots – probably all intellectual or artistic citizens – who were taken to Germany. Less than a hundred of them came back alive.'

'But, though not a blackmailer, you'd like to be paid for not mentioning my father's name – is that it?'

'No, I'd just ask you to give up trying to spoil George

Lambert's dream of bringing his family's old home back to life; that would also mean not frightening people off working for him.' She stared at the man's livid face, and saw in it the rage that had motivated his father all those years ago. 'There will be other lovely places for you to cover with concrete and bright-blue swimming pools. Why not leave Linia to Mr Lambert? 'she suggested quietly.

'Withdraw myself, and then find that you publish the story anyway? I'm not a fool, Miss Rasini.'

'And I'm not a cheat. I shouldn't even tell the Lamberts why you'd changed your mind. Is it so hard for a Greek to shake hands on a bargain? We would have to trust each other, Mr Pandelios.'

It hung in the balance for a moment or two longer; then he gave a little shrug. 'It's a paltry site anyway, scarcely worth bothering with, and I've got much more important things on my mind.' He glared at Anna. 'I'll probably regret this, because I've never liked the English, and I don't like you; but Lambert can have Linia – he'll probably find out in due course that it wasn't worth fighting for.'

'Thank you,' she said, '. . . thank you very much. Now I'll leave you to the things that are so important.' She stood up and held out her hand, and finally he was forced to take it. Then she headed towards the door, but there his voice made her turn round.

'You heard only the German's story,' he growled. 'My father was ill-treated by the Kladis family and it's always been our way here to avenge mortal insults.'

'I'll remember that,' Anna answered, and then walked out.

In the street again, she took a deep breath of fresh air, aware that her legs were trembling with the strain of the interview. A near-by *kafeneio* offered coffee and a much-needed glass of brandy, and also a chance to take stock of her afternoon's work. The bluff had worked, although that was all it had been, because she could never have published Athina's tragic story. She thought George *would* now get his ruin, and Corfu might see less of Loukas Pandelios in future, which would be another good thing; but things were never all black or white, only infinite shades of grey, and Loukas Pandelios's defence of his father had been a necessary reminder that Greeks had always dealt with right and wrong in their own way. They were different people, and suddenly she was in need of her own kind – it was time now to go home.

She walked back to the hotel, where her luggage was still being guarded by a helpful concierge, booked herself a room for the night, and then asked for a reservation on the next morning's flight to Athens and Rome. Next, a telephone call to her mother briefly explained when she'd be arriving – the story she had to tell, she said, had better wait until she got to Rome. Then she lay down on the bed while she waited for the receptionist to let her know that the Lamberts had returned. There were still things that had to be done before she left in the morning, but for the moment she felt too tired to do more than lie there, watching golden reflected light move slowly across the ceiling as the afternoon declined into evening.

Irene's telephone call came half an hour later and she went downstairs to meet them in the lobby.

'Not dinner, if you'll forgive me,' she said in answer to George's invitation. 'There are some letters I need to write before I leave in the morning. All *you* have to hear is that I saw Loukas Pandelios this afternoon. He won't bid for the Linia property after all, and I think you'll now find that people *are* willing to work for you.'

A contented smile spread slowly over George's face, then – blushing a little – he leaned across the table to kiss Anna's cheek. 'Thank you – more than I know how to say. Are we going to be told how you worked the miracle?'

'I promised that I wouldn't,' she said. 'Thank St Spiridhon instead! The truth is that some of what I used was invention, so that the facts I *did* have couldn't be traced to the Kladis family. It's important that Pandelios doesn't know of our connection.' She smiled at Irene's expression. 'I know it sounds very cloak and daggerish, but Corfu *is* part of Greece; Oxford isn't nearly so exciting!'

'But you're going home anyway,' Irene said wistfully. We'd so love you to stay . . .' Then she stopped because Anna was shaking her head.

'I've had my Greek adventures. Yours are about to begin. Stay in touch with Eleni at Mondhiki – it will be good for both of you to make friends. Hers is one of the letters I still have to write, so I'll say goodbye and go and make a start.'

She was hugged and kissed, but finally allowed to leave them settling down to the joyous task of planning all over again the restoration of their Greek home. Now all that remained before she could climb into bed was to write briefly to Eleni, and to Evgenia Vassilikos at Arachova, and then – with much greater difficulty – to Pierre in Paris.

She made several false starts with this one. The first attempt was surely too intimate in tone; the second went to the other extreme and suggested that she was writing to a total stranger. When that had followed the first one into the waste-paper basket, she began yet again.

Dear Pierre,

I hope you got your Kladis paintings to Paris safely, and found all well there.

I went back to Mondhiki, and accidentally sprained my ankle on the way so that Stefanos Kladis had to let me stay. Before I left this morning I learned what happened all those years ago. Steven Curtis and Athina Kladis, Niko's sister, loved one another – hopelessly, of course, because she was about to be married to Yorgos Pandelios, and Steven knew that she couldn't be transplanted to a life in Oxford. But they spent one night together before he went home, with the result that she was already pregnant at the time of the wedding. The child, who became Eleni's mother, was very obviously not Pandelios's, and he believed that Nikos, if not his parents as well, had known that. He waited for the perfect moment for revenge, betrayed Nikos and his Jewish wife and parents-in-law to the Germans and, when they'd been deported, told Athina what he'd done. She took the child back to Mondhiki, and then drowned herself. A complete and terrible Greek tragedy. You'll think that what I did was make old wounds bleed again, but now that they all know the truth I believe there's a chance for them to be happy again at Mondhiki.

I wouldn't have written to tell you this except for one thing. There are a dozen beautiful paintings still in the house, that Petros apologized for not telling you about. They'll never be for sale, but Stefanos finally agreed you should at least be told that they exist. If you ever come back to Corfu you would be welcome to go and look at them.

So far, so adequate, but now Anna had to chew her pen. Then she added her final paragraph.

One way and another these past weeks have been the most eventful – and unforgettable – of my life. But I've decided now that it's time to return to swimming in calmer waters, and Oxford is nothing if not calm!

I hope you decided to keep the Kladis paintings you found; I shall break Rupert Whittaker's heart by never selling mine.

Yours,
Anna Rasini

It was finished at last and, without reading it again, she sealed the envelope and went to bed. She had used hotel note-paper, and not included her own address deliberately. It meant that he wouldn't be able to write back; but that was how it should be. The process of forgetting had begun and must continue; the pity of it was that, like the grinding of the wheels of God, it was as slow as it was inevitable.

Sixteen

When she'd left Rome a day or two before Easter, spring had only just begun to arrive; now, the temperature and tempo of the city had moved into a different gear, and the inward trickle of tourists was becoming a tidal wave. Calculating how long she'd been away, Anna found it hard to believe that what felt like half a life-time was in fact little more than a month; even now it was only the first day of May.

On the taxi-ride into the city she read the signs they passed with a feeling of relief; here she was back where she could communicate and understand, and the people were agreeably familiar. Even Rome's early-evening traffic, though terrifying to a foreign driver, obeyed more or less the same rules as traffic at home. She'd just come from a country that was neither east nor west but peculiarly itself. By contrast Italy felt comfortable.

She said this as she walked into her mother's apartment and found Nicola waiting for her with chilled wine and tempting canapés laid out on the terrace. Away to the west behind St Peter's dome a spectacular Roman sunset was beginning, and the insistent chiming of church bells floated across the noise of the evening traffic.

'You look in need of comfort and you sound tired,' Nicola said. 'I thought the trip to Greece was meant to be a holiday.'

'It was, but it turned out to be an emotional marathon – that's what was so tiring. I've got a lot to tell you – shall I make a start straightaway?'

'Certainly not,' her mother insisted. 'First you can relax

– sip your wine and enjoy the view; then we'll have supper. You can talk after that.'

Anna did as she was told, not arguing with a programme that sounded sensible. Only when the terrace doors were closed for the night and they were comfortably settled indoors did she plunge into the tale she had to tell, beginning at the beginning with the train journey down to Brindisi and her first meeting with the Lamberts. It seemed a long time later that she stopped talking and took a sip of wine to cure the dryness in her throat. The expedition to Delphi had had to be touched on; Epidaurus hadn't been mentioned at all.

Nicola finally managed to murmur something herself. 'My God, what a story! I know that bits of it are very tragic, but all I can take in right now is the fact that I've got an unknown half-sister shut up in a convent in Athens – it isn't the sort of news you get every day. Miranda is very little older than me, and she's been lost to the world for nearly twenty years. What a terrible waste of a life!'

'Perhaps not,' Anna was inclined to argue. 'Who are we to say that time spent in prayer and contemplation is wasted. In any case I don't think the poor girl belonged anywhere else. Stefanos Kladis said that even as a child she felt different from the rest of them.' Then she smiled at her mother. 'It's odd but rather nice to find ourselves related to people we didn't even know existed a few weeks ago. We *were* rather short of family connections before.'

'What happens now – are you going to keep in touch with them?'

'I expect so,' Anna answered, sounding vague, '. . . but I'm not sure of anything at the moment.'

'What about the Frenchman, then? He's surely worth not losing sight of.'

'I've written to tell him about the paintings of course, and I hope he'll go and look at them. There'll be no reason for *us* to meet again . . . no chance of it either.' She was pleased with herself for sounding so calm about it; even Nicola, who was surprisingly good at hearing what hadn't been said, seemed convinced that Pierre's path had crossed hers accidentally and then diverged again.

'So the journey into the past is over,' her mother said. 'You've got it out of your system, you know what sort of man your grandfather was, and you understand his passion for Greece. Now perhaps you'll get on with your own life. What are you going to do – sink back into the academic quagmire of North Oxford?'

'You're very harsh,' Anna protested with a rueful smile. 'It's not nearly as bad as you make it sound.' Then she grew serious again. 'I'd more or less decided to sell the house, as a matter of fact; it seemed the moment to make a fresh start, and I wondered what you'd feel if I suggested coming to Rome to live – I don't mean here; I thought I might find an apartment nearby.'

'Darling, I should be overjoyed, but would you really enjoy flat life? A few well-placed pots on a terrace don't exactly make what you consider to be a garden.'

'I know.' Anna was silent for a moment, then went on again more hesitantly. 'As a matter of fact I rather suddenly went off that plan myself. Maybe I should find a cottage in an outlying village – not too far from Oxford. I rather like the idea of settling in a small community where people know each other and feel kindly towards their neighbours. You might even think that you could bear to come and visit me there!' Her voice faded into silence again, and she sat looking at her hands, clasped together in her lap.

Nicola watched her for a moment, registering the hollows under her cheek-bones and the air of strain and weariness about her.

'You're not just slender, you're downright thin,' she said firmly, 'and I get the impression that there's something I haven't been told. I'm suddenly afraid that you're unwell; if so, I want to know.'

Anna looked up and stared at her mother. 'I'm perfectly well, but I think I might be pregnant!' She smiled at the change of expression on her mother's face – where concern had now given way to consternation 'You *did* tell me to join the human race instead of just watching it – I took your advice!'

'To some purpose, it seems. Let me guess . . . the Frenchman?'

Anna nodded, wishing that she didn't want to burst into tears. 'History repeating itself, I'm afraid, in the strangest way. We only spent one night together, just as my grandfather and Athina Kladis did; I may be wrong about the result, but I don't think so . . . I *feel* different.'

'Hence the cottage in a friendly village,' Nicola said slowly. 'It seems to suggest that you'll keep the child, and that you'll be doing it on your own. What about Pierre Bouchard?'

'He won't – mustn't – know. It may only be a marriage of convenience now that he has with his wife in Paris, but he's devoted to his ten-year-old daughter and believes that she needs him to counterbalance the other influences in her young life. That wasn't something I learned afterwards, by the way . . . I knew that the day and night we spent together was all there would be. Just for now I'm feeling a bit frightened and lonely; but I shall get over that. When everything's been sorted out, I shall be very glad about what's happened.'

'There's something you haven't thought of. Suppose Pierre is feeling as lonely as you are . . . Don't you think his wife will guess the reason? However convenient the marriage, she'll find it hard to know that he's longing all the time to be with another woman.'

Anna's mind went back to the visit to Epidaurus and the night that followed it. Already she was teaching herself to think that what had been unforgettable for her might not seem like that in Pierre's recollection of it. Even for him, she felt sure, it hadn't been just an opportunist grab at pleasure; when they'd gone their separate ways in Athens he'd been genuinely desolate. But men's hearts were known to be less constant than women's.

'I doubt if Pierre will be left lonely for long!' Anna said at last. 'You may be right about his wife, but she's a highly celebrated political commentator, and it suits her very well to have an outwardly successful marriage . . . she's the perfect modern woman – career, marriage, motherhood all being effortlessly juggled with. Pierre accepts the sham in order to stay close to Amélie. He wants her to grow up aware of other things than the shoddy glamour and intrigue of the great and not so good.'

'Poor man,' Nicola murmured, 'and poor you, my darling Anna. I can't wave a wand and make you happy, unfortunately, but I can come whenever you want me to. God knows it's time I did *something* maternal for you.'

'Offer gratefully accepted,' Anna said. 'Once I've sold my house to my tenants who I know want it, and I've found my country cottage, come as often as you can put up with our climate!'

Nicola was now remembering something else. 'You sounded vague about keeping in touch with the Kladis family. Was that because of the child?'

Anna nodded. 'They live in a society that insists on rules we seem to have forgotten; an illegitimate child is something they'd *still* find shocking. But there's another reason as well. I'm sure Pierre won't be able to resist going to see the paintings. He might ask Eleni about me, and if she knows nothing I don't have to ask her to lie for me. Later on it won't matter, when he no longer has a reason to revisit Corfu. Eventually I'd like to get in touch and know there'd been some happy endings – Petros and Eleni together, Stefanos not embittered any more, and the Lamberts enjoying life in Linia.' Then she smiled at her mother. 'Don't you think we've talked enough for one night? It's time for bed and I've got an early flight in the morning.'

Nicola thought about trying to persuade her to stay, but realized that if her daughter had to begin reorganizing her life, the sooner she got home the better.

'These dawn departures are a bad habit I wish you'd grow out of,' she pointed out sharply. 'I hate getting up early.' Then her face crumpled into tears. 'I only sound cross because

I'm anxious about you. I wanted you to be happy . . . you deserve to be . . . but instead of that . . .' Her voice faded away and she lifted her hands in a little gesture of despair.

Anna had got up to leave the room but stopped by her mother's chair to give her a little hug. 'Don't worry about me, please – there's no need. Single mothers are two a penny nowadays; they probably outnumber the married ones, so no one will mind that I don't have a husband. I know it's not an ideal way, to bring up a child alone; but I shall do the best I can and love it with all my heart.'

'Then luckier child than you or I were, say I,' Nicola answered. 'Now go to bed, please. I shall rise with the birds to see you off, and not even begrudge the effort.'

'You're a treasure,' Anna said, blowing her a kiss as she walked to the door.

By mid-afternoon the following day she was unlocking her own front door. It had been the middle of March when she left for Rome and, apart from some impetuous daffodils shivering in the cold winds and the forsythia against the house beginning to be tipped with gold, there'd been little sign of spring. Now she returned to a different garden – the trees were veiled in the first vivid green of the year, and the lawn, already starred with daisies, badly needed cutting.

But these were seasonal changes; the house itself was as it had always been – solid, spacious, and altogether sure of itself, like everything else that belonged to Victoria's reign. The difference was in herself; the Greek experience had been brief but shattering. She'd suffered the sea-change that Lawrence Durell once said befell all travellers who crossed from the Adriatic into the Ionian Sea. The detached observer of other people's lives had joined the herd at last, so it seemed all the more unfair that she should feel lonely right among it now when she never had before.

In an effort to make herself properly at home again she wandered from room to room, touching things that were long familiar; but even when her hands held the well-worn teddy bear that still sat beside her bed, as it had since childhood, her mind was on the beloved her house knew nothing about. The struggle *not* to think about him was not only very tiring, it was also wrong, she was slowly realizing. What she must do instead was allow the thought of him to keep her company; in that way she could draw out the worst poison of her loneliness, and before long the effort needed to remake her life would fill her waking hours completely. She stroked the nose of the bear she was still holding, told him that somehow they'd manage very well, and then went downstairs to telephone Victor Melksham and tell him that she was back in Oxford.

In Paris, Pierre was for once being visited by his wife; Madeleine more usually asked him to climb the stairs to *her* apartment if there was something to discuss. She was, he knew, exactly the same age as himself, but she looked younger than forty-one. Frequent appearances in front of cameras required perfect grooming, of course, but he'd never known her anything but immaculately turned out – her sense of style was what had first attracted him because it had been much more rare than youthful prettiness.

'A new hair-cut,' he remarked as she perched on the edge of his desk.

'You're supposed to say more than that,' she pointed out with the little teasing smile he'd once enjoyed before the world at large had learned to enjoy it too. 'Something complimentary would do!' But she didn't press the point, having some doubt herself about the success of the style she'd been talked into.

She picked up a letter on his desk and idly noticed its heading, the Corfu Palace Hotel. 'You were away for longer than I expected. Did it take that long to decide that the paintings you were looking for didn't exist?'

Pierre took the letter out of her hand and put it down. 'You've been too busy since I got back to hear that the Kladis paintings *do* exist; I even managed to buy two of them. There are others that I've been told about since – not for sale, unfortunately, but I shall go and see them as soon as I can.'

Madeleine Bouchard stared at him for a moment, wondering if she imagined some change in him that even she, skilled as she was in dissecting anyone she talked to, wasn't able to pin down. It was a long time since she'd given any serious thought to their relationship; it now worked, she believed, in a way that suited them both. She accepted that Pierre probably enjoyed the company of other women – was fair-minded enough to know that their arrangement entitled him to; but she'd never doubted for a moment that concern for Amélie wouldn't be enough to keep him with them in the house in the Rue Jacob. She didn't really doubt it now . . . probably it was something about the paintings that troubled him.

'Show me what you bought,' she suggested carelessly after a moment. 'I'd like to know why you're making such a thing about this unknown, unimportant artist.'

He had to deal first with a sudden urge to shout at her. 'I brought them back unframed – they're away at the moment, I'm afraid. You can see them when I get them back. The artist, unknown but very definitely *not* unimportant, was a Corfiot called Nikos Kladis; he was taken to a German concentration camp because his wife and parents-in-law were Jewish. He was thirty-five when he died there, with them.'

'And you're angry about that, as well as sad,' Madeleine said, satisfied to know that she'd been right about the cause of his edginess. 'I'll explain to Jules Gramont – I saw him yesterday and he complained that you were very unlike yourself when he met you in some restaurant or other; you bit his head off, I rather gathered.'

'If I did it's no more than he deserves; spreading salacious gossip about people in high places for money isn't a fit occupation for any man in my opinion.'

She was taken aback for a moment by the contempt in his voice. 'You're very severe, my dear Pierre. At least admit that his gossip is amusing and usually well founded.' She glanced at her watch, and stood up. 'I must go and change . . . I'm dining out tonight. Celestine is picking Amélie up from her dancing lesson; you could go up and say good night to her if you're staying in.'

Pierre stared at her, trying to see in this now thoroughly professional woman the eager, intense girl he'd fallen in love with a long time ago. 'Don't you get tired of it?' he asked curiously. 'The endless round of restaurants, receptions, political skirmishing and chicanery?'

She seemed genuinely surprised at the question. 'It's fascinating . . . how could I possibly get tired of what I'm so good at? Anyway, it amuses me to know that quite important people are a little bit afraid of me . . . I perform a public service in my own way!'

'So you do . . . I was forgetting that.'

She hesitated, held there by something in his expression that looked for a moment like intolerable sadness. 'Are you all right?' she asked, sounding almost uncertain for once.

He picked up the letter he'd put down, as if it needed reading again, and gave her a brief smile. 'Perfectly all right, but thank you for asking. I'll go up and see Amélie. Enjoy your dinner.'

Irritated by the feeling that she'd been dismissed, Madeleine promised that she would and went away. It was tragic, of course, that anyone should have perished in a concentration camp, but she couldn't help thinking that Pierre was slightly obsessed with the fate of a single victim, even if he had been a talented artist. It was a pity that Bouchard *père* had ever discovered the paintings of Nikos Kladis, and it would certainly be inconvenient to have Pierre dashing off to Corfu again the moment he got the chance.

When she'd left the room her husband read Anna's letter yet again. He'd done that many times already, but still he could find in it no hint of regret, no tinge of warmth, no faint suggestion that she even remembered the night they'd spent together. He'd removed the letter from Madeleine's hand soon enough, but not because it contained anything she shouldn't read. As clearly as if she'd written the words, Anna was saying that a very brief relationship was over . . . repeating it, in fact; it was exactly what she'd said when they'd parted at the entrance of the Phoenix Hotel.

He put the letter back in a drawer of his desk, and promised himself that he wouldn't look at it again. Nor could he do anything about going back to Corfu, beyond writing to let Stefanos Kladis know how much the permission to look at his father's paintings had been appreciated. The summer ahead looked over-full already, with his own gallery to run, and two international exhibitions to arrange – one in New York, and the other on the far side of the world in Sydney – but before the end of the year he would somehow get to Mondhiki. That was another promise he made to himself.

Seventeen

With her pregnancy confirmed, Anna felt better; it was uncertainty that was tiring, she told her old friend, Victor Melksham, over the home-coming supper she'd invited him to. He'd taken the news surprisingly well, she thought, until she remembered that he was a lawyer, experienced in the problems people created for themselves.

'Moving house is going to be even more exhausting,' he pointed out. 'Must you do it at this moment of your life?'

'This is the moment to do it,' she insisted, smiling at him. 'Everything has to change now, and for the next few months I shall be full of energy – at least, if all the stories I hear about pregnant women are true!'

Victor Melksham nodded, reverting in his mind to the brief account she'd given him of her visit to Corfu. 'You mean you've laid your grandfather's ghost to rest, and Lavinia's house can safely be left in someone else's hands?'

'That's how it feels,' she agreed, 'as if it's right to be moving out.' After a moment's thought she went on. 'I didn't just visit Corfu. With the help of a friend who directed me to the right department in Athens, I found a lovely old man who'd been in Grandfather's group of partisans. He spoke of him with a kind of reverence, and insisted on giving me the dog-eared paperbacks that he'd kept after Steven died – *The Odyssey* and *The Iliad*, as if you couldn't guess! Their hunting-ground was up on Parnassus itself, so I went there as well, and of course to visit Delphi. It was very moving . . . unforgettable, in fact.'

Victor Melksham stared at her across the supper-table.

He'd known her all his life, watched her grow into the woman she'd become; it seemed to him that in her self-reliance and uncomplaining acceptance of what had happened she fitted very well into the group of people that included Steven Curtis, his friend Nikos, and their fellow-partisans; even Lavinia Curtis, unlikable though she'd often seemed, had been in the same courageous mold.

'You also mentioned a painting,' he remembered suddenly. 'Did you bring that back as well?'

She left the table to pull it out of a bureau drawer. 'I offered this to my mother, but she insisted that I keep it. I haven't had a chance to get it framed yet.' She handed him Nikos's sketch, and waited for what his response would be; when it came she wasn't disappointed.

'He puts me in mind of Byron's "Corsair" – "the mildest-mannered man that ever scuttled ship or slit a throat"! What an artist Nikos Kladis was – in a few brush strokes he lays out for you the complicated character of a gentle scholar-turned-warrior! No wonder Steven was so much loved.'

Victor handed her back the sketch, and reverted again to her own affairs. 'Are you determined not to let Pierre Bouchard know about his child? Is that quite fair, Anna?'

'It may not be fair,' she answered quietly, 'but there isn't any alternative. Pierre's life is in Paris with his wife and daughter. He was perfectly entitled to think that if I agreed to sleep with him I'd taken the necessary precautions. I hadn't, as it happened, but I don't regret it. I want the child very much.'

'Then I shan't go on trying to persuade you to get in touch with him,' Victor Melksham said, 'but let my people in the office take care of the sale of this house; since you already have a buyer lined up you won't need an estate agent for that. But you *will* need one, probably, when it comes to looking for something to buy.'

In the following days Anna discovered that he'd been right – even thinking about moving house was an exhausting business, especially when the house was one she'd lived in all her life. But *she*'d been right, too – it left her no time at least to dwell on any part of the past; it was concern for the future that now filled her waking hours, and at night sheer tiredness mercifully sent her to sleep.

Then one morning she remembered with a slight pang of conscience the man whose gallery window had begun the series of events that changed her life – it was high time she called on Rupert Whittaker again.

His face lit up when she walked in but she smilingly shook her head. 'The answer's still no, I'm afraid; I only came to tell you what I now know about Nikos Kladis.' She recounted only what had happened during the war but thought the art-dealer also ought to be told that more paintings had survived than they'd known about. 'They aren't for sale either; Nikos's son and grandson insist on keeping them. But I *was* allowed a visit, and they're simply beautiful.'

'I think I should at least let Pierre Bouchard know that,' Rupert Whittaker suggested.

Anna shook her head. 'There's no need – he knows already; he was on Corfu when I was there, but he didn't get to see the paintings . . . I was lucky enough to have a sort of family connection.' She smiled suddenly at the man facing her. 'You can come and see mine if you like – that would be easier than bringing it to you.'

He was so eager that he called at the house the next evening, and spent a long time looking at the painting. 'It's an extraordinary technique,' he said at last, '. . . not something that Kladis was ever taught, I suspect; he was simply a natural, instinctive, *born* painter.'

Over the whisky that Anna then offered her visitor, she explained that she would be leaving the house as soon as she could find the new home she wanted.

'Still in Oxford, I hope,' said Rupert Whittaker, who'd discovered that he wanted very much not to lose track of her.

'Not far from, at least . . . but I want to find a village

house, not go on living in a city. I've inspected three so far – two of them on the verge of falling to pieces, the third one renovated to death. I shall just have to go on looking.'

He considered this for a moment, then diffidently made a suggestion of his own. 'I know of a cottage just going on the market in Long Wittenham. The owner died recently and his widow asked me to go and look at some pictures she wanted to sell. It looked rather charming to me. If you liked, I'm sure I could arrange a visit. It's not late . . . I could even ring her now.'

Anna accepted the offer gratefully, listened to his telephone conversation, and found that she would be expected at The Clerk's Cottage the following morning.

It proved to be even better than Rupert's modest claim for it. The thatched cottage was certainly old, but not antiquated, attractive without being self-consciously picturesque, and it had obviously been loved and cared for.

'You must hate the thought of leaving it,' Anna suggested to its present owner.

Audrey Graham smiled ruefully. 'When you get to my age your children know best – I'm to be accommodated in a granny-flat next to my daughter! I don't mind too much, and I shall love seeing my grandchildren growing up. But I shall be happier about going if *you* buy the cottage; I have the feeling that you'd love it as my husband and I did.'

Anna had the feeling too, and drove away from Long Wittenham certain that her new home had been found, thanks to Rupert Whittaker. Life moved in mysterious ways its miracles to perform, but there was no doubt that he'd been involved in two of its most crucial turning-points as far as she was concerned.

She moved out of Oxford a month later and, unlike Audrey Graham, closed the front door for the last time without any trace of regret.

A glorious Indian summer was only a memory by the time she drove to Didcot station to meet the train from London.

It was the kind of grey December day, cold and damp, that Nicola would particularly hate; before she'd even arrived she'd be regretting having left Rome to spend Christmas in England. But having been helped out of the train by a kind young man, who insisted on waiting while she hugged her daughter, she managed to smile bravely despite the atmospheric gloom. It wasn't even necessary to implore him to carry her luggage out of the station – he couldn't miss Anna's by now advanced state of pregnancy, and asked cheerfully to be directed to her car.

'You're looking well . . . blooming, in fact,' Nicola announced as they drove out of the car-park a few minutes later. 'If your cottage isn't *too* desperately medieval, I shall love being here.'

'You'll be pleasantly surprised,' Anna said, tongue in cheek. 'It's got running water, electric light, and even a lavatory indoors; no need to run to the bottom of the garden!'

Nicola thought wistfully of Rome . . . of the chilled wine she drank as an aperitif, and the heated bathroom she liked to linger in each morning; but Anna needed her, she reminded herself. That was the very good reason she was here.

'Who was the Clerk?' she asked, remembering the strange name of the cottage.

'My part of the village was owned by one of the Oxford colleges. The Clerk kept an eye on property and collected the rents. Rather more recently the cottage was owned by a military man who modernized it without spoiling it. I've grown to love living there.'

Driving through the gateway a little later, Nicola admitted that it looked nice, even with the branches of the wistaria now bare against its white-washed walls. Inside, she admired a stone fireplace in the sitting-room that could roast the proverbial ox, but was relieved to see the discreetly positioned radiators as well. If the kitchen boasted a refrigerator and a dish-washing machine she'd reckon that the clerk and the military man between them had organized things quite well.

When she came downstairs from inspecting her room, there *was* cooled Riesling waiting for her, and she sank into an armchair by the fire with a little sigh of pleasure.

'Nice neighbours?' she asked.

'Very nice. There may be some little feuds I'm not yet privy to, but everyone I've met has made me feel welcome. My Oxford friends drive out to visit me, and dear Victor Melksham keeps a fatherly eye on me.' She smiled at Nicola over the top of her wine-glass. 'I've even had an offer of marriage, despite my all too obvious condition!'

'From an elderly widower hoping for a new lease of life?'

'No, from the man who really began the train of events that brought me here. He owns a picture-gallery in the High.'

'It didn't occur to you to accept, I suppose?'

Anna shook her head. 'He's a nice man, and I enjoy his company, but I don't want to marry him. Anyway, I suspect him of wanting my Kladis painting more than he wants me – he looks wistfully at it each time he comes!'

She leaned forward to refill her mother's glass, then sat back again. 'Seriously, I'll answer the question you can't bear to ask. I haven't stopped loving Pierre and never shall, I now realize, so I no longer pretend that I might find someone else. At least I've got the happiness of bearing his son – you see, I already know it's a boy!'

'And you know what you're going to call him?'

'Henry . . . Hal for short.' Anna hesitated for a moment before going on. 'I hope you won't mind that he and I are both going to be called Curtis soon – by courtesy of deed poll! I thought that a small Henry Rasini in an English school might have a lot to live down.'

Nicola ventured on her next question. 'Are you in touch with the Kladis family yet?'

'Yes, I wrote to Eleni because I was afraid she'd feel hurt at not hearing from me; but she still doesn't know about the child. The only person who does know in Greece is called Evgenia Vassilikos. Pierre took me to meet her and we've become dear friends. She reads other people's hearts very easily, so she guessed the state of mine straightaway and feared that I'd be unhappy. That's why I told her about Henry. But even if Pierre goes to visit her again she'll keep the news from him.'

Anna took a sip from her glass and smiled at her mother. 'There's happiness now at Mondhiki, by the way. Petros and Eleni were married a month ago, and I think I can take a little of the credit for that.'

'So *she* knows where you are, too?'

'Yes, but it doesn't matter. Pierre has never gone to see the Kladis paintings. Perhaps things that he knows he won't be able to buy don't seem worth a complicated journey; or perhaps he's always just too busy. I read not long ago that he'd organized a hugely successful French Impressionist exhibition in New York; compared with that a handful of Kladis paintings might seem very small beer.'

In the firelight her face looked sad for a moment, but she saw Nicola staring at her and went on cheerfully. 'There's another piece of good news . . . Do you remember me mentioning the American couple I met going down to Brindisi? It's a long story, but they finally managed to buy the ruin that belonged to George's family, together with a sizeable piece of land – not very far from Mondhiki, as it happens. They're back in America at the moment, but they'll start rebuilding in the early spring, and my guess is that they'll end up living there all the time. There's something very seductive about Prospero's island!' Then she heaved her heavy body out of the chair. 'Drink up . . . supper's ready. I hope you won't be too bored with village life for the next few weeks. From my point of view it's lovely to have you here.'

'I should have come sooner,' her mother said, 'and I'm never bored.'

Rather to Anna's surprise, that turned out to be true. For one thing, Nicola insisted on taking over the kitchen, and revealed herself to be an inspired cook. When her daughter confessed that this was unexpected she pointed out that no woman who wished to keep an Italian happy for thirty years, as she had kept Enrico Caetani happy, neglected to learn how to cook.

Then in one of her walks about Long Wittenham, she met the head-teacher of the village school and discovered that he not only remembered the name of Nicola Rasini but possessed all the recordings she'd ever made.

'He was quite overcome,' she explained when she got back to the cottage, '. . . and he was so nice that I've agreed to something I shall certainly regret.'

'You've said you'll sing at their carol concert,' Anna suggested, smiling at her.

'Worse – I've promised to go and help the children rehearse, in the hope that the audience will recognize the carols they have to sit through at the actual performance.'

With the concert only a week away there was no time to be lost, and Nicola set off for the school the following morning. When she came home Anna half-expected to hear that she'd thrown in her hand and found some excuse not to go back. Instead, a famous diva had decided that, come hell, come high water, the children were going to *sing* – in tune, in time, and all together. But in the course of the next few days it became obvious that she was also enjoying herself.

'You're loving it, aren't you?' Anna said one evening when they were sitting over supper. 'I think you've discovered that you really can teach . . . it isn't just a boring chore you've taken on.'

'Well, they're all delightful and worth being given some proper coaching, but there's one child there, Sandra Blott by dreadful name, with a voice so pure, so perfect in pitch, that I can't believe she isn't a real singer in the making. I guarantee that when she's finished "Away in a Manager" strong men will be weeping.'

And when the evening of the carol concert arrived, Anna saw what she meant. No one in the crowded hall stirred or coughed or cleared their throats, and then came the final memory to take away – Nicola's still-beautiful voice leading the children in 'Silent Night, Holy Night', which she'd taught them to sing in German.

'It feels like Christmas already,' Anna said as they walked home. 'And there's something else this evening has shown me – you gave up singing much too soon. Perhaps you don't want the strain of public performance any more, but shouldn't you think of more teaching . . . master-classes maybe, for advanced students? Will you think about it?'

'I might,' Nicola agreed cautiously, 'but not yet. We have to get your performance over first.'

'Christmas, *then* me,' Anna agreed. 'I've asked two lonely men – Victor Melksham and Rupert – to share the turkey with us, by the way. There isn't room at the moment for both of us in the kitchen, so who's going to cook it, you or me?'

'Me . . . and I shall be wishing that Enrico was here to taste the forcemeat balls and chestnut stuffing.' Then she glanced at her daughter in the light of the street-lamp they were passing. 'Thoughtless of me, darling. We could do with your Frenchman here as well, of course.'

'Definitely not *my* Frenchman,' Anna managed to say firmly. 'I doubt if he can even remember my name! I mention him in my prayers, but his brief part in my life was over before we left Athens.' It wasn't true, of course, because he was still the companion of her mind and heart, but Nicola needed to be reassured that she could return to Rome without leaving a desperate daughter behind.

Despite the freezing night they attended midnight mass on Christmas Eve to give the cook plenty of time the following day to work her miracles. They walked home through a hoar-frosted white wonderland, and told each other smugly that the Clerk's Cottage *looked* festive and *felt* warm and welcoming; their guests should feel themselves fortunate.

'It's a very different Christmas from last year,' Anna also pointed out thoughtfully. 'Then Granny was just dead, you were hating every minute you spent in her house, and I hadn't the slightest inkling of all that this year would bring. Look at us now . . . happy as sandboys, whatever sandboys are.'

She kissed her mother goodnight and hauled herself up the stairs to bed, leaving Nicola to struggle with a very rare longing to burst into tears. It wasn't the time of unadulterated gloom that last Christmas had been, that was true enough; but not all Anna's gallantry could make it right for her to be facing childbirth and the long years ahead alone. Nicola still remembered the despair she'd been rescued from herself by Enrico. Whatever the feminists might say – and as a breed they were inclined to talk far too much and too often – a woman needed a man to make her feel complete and beautiful; that had been the case from the beginning of time, and any female who denied the fact was a fool.

There was clearly nothing to be hoped for from Pierre Bouchard and, remembering her own ex-husband, Nicola had to give him a grudging good mark for not wanting to leave his daughter; but *someone* was needed to replace him in Anna's prayers. She didn't despair of Rupert Whittaker but she'd reserve judgement until she'd met him over the roast turkey. 'Joy cometh in the morning,' Scripture said; Nicola wasn't yet convinced of this, but at least she felt slightly cheered as she turned out the light and climbed the stairs.

Eighteen

The feast was memorable, the guests – meeting for the first time – liked one another, and, best of all in Anna's opinion, they both seemed prepared to fall under her mother's spell. She'd expected this of Rupert Whittaker, but Victor had always been stubbornly resistant to Nicola's charm. He'd acknowledge her beauty and admitted that her operatic success had been deserved, but how could one approve of a woman who had not one charitable word to say of her mother, virtually abandoned her own child, and lived in sin for years with a very colourful Italian?

Now, though, Nicola's faults were obviously being forgiven and he didn't even seem to mind that, aware of the thaw, she was teasing him a little. She was more interested in their other guest, unable to decide whether his slightly precious air came from choice or from habit. The flamboyant clothes, scarlet silk handkerchief cascading from the pocket of a dark-blue smoking-jacket, pleased her – Enrico had been a sharp dresser too – but, kind and civilized though Rupert Whittaker clearly was, she couldn't see him dislodging the image of Pierre Bouchard in her daughter's stubborn heart. Still, at least she could mark him down as a true friend.

The leisurely meal was over and they were sipping coffee by the fire when Victor Melksham asked whether Anna would be able to go on writing after her child was born.

'Oh, I hope so,' she said, 'but it depends whether I get a contented baby who eats and sleeps as required! All I have to show for the past year is a collection of short-stories – enjoyable to do, for a change, but not what I've got in mind.'

Rupert pounced on this. 'You've got something fizzing away in your imagination . . . an enviable state of affairs for a writer, but frustrating if she isn't able to come to grips with it!'

Anna's smile agreed that this was so. 'As it happens you can double the frustration – I've got *two* ideas' she explained, 'but one of them I might never be able to write about. It's the story in part of my own family and involves people who'd rather not be written about.'

'Wouldn't a change of names remove the objection?' Victor suggested.

Anna thought of the Kladis family and Loukas Pandelios and shook her head. 'I'm afraid the people would still be recognizable. In any case, I used a promise *not* to publish as a kind of blackmail!' Their astonished faces made her smile, but required her to go on. 'Don't look so horrified! There was a man I had to prevent destroying someone else's dream . . . If I'd written the story *his* father would have been exposed for what he did in war-time Corfu.'

'So reasonable in the circumstances, don't you think . . . a little blackmail?' Nicola enquired mildly of their guests. 'You know I can just remember a time when my daughter's sheltered existence in Oxford worried me. Now I can't decide whether a few weeks in Greece were the making of her or ruined her character for ever.'

It was Rupert who answered with unexpected firmness. 'There's no doubt about it at all – Anna came back liberated . . . it's the true Greek experience.'

'And my grandfather would have approved of it,' she suggested, smiling at him.

'I agree,' Victor's deep voice chimed in, 'but you said you had two ideas, Anna – what's the other one?'

'Well, that's the story of a Grecian lady whose life begs to be written. Since I came back from Greece I've been receiving instalments of her history, which is also the recent history of Greece itself. I must turn it into a work of fiction, of course, but it's a gift to make any author's mouth water.

The responsibility is also huge. Brave, beautiful Evgenia deserves to be immortalized, and I just have to hope that I can do her justice – but the people concerned must be disguised.'

Rupert was the first to get in with a question. 'I suppose she lives in Athens . . . would she like to be visited by an insignificant, nearly middle-aged Englishman who especially admires courage and beauty when they occur in a Grecian lady?'

Laughing, Anna corrected him. 'Not Athens, Rupert. She now lives high up in the village of Arachova, overlooking Delphi and the Pleistos Valley, and I can't describe the splendour of the view from her verandah.'

He was silenced by what he could see in his imagination, and it was Victor who suggested that it was time to bring a memorable evening to a close. Rupert reluctantly agreed, but in case he should seem not to have admired local rather than Greek beauty enough, he warmly invited Nicola to visit his gallery and be given lunch before she returned to Rome.

'If I can't avoid going into Oxford I'll be sure to let you know,' she agreed.

He smiled but felt bound to protest. 'Dear lady, you're being unkind about a city I love! It has its unsightlinesses, I grant you, but think of Christ Church meadows at dawn on a summer's day, and think of the High, lamplit, on a misty autumn evening . . . I could go on and on, of course.'

Nicola hoped he wouldn't, because she could see that the younger of his hostesses was now very tired. Skilfully shepherded to the door, both guests finally said goodnight and went out into the frosty night, and she went back into the sitting-room to find Anna gratefully sunk in an armchair by the still-glowing fire.

'Unwind a little,' she said, 'then you must go to bed – you look exhausted.'

'But you did most of the work! They both had a lovely time. Rupert has gone away more than half in love with *you*;

not me, which is as it should be, and even Victor was quite won over at last.'

Accustomed to the effect she had on mature but still impressionable men, Nicola didn't bother to dispute this; she had something else on her mind.

'You talked about Greece this evening. I've been waiting for the right moment to tell you something and I think this is it: I tried to get in touch with my half-sister.'

'Tried . . . how?' Anna asked in astonishment.

'By getting my highly-placed Catholic contacts to do some ferreting for me! There turned out to be only one convent in Athens where Miranda could have gone. Then I wrote to the Mother Superior – explained who I was and asked whether I could meet my sister, supposing she was still there.'

'What happened – did you get a reply?'

'Of course, nuns can't help being polite! The Mother Superior wasn't there when Miranda – now Soeur Monique – arrived twenty-five years ago, but she knows her history. The poor girl *is* still there, but visitors aren't allowed; the Order is strictly enclosed.'

Anna thought back to her conversation with Stefano Kladis. Miranda had always felt different from the rest of them, even as a child, but that wasn't the same as saying that she'd known who her real father was.

'Suppose she *wasn't* told why they all died – her mother, Nikos, Katerina . . . What a shock to learn the truth now.'

But Nicola shook her head. 'Miranda certainly did know, and blamed herself. As she saw it, *she* was to blame; if she hadn't been born the tragedies wouldn't have happened.'

There was one more question to ask. 'Was Miranda – Soeur Monique – told that you'd written?'

'Yes, and I think the Mother Superior might even have stretched a point and let me meet her, but Miranda herself refused. God knows what we'd have talked about, or in what language, but I can't help feeling terribly let down that it didn't happen.'

Anna thought about this for a moment. 'There's something you've forgotten,' she finally pointed out. 'Miranda withdrew from the world, as she saw it, to keep the people near her safe from more harm . . . especially Eleni. I think she probably had the same idea about you – that you were better off not knowing her. She sounds to me exactly like Steven Curtis's daughter.'

Nicola slowly nodded. 'That would explain the last thing that happened. I wrote to thank the Mother Superior for her help and assumed that would be the end of it; then some time afterwards an envelope arrived. There was no note inside, only a carefully wrapped and beautifully carved ivory rosary.'

'A gift from your sister,' Anna said gently. 'How lovely!'

There was silence in the room for a moment until Nicola put another thought into words. 'Rupert talked about your liberating Greek experience this evening; he was right, of course, but there was something else he didn't know about. It may sound harsh and I don't mean it to, but it was Lavinia's death that liberated us both.' Then she pointed at the ceiling. 'Now, upstairs for you . . . you look done in. Are you feeling all right?

'Tired but fine, thank you, and so glad you're here. Have I mentioned that before?'

'Yes, but I don't mind you repeating yourself.' She pulled Anna to her feet and kissed her goodnight. 'One way and another it's been quite a year.'

'But quite a good year, wouldn't you say? Only think of little Sandra Blott!'

'I do, quite a lot,' Nicola said seriously. 'Now please go to bed.'

Henry Peter Curtis made his appearance three weeks later, after a long and difficult labour, but he was worth every minute of it, Anna said, when she was given him to hold.

'Not fair like you,' the smiling nurse pointed out, looking at his mop of dark hair, 'but that'll probably change soon enough.'

She wasn't to know, Anna thought, that it might not, nor that his tiny fists would eventually become the long-fingered brown hands that his father had. Looking down at him, she was flooded with joy, but suddenly conscious, too, of very real fear. It was one thing to accept in principle the idea of bringing up a child alone; the reality was this small scrap of humanity in her arms, totally dependent for quite a long time to come simply on *her*. What if she fell sick before he was able to fend for himself? Friends were only friends; once Nicola went back to Rome, how would she manage if things went wrong?

'You're supposed to look happy and triumphant, not about to burst into tears,' said a voice beside her.

She opened her eyes to find Nicola smiling at her. 'You've got a gorgeous son – what's wrong with that?'

'Nothing at all,' Anna said, as she relinquished Henry to the nurse, '. . . absolutely nothing at all. We just need a little time to get used to each other.'

'Rupert's waiting outside to take me to lunch. He was steeling himself to come in, but I said you wouldn't be quite up to entertaining visitors just yet. Even fathers aren't wanted in maternity wards, in my opinion, much less male friends.'

'Quite right,' Anna agreed, now able to smile at her. 'Go away and enjoy your lunch . . . I shall go back to sleep.'

She was allowed home three days later, able to tell Victor Melksham, who insisted on collecting her from the hospital, that the enforced rest had done her a power of good.

'I was panicky for a while . . . afraid of not being able to cope,' she admitted. 'Quite daft, but I expect I was just feeling a bit low at the time; I'm all right again now.' She smiled affectionately at her old friend. 'Hal's a bit short of family – may he look on you as an honorary uncle?'

'Grandfather would be more appropriate perhaps,' Victor amended ruefully. 'But yes, of course he may; I shall count it a privilege. All the same, a confirmed and rather elderly bachelor will be of very limited use to you, my dear. I wish you'd think of finding someone else – a live-in nurse – for when your mother goes back to Rome.'

'I am thinking about it,' Anna said. 'It's not fair to Nicola as things are – she'd like to go home, I'm sure, but doesn't want to leave me and Hal on our own.'

'And you won't get your Greek lady's story written if you don't have some help.'

'There's that as well,' she agreed with a smile. 'I do want to get on with it, and my publishers are very keen on the idea too. They reckon I've been idle for too long.'

She left Victor to negotiate the traffic in peace, and nothing more was said until they were at the cottage gate. Then he spoke again. 'Has Rupert told you he's going to Paris for a day or two? There's an exhibition there he wants to see.'

'I know, he told me; it sounds wonderful – fourteenth-century Siennese masterpieces that Pierre has rounded up from all round the world. Rupert's rather touched to have been sent an invitation to the official preview.' She turned to look steadily at Victor. 'He understands about not mentioning the baby if he should happen to talk to Pierre. Now, shall we introduce our young man to his home?'

Unable to persist with a subject he knew she wouldn't want continued, Victor lifted the baby's basket out of the car and followed her indoors.

A week later, when Rupert returned from Paris and came to see them at the cottage, he described the splendours of the exhibition first, and then the glossy attendance at the preview. 'Ministers and ambassadors thick on the ground, I gathered, and very few plebs like me.'

'I hope you got a chance to speak to Pierre,' Anna said calmly.

'Yes, I did. He also introduced me to his mother, a charming aristocratic lady, who rarely visits Paris, she told me. But she's very proud of her son!' Rupert hesitated for a moment before going on. 'I met Pierre's wife as well – *very* elegant, and very much at home in high society.'

'Yes, I believe she is,' Anna agreed, and then talked of something else.

But the next day brought another reminder of Pierre in the shape of a letter from Evgenia, full of love and congratulations on the safe arrival of the baby. Also inside the bulky package was all the remaining material that she'd collected over a long life. Her letter explained that she was sending it now because she wanted to be sure that Anna received it safely. There was a casual hint that she'd been feeling unwell, and a reminder that octogenarians couldn't expect to live for ever. Nevertheless she promised to do her best to survive until she could see Anna again and make the acquaintance of Hal Curtis. The tone of the letter was so typical of its sender that Evgenia seemed to be there in person, loving and funny and wise, but there was something faintly elegiac about it as well that Anna found worrying.

'It's the sadness of old age,' Nicola said when she was asked to read it. 'I get quite pensive myself at times and I'm only sixty-two! God knows what I shall be like by the time I'm Evgenia's age.'

Anna smiled, as she was meant to do, but grew serious again. 'I think you're getting pensive for your own home. You must, *please*, plan to go back to Rome soon. You've stayed far longer already than you meant to, and I shall manage very well now with the day-time help of dear Mrs Blott.'

Mrs Blott, mother of Sandra, had been pounced on by Nicola when discovered to be looking for work to keep her occupied now that her three elder children were 'off her hands'. She was experienced, kind, and sensible . . . just the sort of woman who was needed at The Clerk's Cottage.

Nicola waited a day or two more, saw that the new arrangement was working smoothly, and finally agreed to book her flight back to Rome.

'It's not the other side of the world,' she insisted almost tearfully when the moment came to say goodbye. 'I can be here in less than a day, and I shall be back in any case for Hal's christening. I shall also check with Rupert in case you aren't always truthful when I ring.'

About to say that she was always truthful, Anna blushed at the memory of certain 'charming inventions', as Evgenia had kindly put it. 'I'm more often truthful that not,' she said cautiously,' 'and I promise to say if I need you. Will that do?'

With this agreed, Nicola gave her a last hug, climbed into the waiting taxi and was driven away to the station. Anna checked that Hal was asleep, and Mrs Blott happily engaged in spring-cleaning cupboards, a job she particularly enjoyed, it seemed. With The Clerk's Cottage peaceful, she could return to Evgenia's diaries.

Apart from attending to Hal's regular requirements she spent most of the day reading and re-reading the diaries. They covered the years after the war; married by then, Evgenia lived in Paris with her husband, a Greek professor teaching at the Sorbonne. Stavros Vassilikos, she made it plain, had been a kind, vague academic who was more father than lover to his tempestuous wife. Inevitably Evgenia had embarked on a passionate affair with someone else – a Frenchman married to a delicate aristocrat unable to give him children. The strangest aspect of the affair was that it left both marriages intact: the Frenchman continued to love his frail wife, and Evgenia remained devoted to Stavros. Even the birth of her son – in the house at Arachova – was quietly dealt with. The child was given up to his father and his father's wife. Evegenia returned to Paris and watched him grow up as someone else's son.

Even reading her account of it was painful; what miracle of love and self-discipline all round, Anna wondered, had made the actual situation bearable? With life's usual irony, the frail wife had outlived her husband, and Evgenia had nursed Stavros until he died.

Anna put down the diaries at last with hands that shook slightly; the idea that was taking root in her mind was too incredible to be true . . . and yet . . . and yet, if it *were* true, it would explain so many things. Evgenia had changed the names of everyone except Stavros and herself, and had insisted that her story should become an imaginary piece of fiction. But it *had* all happened, and Anna believed she now knew who had lived it with Evgenia – surely her lover had been René Bouchard, and Pierre was her son.

It explained, as nothing else could, the bond between them that had been so obvious at Arachova; it explained why she herself had found it so easy to love Evgenia; and it finally explained why she'd been given the diaries at all. Bound never to tell Pierre the truth, at least while his *soi-distant* mother was still alive, Evgenia had needed *someone* to know and who better than the girl she knew loved Pierre?

Anna came at last to the final question to be thought about: what to do with the story she'd been entrusted with. Her conviction was still strong that Evgenia wanted her to use what she'd been given, and slowly she made up her mind – the novel would be about imagined people with invented names that no one need associate with anyone still alive. But it would be dedicated – anonymously – to a brave and lovely woman, a true heroine of Greece.

Nineteen

The winter had been even wetter than usual but Petros found nothing to complain of in that. Now, with the return of spring, the hillsides were already green and his new vines dotting the sweep of ground in front of him were sprouting just as they should. It was the time of the year when everything seemed possible, and failure needn't even be thought of.

Walking back towards the house, because it was almost lunch-time, he looked from force of habit at the spot where he'd found Anna in the ditch. There was no real expectation in his mind that he would ever find her there again, but there *was* always the memory of her bright hair shining in the sunlight, and her smile when she'd stopped berating him for leaving stones lying about the track.

Largely thanks to her, he now had a loving wife, and he and Eleni looked forward to the birth of their first child. Mondhiki was coming properly alive again; even his father had put away bitterness and left the past behind. He knew that he, Petros Kladis, was a fortunate man, so it did no harm to Eleni that, in a deep corner of his mind, he still cherished the memory of the Englishman's other granddaughter.

As he reached the house Eleni was laying the table on the terrace for lunch – the first time it had been warm enough to eat out-of-doors. When she smiled at him he was suddenly reminded of the day Anna had brought her back from Corfu Town, transformed by her new clothes, and smiling as she was now.

'Petros, your father's indoors . . . looking at the paintings.'

Something in her voice told him there was more to come. 'Do you remember the Frenchman, Pierre Bouchard?'

'Of course – I went to see him in town one day.' Of course, he might have said, 'He is the man Anna told me she'd fallen in love with.'

'Well, he telephoned a little while ago. He's arrived from Paris, and wants to see your grandfather's paintings. Cousin Stefanos said that he could, and we're to expect him tomorrow morning.' Then she hesitated before going on, not sure whether she was giving away something that should be kept to herself. 'Anna did say in the first letter she wrote to me that he might come to Mondhiki, and if he did, she wished him not to know where she was. But that was a long time ago . . . perhaps it doesn't matter now.'

'How can it when she must have been in touch with him herself?' Petros suggested. 'Bouchard would have known nothing about the paintings otherwise.'

Eleni smiled with relief. 'Yes, that's true, of course; then I needn't worry.' She made a minute adjustment to something on the table, nodded as if to say that it now looked right, and then thought of another troubling question. 'Shall we need to offer the Frenchman food? Is our normal lunch too simple for him?'

'Our normal lunch is what will be offered, if anything is.' He smiled at her anxious expression. 'The man is an art expert interested in my grandfather's paintings, not the President of the Republic, Eleni, love. My guess is that he'll make his inspection and then leave. Now, may we start on *today*'s lunch? I've a lot of work still to do.'

Gently called to order, she went indoors to check with Maria that everything was ready, and Petros went in search of his father. He found Stefanos in what they called the 'painting room', still staring at the pictures hanging on the walls.

'I wish I understood why men like Mr Bouchard want to come and see them. They just copy what's here – the house, the olive-groves, the sea down in the bay . . .'

'I know, but they're not meant for us,' Petros said gently. 'They're to show people not lucky enough to live here what a small Greek island has to offer.' Then he smiled at his father. 'Eleni sent me to tell you that lunch is ready.'

The following morning, aware that his father and his wife were nervous, Petros changed the normal pattern of his working day so that he'd be near the house when Pierre Bouchard arrived. At least he'd met the Frenchman before – that would ease things surely.

The visitor arrived promptly, and looked round with obvious pleasure as he got out of his car.

'Good morning,' Petros found himself saying in English, as if it seemed fairer for them both to be using something other than their mother tongue. 'You found Mondhiki without trouble, I hope.'

'It's well-hidden,' Pierre replied, 'but I can't blame you for that. If it were mine I'd make it hard to find as well!'

They shook hands, taking stock of one another. To the visitor, it seemed a different man who stood in front of him from the one he'd met in Corfu Town. This Petros Kladis had the advantage of being on his own ground, but it was more than that – he was relaxed now, and unsuspicious. Petros, in turn, studied the Frenchman and found a change in *him* – Bouchard was still elegant even in the casual clothes he wore, still able to take charge in any situation, but he looked thin, and the pleasant smile quickly faded to leave his face reticent again.

'My wife, Eleni, and my father are indoors,' Petros said. 'Come and meet them.'

He was introduced first to the smiling, dark-haired girl who was Petros's wife – Eleni Kladis, as she now was, looked far removed from the sad drudge of Anna's description of her. Marriage and the first unmistakable signs of motherhood had given her poise and even a kind of beauty.

'Welcome to Mondhiki,' she said as he bowed over her hand. 'Like Petros, *monsieur*, I speak English but not French.'

'Alas, like half the world, *madame*,' he said ruefully. 'We're getting used to it, we French!'

She liked him instinctively and decided that lunch could be managed very well if Petros was wrong about him not wanting to stay. Then Stefanos Kladis appeared and she could safely leave the visitor to her father-in-law.

'You're welcome, Mr Bouchard,' he said. 'When Anna Rasini first asked me to let you come I refused. I think now I was wrong to do that. Mondhiki is friendlier than it was then, but you have Anna to thank for it, not me.'

'Nevertheless you're my host,' Pierre pointed out tactfully, 'so I'm grateful to you both.'

With the courtesies adequately taken care of, he was taken to the 'painting room' and left alone, after permission had been given for him to photograph and measure the canvases. An hour later Petros was sent to enquire whether the visitor was in need of food; if so, would he join them on the terrace? Pierre reluctantly agreed that he'd been there long enough and followed Petros outside.

While Maria served lunch conversation was general, but at last impatience got the better of Stefanos. 'What do you think of the paintings, Mr Bouchard – you're the expert.'

The expert raised his hands in a little gesture of despair. 'I don't know where to begin. Individually, each canvas would be stunning enough; as a group, they're almost overwhelming. The second thing to say is that their value in today's international market would be very high. I accept that you intend to keep them, but I must stress that selling them would make you rich.'

Stefanos first looked at his son, who shook his head, and then answered for them both. 'We don't need to be rich. Our land and livestock are here to be looked after – they provide all we want.'

It was an unfashionable view, Pierre thought, but his host was a very unfashionable man. 'Then there's only one more thing to point out,' he went on, 'and that's the preservation of the paintings. The room they're in is thankfully shaded, and Corfu's climate protects them from the worst variations in temperature; but they *will* gradually deteriorate outside the carefully controlled conditions of an art gallery. In my opinion that would be nothing less than a tragedy.'

Seeing that his father wasn't ready to speak, Petros asked a question. 'What are you suggesting – that we let you take them to a gallery in Paris?'

'Certainly not – they should stay on this island where they belong. But what I'd dearly like to happen is for the Municipal Gallery in Corfu Town to have them on loan, where they would be professionally cared for, and where everyone – citizen and visitor alike – would be able to see them. I'd like there to be a special Nikos Kladis display within the gallery that would give him proper recognition at last.'

In the silence that followed he studied their faces, kept deliberately blank while they considered the idea. 'You'll want to think about it, of course,' Pierre went on, 'and perhaps you'll decide to turn the suggestion down. But if you agree, I'll be glad to talk to the curator of the gallery, and I imagine that such a loan would be received with open arms.' There was one last hurdle to jump which he found the most difficult of all. 'Anna told me briefly why your father's life ended so prematurely. Any catalogue reference could merely record *when* he died, not how and why; that would be for you to decide.'

Then he stood up, thanked Eleni for her delicious lunch, and prepared to leave. But Stefanos, now also on his feet, wasn't yet ready to see him go.

'Wait, please, while I talk to my son indoors . . . We shan't keep you long.'

When Petros had followed him into the house, Pierre sat down again, smiling at Eleni. 'What is your guess, *madame*? You know Kyrie Stefanos much better than I do.'

Pleased to be asked, Eleni gravely considered the question. 'I think a loan is very possible,' she said at last. 'It would be the right way to honour the memory of his father; I'm sure Kyrie Stefanos understands that.'

Pierre nodded, then asked another question as casually as he could. 'He spoke of Anna Rasini as a good friend of the Kladis family . . . I hope you're still in touch with her?'

'Of course we are,' Eleni said with pride, '. . . I heard only the other day. Anna wrote to me of the "new man in her life" – that's just how she put it! His name is Henry, which she couldn't translate into Greek, but she said how happy they are to be living together. That pleases *me* very much, because I owe her a great deal, but I haven't mentioned it to Petros or his father because she doesn't yet speak of their marriage.'

Pierre stared out across the terrace, now not seeing any of its charm. He was remembering instead Anna's entranced face when he'd climbed the steps of the theatre at Epidaurus to guide her down to ground level again. He'd known *then* that he'd love her for the rest of his life; the night that followed had only confirmed it for him.

He became aware that Eleni was speaking again, and forced himself to make sense of what she said.

'We have a complicated family history,' she was explaining shyly. 'It happens that Anna and I share a grandfather, so we are related to each other . . . She told me to feel glad about that, and I am.'

'Your grandfather being someone called Steven Curtis,' Pierre managed to say. 'Yes, I think you should both be glad about that; by all accounts he was a splendid man.'

But it seemed to Eleni that her guest had lost interest in a conversation that she feared was too much about herself, and she was relieved to see Petros and her father-in-law walking back towards them. As usual Stefanos needed few words to make a decision known.

'We agree to the loan, Petros and I . . . my father's paintings must be properly taken care of. We will leave you to arrange it with the gallery.'

Pierre promised to do whatever was necessary, hoping that he sounded adequately pleased. At least there was now the best possible excuse to leave Mondhiki at once and head back to Corfu Town. Goodbyes were said, and then he was escorted to his car by Petros and waved away.

Twenty-four hours later, with the Municipal Gallery happy to start preparing a suitable area for its precious new exhibits, he began his journey back to Paris. From a professional point of view it had been a very successful visit, and that, he told himself, as the plane climbed and turned away from the island that lay so greenly in its sapphire sea, was all that mattered. He would come back to make sure that the paintings had been properly housed and hung, and by then his present sense of desolation would have faded. She wasn't any more lost to him now than when they'd parted a year ago . . . it just felt as if she was, that was all.

In Paris again, even a brief absence meant a backlog of work awaiting him. He was still at his desk at home one evening when Madeleine gave a knock at the door and walked in.

'My dear Pierre, I know I work strange hours, but that's the nature of my job. Surely you needn't still be glued to your desk at this hour of the evening?'

'Perhaps I couldn't think of anything more exciting to do. You clearly can, because you're dressed to go out. You mustn't let concern for me make you late!'

He smiled as he spoke but, as usual nowadays, she couldn't be sure how to take what he said. Behind the note of affable teasing lay something darker that she couldn't penetrate, and she found that professionally as well as personally irritating.

'It's concern for Amélie that brings me here,' she admitted, direct for once. 'You're often away from Paris, I'm away from home. It means that a child of nearly twelve is left to a servant far too much. Celestine is excellent, but Amélie needs more than her company.'

'So what are you suggesting – that we take it in turns to stay here?'

The question was meant to provoke, she thought, and it did. 'Be serious, please. We each do what we have to do. In any case what Amélie needs is companionship of her own age. The obvious answer is to let her go away to school.'

Knowing his wife very well, Pierre understood that the idea hadn't just occurred to her. The vague suggestion wasn't vague at all, and she probably had the school marked out already. But rather than make it easy for her, he said nothing and she was forced to go on.

'While you were away I took her to see a European School at Lausanne – lovely buildings, good facilities of every kind, and an excellent academic record.'

'Amélie appreciated all those things?'

She bridled a little at another dry question but answered with more patience than usual. 'What she appreciated most was a lot of children like herself obviously enjoying themselves. Well, they aren't children, of course; they're semi-adults, the product of sophisticated, intelligent parents from all over Europe. They learn each other's languages without any effort at all and grow up as European citizens, which we should all be instead of insisting that we're French, or German – or even Lithuanian nowadays.'

It sounded reasonable, of course, even though he could have insisted that French was, after all, what they were. Madeleine would have liked nothing better than the chance to defend her point of view, but it was Amélie's future they needed to thrash out.

'No snags at all?' he enquired.

'Only the cost!' she said ruefully. 'Since we're not having to live outside our own country for the general good of France, the fees for Amélie would be high. But if we share them they'd be bearable.' She looked at him for a moment, suddenly aware that without her noticing it before he now looked older than his real age . . . older and somehow more unfamiliar. 'I know you'll miss her,' she said more gently, 'but it *is* the best thing we can do for her, and she's wildly excited at the thought of going. We shall have her home for the vacations.'

The pass had been sold, he realized, before he even knew it needed defending. Amélie had already been infected with the idea of the glamour of a European school. The very word made him sick at heart, because it belonged to the world he'd wanted her *not* to grow up in. Between her celebrated mother and her cosmopolitan, no doubt precocious classmates how little chance she stood of not acquiring the very values he despised.

'I should prefer her to stay here,' he said at last, 'for *her* sake, not mine; but I suspect that I've only been asked to rubber-stamp a decision that has already been taken.'

Madeleine gave a little shrug. 'Not quite that, but it *would* be difficult now to tell Amélie that she's not allowed to go simply because *you* don't like the idea. May we go ahead, Pierre?'

He nodded and watched her consult her watch, the way their conversations usually ended. It was that simple, almost contemptuous action that seemed to provoke what he suddenly said next, without knowing that it had been in his mind.

'With Amélie away most of the time in future, there will be no reason to continue with our sham marriage. I should like to bring it to an end, please.'

There was a stillness in the room while Madeleine considered something that had taken her completely by surprise. She realized too late that she'd been a fool *not* to have anticipated it.

'A divorce . . . is that what you're asking for?' she finally suggested.

'I can't think of doing it in any other way, can you?' He saw the objection in her face and gave her no chance to put it into words. 'I'm serious, Madeleine. I'm tired of pretending to the world at large – your world, that's to say – that we have a real marriage.'

She tried to smile as if it hadn't hurt, just the least little bit. 'I suppose you want to marry someone else.' Then, when he shook his head, 'Live with someone else at least?'

'No, I shall live alone.'

'You'll want to sell this house . . . make me find another home?'

'I shall give you this house. I'll make an apartment for myself above the gallery.'

She lifted her hands in a little gesture of frustration. 'Then I don't understand why we can't just go on as we are. What's wrong with our present arrangement?'

'Simply that I can't bear it any longer.' The starkness of it was like a mirror held up so that she finally had to face the truth. This wasn't a spiteful tit-for-tat to punish her for sending their daughter away; he just wanted to be rid of her.

'Very well then; go – Amélie and I will stay here.' She sounded calm, but it was humiliating that he should want to be the one to leave, and infuriating not to be able to at least understand why their lives were to be so inconveniently disarranged.

'It's something that happened in Greece,' she suggested, '. . . something to do with those paintings you're so obsessed with. You haven't been the same since you started looking for them.'

'They are involved,' he admitted. 'I now know what the Kladis family story was about – real tragedy, real heroism . . . It makes our little charade more shoddy than I can live with any longer.'

A flush of natural colour disturbed the surface of her beautifully made-up face, but she managed to smile. 'That's putting it very bluntly, *mon cher*! But I shan't be difficult about your seeing Amélie – that would be very unfair.'

'Thank you,' he said gravely. 'Now, isn't it time you left for your appointment?'

She was already late, but still held there by an unusual sense of failure and regret. 'It was all so perfect to begin with, but I suppose my career made it all go wrong. I couldn't stop, Pierre, once I discovered how good I am at what I do . . . Can't you accept that?'

His mouth twisted in a wry smile. 'That's part of the trouble, I'm afraid – you see, I hate what you do!'

She gave a little sigh of relief; now she knew at last. He was simply like many another husband with a wife more celebrated than himself. Their failure wasn't her fault . . . it was some lack of generosity in *him*.

With the problem solved, she could sound brisk again. 'I'll see about the school; you must do what you want about the divorce. Goodnight, my dear Pierre.'

She went out and closed the door, leaving him to stare absently at the painting above his desk – the scene of Corfu Town that had been his first Kladis painting bought from Rupert Whittaker in Oxford . . . the beginning of it all. But for once he wasn't seeing its beauty. The conversation he'd just had with Madeleine would effectively empty his life – of child, wife, home and marriage. He had no way of knowing how he would survive that wholesale destruction. The only comfort he could cling to was the knowledge that it had come *after* his visit to Mondhiki, not before. For as long as he hadn't known about the new life Anna had made for herself with 'Henry' – he would hate that name from now on – there might have been an ulterior motive in destroying his existence in the Rue Jacob. But with absolutely nothing to be gained for himself, the decision to leave at least looked forgivable. It wasn't very much to be sure of, but it was something.

Twenty

The season changed more reluctantly in Oxfordshire than in Corfu. Even a later Easter than usual could produce only days of sleety rain that encouraged nothing to burst into bloom and blossom. It wasn't until May was mid-way through that Long Wittenham judged it safe to garden in shirt-sleeves – the surest indicator that the winter was past and the rain over and gone. The voice of the turtle might not be heard in the land, as the *Song of Solomon* promised, but the song of the blackbird certainly was.

It *had* seemed a long drawn-out winter, Anna admitted, when Rupert Whittaker arrived at the cottage one evening and accused her of looking tired.

'I expect you're working too hard,' he said severely, 'but it isn't just that, is it? You're here too much alone. When did you last go further afield than the not very exciting town of Didcot?'

'I've been to Oxford at least twice; that's excitement enough for the moment!' But the concern in his face didn't change, and she held up her hands in a little gesture of defeat. 'All right, I'll agree that my social life at the moment isn't what it was. A four-month-old baby is scarcely welcome at other people's dinner-parties. On the other hand there's the joy of watching Hal thrive and develop – so don't think I'm miserable, Rupert, because I'm not. Old friendships can be picked up later on; meanwhile I manage with dear people like you and Victor who come to admire Hal as well as talk to me.'

'I suppose you're working on the story of your Grecian

lady,' he suggested. 'Is that fun to do . . . is it going well?'

'It was slow to begin with because I had to link Evgenia's own story to the history of Greece after the war – and an incredibly chaotic and tragic history it was. But I've got a grip on it now, and I only stop when Hal needs seeing to.' Her own expression looked worried for a moment. 'I'm concerned about Evgenia, though. Around Christmas-time she hinted at not being well, and she hasn't answered any of my recent letters.'

'No telephone, no email?'

'No email address, and no one answers my calls. She could just be away, but I'd have expected her to say if she wasn't going to be there for some long time.'

Unable to help in any other way, Rupert switched the conversation to someone else. 'What about the man you threatened with blackmail . . . did that story end happily?'

'Oh, indeed it did – George and Irene Lambert, my American friends, are back on Corfu now, starting to work on the rebuilding of his family home. As a matter of fact that success gave rise to *another* problem! Irene kept inviting me to go and stay with them, so in the end I had to tell them about Hal. I hadn't done so thinking that Irene would be shocked by the idea of a child born out of wedlock . . . in a way I suppose I still agree with her!'

'What happened . . . did she suddenly forget that you'd salvaged their dream for them, and decide that she wasn't a friend any longer?'

'Not at all. She very sweetly insisted on coming here for Hal's christening, at which – as his godfather – you're also required to be present! Nicola's coming too, of course, much as she hates travelling alone!'

'I know,' Rupert said absently, '. . . she mentioned that once, I remember. I think I shall go to Rome and escort her back here.'

She inspected his face, and found that he was serious. 'You're a very dear and splendid man,' she remarked gravely, thereby giving him embarrassment and pleasure in roughly equal measure. 'There's nothing she would like better than to travel with a considerate gentleman again.'

'Then consider it done.' His charming smile shone for a moment. 'It gives me pleasure, you know, to help you whenever I can.'

She knew that it was true, but suspected that it would give him even more pleasure to help Nicola. He was in thrall to her spell, that was made up of part-legend and part-actuality, and Anna could foresee a time when he would have to deal with a problem of his own: how to offer to marry the mother, having previously proposed to her daughter. It was a thousand pities, Anna reckoned, that she'd ever mentioned his earlier suggestion.

But her immediate concern in the next week or two was Hal's christening, timed for the middle of June. Not only Nicola but *both* Lamberts as well now needed to be accommodated, and she was intent on both cottage and garden looking their early-summer best. While she toiled outdoors, Edna Blott, assisted by Sandra, worked in the house, washing and polishing and polishing again – just to make sure, said Edna – and when the day of the arrivals came the three of them smugly told each other that The Clerk's Cottage was a joy to behold, inside and out.

The Lamberts, the first to reach them, clearly thought so, and from the moment Hal offered them his grave stare followed by a small, sweet smile, they abandoned whatever doubts they'd had about Anna's fatherless son as well. Irene dealt with the vexed subject in her usual straightforward way.

'Better one lovely parent that two wrong ones is what I say, and George would say the same, Anna, if you asked him . . . wouldn't you George? My dear, it's so good to see you again . . . we never look at what we're doing at Linia without thinking that we wouldn't be doing it at all but for you.'

'When can you move in?' Anna wanted to know, anxious to honour her arrangement with Loukas Pandelios by giving the past a decent burial.

This time it was George who took up the tale. 'We've

brought photographs to show you . . . the work's going so well we'll have the last of the summer there. I haven't quite sold this to Irene yet, but I'd like to spend the winter in the house as well . . . partly to check it out, and partly to decide whether we *could* make it an all-year-round home. I can tell you now, Anna, it's going to be just beautiful . . . and we're both learning Greek!'

She smiled at him, thinking what a sensible and likable man he was; it seemed much more probable than not that they'd become permanent residents before another year was out . . . American Lamberts gradually becoming the Corfiot Lamberkis family again as far as the local people were concerned.

There was barely time to show them the house and garden before Rupert arrived back with Nicola and was pressed to stay for supper. Then the story had to be told again of how a Nikos Kladis painting in his gallery window had begun the adventure of Anna's search for her grandfather's love-affair with Greece. Entrusted with what they hadn't heard before, even Irene could find nothing to say, and she was dabbing away tears by the time Nicola produced from her bag Miranda's rosary that she now always carried with her.

The next day's christening went without a hitch in the presence, it seemed, of most of the village, and afterwards there was tea in the garden, served by the entire Blott family. Hal, with no idea what all the fuss was about, watched the proceedings with the considering stare that seemed to be his particular trademark.

The following day Nicola and Victor Melksham took Anna's American guests off her hands by showing them first his own old College – Christchurch – and then Blenheim Palace; by which time Irene's cup of wonder seemed to be overflowing. George, though, with feet firmly planted on the ground and more philosophically inclined, doubted whether mortal men could ever live happily in such monumental surroundings.

'Give me this place any time,' he said contentedly, when

they were back on Anna's terrace, with pre-dinner wine poured out for them. 'This is exactly the right size!'

They left the following day to go back to Corfu, having promised Anna that in Athens they would ask someone who could speak Greek to ring the house in Arachova and let her know the result.

'Nice people,' Nicola commented when they'd driven away, '. . . the nicest kind of Americans, in fact; but none the less tiring as house-guests for all that. Now we can undo our corsets, so to speak, and what bliss it is!' She shot a glance at her daughter's face, and then went on gently rocking Hal to sleep. 'I suppose you're dying to get back to work, but a good rest would do you more good. You're thin as a rake.'

'I'm fine all the same,' Anna said, 'just worried about Evgenia. It's so unlike her not to answer letters. Maybe I'll hear something from George, but I'm almost tempted to ring Pierre in Paris, even though I promised myself I never would.'

She was quiet for a moment, uncertain about what to say next, but in the end began to speak again.

'It's more complicated than you know, I'm afraid,' she said hesitantly. 'Since you were here last I've received Evgenia's remaining diaries – read and re-read them. There's no doubt in my mind now that although she wanted me to make use of them she sent them with another purpose as well – she needed me to know that Pierre Bouchard is *her* son, not the frail aristocratic lady's that Rupert met in Paris. He was handed over as a baby, and Evgenia had to watch him grow up, apparently as someone else's child.' She threw up her hands at the expression on her mother's face. 'I know – it sounds almost incredible, but given the people and the time and the circumstances it *isn't* unbelievable at all.'

'Pierre himself *doesn't* know?' Nicola managed to ask.

'Of course not; all he knows is that Evgenia was his parents' dear friend, and that what exists between him and her is simply a bond of close and loving friendship.'

'Dear God, I thought *our* family was dysfunctional,' Nicola said helplessly, 'but they can beat us into a cocked hat.' She thought about this for a moment and then put what else was in her mind into words. 'Not much more than a year ago we didn't know any of these people existed. Now, because my father had a love-affair with Greece, we seem to have become deeply involved in their lives, and *our* lives have changed as a result.'

'Mine has, certainly,' Anna agreed, smiling at her, 'and you've acquired a beautiful grandson you probably never expected to have.'

'It's more of a change than that. I'm going to come back to England,' Nicola suddenly confessed.

'Not because of us . . . *not* because of Hal and me,' Anna entreated her after a moment's shocked silence. 'You've loved living in Rome . . . you *know* that.'

Her mother's expressive face had become a mask of sadness. 'I loved being there with Enrico . . . now it's time to come home; it's as simple as that.'

Anna refused to be convinced. 'I think you're afraid I can't manage. Rupert's been worrying you with the notion that I'm too alone here. He means to be kind, but it's *not* kind to you. Of course it's lovely when you come, but you're not to upheave your life because I've upheaved mine; I won't have it.'

Nicola hushed her agitated daughter by taking hold of her hands. 'Darling, just stop talking, please, and listen. I've enjoyed Rome in the past, now I don't any more; I've disliked Oxford, now I don't even do that. I'm happier here than I could be anywhere without Enrico. I was fool enough to miss most of *your* childhood, and at least I want to watch Hal grow up. So don't, please, say I can't.'

Anna regarded her in silence for a moment, then suddenly smiled. 'Rupert's deeply in love with you, but I expect you know that.'

'Yes, I do,' Nicola agreed calmly. 'I shan't marry him . . . much to his relief, I think, because he's not really a marrying man, but we shall both enjoy our relationship very much –

not quite a love-affair, but much more than friendship. And I shall let him take care of me in my old age!'

She grinned herself as Anna burst out laughing, but then grew serious again. 'I'm not proposing to live with you – that wouldn't do at all – but I'll find a small house nearby. Dear Victor can help with that. First, though, I must go back and settle my affairs in Rome. It won't take long – I'm very good at getting other people to help me sort myself out.'

Anna smiled at her with a mixture of affection and respect. 'You're very good altogether! Are you going to keep an eye on Sandra Blott as well once you're here?'

'Of course – the child must be properly trained, and I shall see to it that she is. She won't be a *Wunderkind* prodigy if I can help it, discovered one moment, then ruined the next.'

Now accustomed to the efficiency that lay concealed under Nicola's outward helplessness, Anna wasn't surprised to find that within another day or two her mother's future was neatly planned. She would go back to Rome to close that chapter of her life while Rupert and Victor between them were given the privilege of finding her the house that she would like to buy somewhere near Long Wittenham. She kissed Anna a temporary goodbye, told Hal confidently that she'd be back with him before the summer was over, and then was driven away to the airport, wondering which of her Roman friends she would call on for help first.

Anna closed the front door, still smiling; then the telephone rang, and she heard George Lambert's voice at the other end of the line, calling from Athens with the message that she half-expected. Evgenia's servant at Arachova *had* finally been spoken to and had tearfully explained that her mistress was in a hospital in Athens. Irene had gone there, but been told that Evgenia was not well enough for visitors she didn't know. With the hospital address jotted down, Anna thanked George, and then at once began another letter to her friend.

Evgenia was dying – as she said calmly to Pierre while he sat beside her, holding her hand – but as usual she was peaceful and unafraid. 'I'm so glad you're here now, darling, to say goodbye, but then you must go home, *not* wait about here.' Her voice was a mere thread of sound, but still he heard an echo of its old authority.

'I'm on my way to Sydney, not going home,' he explained gently. 'I went back to Corfu Town for the opening of the Kladis Room, which looks splendid, and then I rang Arachova and Thekli told me you were here. Why didn't I know sooner; I'm very angry with you, much as I also love you.'

'There was nothing for you to do,' she murmured, smiling at that. 'I'm beautifully looked after. How are *you*, my darling? That's all I want to know.'

'Settling down again! Amélie has had a trial term at the school in Lausanne and loved it – Madeleine was quite right to send her, I now realize. Our divorce is going through, and at least *I* was right about that.'

Evgenia's smile again transfigured her worn face. 'Everything will be all right, then,' she whispered. '. . . I'm glad it's all arranged.'

He wanted to ask what she meant by that, but her eyes were closing and the nurse came in to say that he'd stayed long enough – it was time for Madame Vassilokos to rest now. He leaned over to kiss her cheek and then headed blindly for the door.

Ten minutes later, outwardly himself again, he listened to the sister explain that Evgenia's life was, indeed, drawing to a close. No, she said in answer to his question, she couldn't tell him when it would be – perhaps a week from now, perhaps a little longer. But Madame Vassilikos had arranged everything . . . there was nothing for him to do but go on with his life as he must and remember her with love.

'I'm needed . . . expected . . . on the other side of the world the day after tomorrow,' Pierre said unsteadily.

'Then you must go,' the sister insisted, 'she would want you to.' Then she smiled at him. 'We love looking after her, you know – you can safely leave her with us.'

Pierre fumbled in his pocket. 'Here are some telephone

numbers. Call me, will you please, if there's any change, and thank you a thousand times for your kindness.'

He left Athens that evening, and arrived in Sydney late the following night. A message awaited him from the hospital to say that Evgenia had died, it seemed, almost as his plane had been taking off.

Twenty-One

The lawyer's letter reached Anna a month later – the wheels of an Athenian law office grinding slowly, so much as a matter of course, apparently, that no apology for the delay was thought necessary. In English that had been rather strangely translated, it announced the death of Evgenia Vassilikos after a short illness. The date given for this meant, Anna calculated thankfully, that her last letter, addressed to the hospital, should have arrived before Evgenia died; but there was no way of knowing whether by then she'd been able to read and understand it.

She mopped away the tears that were now trickling down her face, and went back to the lawyer's letter to finish reading it. Her friend's estate was small, and the money that *was* remaining had been left to her servant. Then came the final heart-stopping paragraph: the house at Arachova was bequeathed jointly to Monsieur Pierre Bouchard in Paris and Miss Anna Curtis in England, and beneath the formal wording Anna thought she detected the lawyer's disapproval for so unusual an arrangement, but the gift was typical of Evgenia's special brand of generosity – instinctive, totally impractical, and full of love.

Inclined to start weeping all over again, Anna sat down at once to write to the lawyer, insisting that the legacy couldn't be accepted – the house must belong outright to Pierre Bouchard; she, Anna Curtis, was formally renouncing her share of it. Then, with Hal bundled into his pushchair for the short trip to the letterbox and her decision on its way, she felt able to relax again.

On the journey home she went into the church, to pray for Evgenia and to thank God for the privilege of having known her, and then walked back to The Clerk's Cottage. It wasn't until Hal had been bathed and put to bed that she allowed herself to think again about the house at Arachova. As seldom as Pierre would probably be able to enjoy it, she couldn't imagine him disposing of what had been Evgenia's home, and it gave her a kind of sad pleasure to think of him watching the moon rise from its airy verandah perched half-way between heaven and earth.

No further word came from the lawyer as the weeks of summer passed, and she thought it safe to assume that the house had been assigned to its new owner. But at least there was *good* news arriving from Corfu. George and Irene were installed in their new home; Eleni had given birth to a son, to be called Yanni after great-aunt Theodora's late husband; and they'd all gone to Corfu Town for the official opening of the Kladis Room that now housed Nikos's paintings. They sent Anna their love, and insisted that she should be the baby's godmother, or *koumbara*. And Eleni's P.S. said that she'd forgotten to mention that they owed the Kladis Room to Pierre Bouchard, the very nice Frenchman Anna had sent to Mondhiki.

This letter from Eleni still remained unanswered by the time Nicola returned to England for good, to assume ownership of her new home. A pretty cottage in the next-door village of Clifton Hamden had been tracked down by Rupert and negotiated for by Victor Melksham. But Nicola had agreed to the purchase with only photographs and details to go by, and it was a nervous Rupert, supported by Anna and Hal, who conducted her to see it for the first time. But the local combination of mellow red brick and flint appealed to her, and anxiety faded away.

'Darlings, you've been *very* clever,' she said at once. 'I love it already, and it's the ideal distance from The Clerk's Cottage – we'll be close at hand without overcrowding each other.'

Anna left her mother and Rupert arguing amicably about where her furniture should go when it arrived, and walked home with Hal, still wondering how to deal with Eleni's unanswered letter. Later that evening, after Rupert had gone home, she told Nicola about it.

'I think I have to refuse; a Greek christening certainly requires a godparent to be present, and that's out of the question, I'm afraid. But Eleni will be deeply offended and I find that upsetting . . . I so wanted to keep their friendship.'

Nicola was now looking offended in her turn. '*Why* can't you spend a few days in Corfu? Aren't I and Rupert and Mrs B capable of looking after one small child for that length of time? I've got nothing to do except keep changing my mind about where everything is to go. Say you'll be there, *please*, Anna?'

And so she went, trying hard not to look anxious, nor to leave her deputies with a list of instructions they'd probably manage better without. She saw Mondhiki this time in the mellow light of late-summer when the fiercest heat of the year was over, and Petros's vines were swagged with purple fruit. He and Eleni looked very content with life, and with each other, and Stefanos Kladis seemed to Anna to be a changed man, relaxed and almost gentle. He welcomed her kindly, and spoke of the care Pierre had taken over the Kladis Room.

'You'll see it for yourself, of course, but I think he is a good man.'

'I think so too,' she agreed, trying to smile at him, 'and everything at Mondhiki looks good to me, as well.'

Stefanos nodded his grey head. 'It's out of the shadows, Anna – back in the sunlight again.'

It seemed for the down-to-earth countryman that he had an unexpectedly poetic way of putting it – surely another sign of the change in him.

They went, of course, to see the paintings – beautifully placed and hung – and after the complete day of rejoicing that Yannis's christening became, drove to Linia to see George and Irene, who were already laying out what would soon be their kitchen garden and olive-grove.

'It'll be vines next,' Irene said cheerfully. 'George is ready to try his hand at anything.'

Anna smiled at her tanned face and simply cut hair – here was someone else who'd been altered by the Greek experience. 'It's working out, isn't it . . . not too many regrets?' she asked.

'No regrets,' Irene insisted, 'except that I lived with George all those years not knowing that *this* life was in his blood; he's a happy man now. I'm not so quick with the language as he is, but I'll get there.' She looked affectionately at her friend. 'Bring Hal out next summer Anna – he'll be old enough to enjoy the beach by then.'

She promised that she would; then after the delicious lunch Irene had prepared, it was time to leave and drive back to Mondhiki. Later that evening, while Petros and Stefanos were outside on their nightly stroll to make sure that all was well, Anna took out the photographs of Hal that she'd brought and showed them to Eleni.

'Mine!' she said with a proud smile. 'You aren't the only one with a gorgeous son, though I have to admit that I don't have a gorgeous husband to go with him!'

Eleni studied the photographs for a moment, then handed them back. 'He's beautiful, Anna . . . now I know why you look different, and why you didn't come to see us before. I suppose his father is looking after him.'

'No, my mother is. Apart from her, I bring up Hal alone. I know Petros and your father-in-law wouldn't approve of that; it's why I haven't told you before.'

Eleni didn't miss the note of sadness in her voice, and took hold of Anna's thin hands. 'Perhaps one day his father *can* be there?'

'No, I'm afraid not; but we manage very well without him.' She put the photographs away and smiled at her friend. 'I'm glad *you* know; you needn't tell the others.'

'I *shall* tell them,' Eleni said firmly, 'when the moment is right,' And, looking at her, Anna mentally chalked up one more transformation – Eleni Kladis was her own woman at last, poised and confident.

The next day Petros was only allowed to drive her away when she'd repeated her promise to return the following summer. By late-afternoon she was already back on English soil, to find that Rupert had brought her mother and Hal to meet her at the airport.

'You look better,' Nicola said at once, 'rested and relaxed; Rupert and I are not exactly rested, but we've all had a marvellous time.'

'I have, too,' Anna admitted, hugging her son, 'but I'm so glad to be home!'

By the time Christmas came round again Nicola was comfortably ensconced in her new home, fully in charge of the forthcoming carol concert, and with two new pupils in addition to Sandra Blott. It was hard to remember a time when she hadn't been there and, apart from grumbling at the struggle for survival that an English winter seemed to represent, she expressed no regret at having exchanged the grandeur that was Rome for the contentment that was Clifton Hamden.

Hal celebrated his first birthday with the novel experience of cramming beautiful cold snowflakes into his mouth and laughing at the taste, and this time round Anna also found herself enjoying the winter. She supposed that every parent shared her own delight in watching a child's discovery of the world around him; each day that passed added to Hal's awareness of why and what things were and, as with the coming of spring, she wanted to slow time down for fear of missing something.

The change of season brought a spell of grey, rainy days, but one morning they awoke to the return of the sun, and Anna went outside to pick late daffodils for the house. A car was drawn up further along the road, the driver apparently asking directions of Ada Jenkins, just arriving to do her daily 'clean' for Mrs Marchmount. Mildly interested, because strangers needing guidance weren't all that common in Long Wittenham, Anna saw Ada's arm lifted in her own direction; then she saw who it was that now got out of the car.

She bent down, to pick another bloom it might seem, but in reality to recover from the dizziness that swept over her. When Pierre's voice spoke from the gate, she was more or less herself again even though her hands were clammy and her heart was beating much too fast.

'Good morning, Anna – do you remember me?' he asked.

She straightened up slowly, managed to look at him, and even to find her voice. 'Let me see . . . the Athenian business man who spoke very good French?'

'The very same.' She waited for what he would say next, but he seemed intent on simply staring at her as she stood there with her hands full of golden flowers, and the breeze ruffling her bright hair.

'I suppose you're passing through on your way to or from Oxford,' she finally suggested, for something to fill the awkward pause.

'No, I came to see you. Your house looks charming from here, but may I come in?'

She unlatched the gate and held it open for him. 'I can offer you coffee, but not invite you to stay very long, I'm afraid.'

His eyes, deep-set in a face that looked older and far too tired, still watched her intently. 'Guests expected . . . much to do before they arrive, or am I not welcome?'

'Much to do,' she agreed. 'Excuse the kitchen approach, but I haven't unlocked the front door yet.' She led him round the side of the house to the garden door that opened on to a back porch and then a warm and welcoming kitchen. Mindful of Hal's toys stacked neatly in a corner, she walked quickly through into a wide stone-flagged hall, and then into the sitting-room – with its long windows overlooking the garden, comfortable chintz-covered chairs, book-shelves lining the walls, and bowls of spring flowers scenting the air.

'The coffee doesn't matter,' Pierre said, '. . . I'd rather talk to you.'

Anna found that she was still holding the daffodils. 'Then I'll just put these in water . . . Sit down, please, Pierre.' She put them in the cloakroom, and saw her white face in the mirror above the basin. It was by God's mercy that she'd put Hal down for his morning nap just before going out into the garden, but he never slept for very long; and, sweet-tempered though he was, he always awoke cross and noisy till she went to get him up.

She went back to the sitting-room and found Pierre standing in front of a framed pencil-sketch of a child's head – Hal at one year old.

'It's very good,' the expert said, '. . . charming, in fact.'

'The work of a local artist,' Anna explained hurriedly. 'She's a friend of mine.' Then, to lead them to what she supposed he'd come about – though why after all this time? – she spoke of Evgenia. 'I miss her still, very much; it must be even worse for you.'

He nodded by way of answer, then asked a sudden question himself. 'Why did you refuse her gift? She would have been hurt by that.'

'It was obvious that her house should belong to you,' Anna managed to say calmly. 'And in any case, this is where I live . . . much too far away from Arachova.' Again, to skirt a dangerous subject she spoke of something else. 'I went back to Mondhiki last summer for the christening of Eleni and Petros's son. They took me to see the Kladis paintings . . . thank you for getting the room arranged so beautifully.'

'It's what I do,' Pierre commented, 'see that paintings are displayed as they deserve.'

What to talk about now? Anna wondered desperately. She was about to mention her mother's attempt to get in touch with Miranda when he suddenly took charge of the conversation himself.

'I didn't intend to inflict myself on you – an infliction is what I'm afraid it is – but something made me change my mind. I've just been in London, visiting Burlington House. There's a bookshop almost opposite it in Piccadilly, with a window full of copies of your Greek novel. The assistant said they're selling very well.'

'Yes, I believe so,' Anna mumbled, and found herself praying that he hadn't bought one.

'It's a beautifully written piece of work – I finished it at three o'clock this morning, unable to put it down once I'd started.'

'What every author hopes for,' she said, trying to smile.

Pierre brushed the nervous comment aside. 'It's Evegenia's story, isn't it? She fairly leaps off the page, even though you've changed her name.'

'I used the material she sent me and wove a novel out of it. My heroine wasn't meant to be her, but she kept taking the story over. Perhaps I should have expected that she would!'

Pierre moved from where he'd been standing in front of Hal's picture and propped himself against the stone fireplace. 'The heroine's child in the book *was* Evgenia's, wasn't it . . . that wasn't fiction?'

Anna nodded, terribly afraid that she could guess what would come next. Anxious about that, she'd even forgotten that at any moment now Hal would wake up, and then the morning would finally descend into chaos. Pierre saw the apprehension in her face, and didn't even bother to phrase what he was going to say as a question, because he already knew the answer.

'The child was me . . . she wasn't just my father's friend – she was his lover. Clothilde Bouchard, my father's wife, never had a child at all.'

Anna nodded again; it was all she seemed capable of now. But the grief in his voice made her struggle to explain. 'There's no proof because Evgenia disguised the people she wrote about. You must read the diaries and decide for yourself – they properly belong to you anyway. She only sent them to me, I think, because she couldn't bear to die without *someone* guessing the truth. I'll get them for you.' Without waiting for him to reply, she walked out of the room and returned a moment later with a large folder of material, but there seemed to be one more thing to say.

'She wanted me to use this in whatever way I liked as long as living people were protected – that's why even the dedication to her is anonymous. If . . . if Madame Bouchard by any remote chance saw the book, would she . . . recognize any of it . . . be hurt by it? I thought I'd made sure that wouldn't happen.'

'My mother . . .' Pierre grimaced at the word, but then repeated it, 'my mother lives in a remote part of France and her memory of the past is very faint. Even if she were given the book she wouldn't be troubled by it; as far as she's concerned, I *am* her son, and of course I must remain so.'

Anna let out a sigh of relief, then looked at her watch, with just enough emphasis, she hoped, to remind him that time was passing. He acknowledged the gesture by picking up the folder she'd placed on the table.

'Now, I think, you want me to go.'

She needed him to go . . . couldn't bear the suspense and tension of his presence much longer. When he was safely out of the house she could weep, collapse, fall on her knees and pray to God to make him less unhappy-seeming and withdrawn somewhere deep inside himself; but now she needed him to go before his son woke up.

'I *do* have things to do,' she agreed with a kind of mad cheerfulness, 'and you're always *en route* for somewhere else. I'll let you out by the front door – it's this way.'

She led him along the hall to the door, and opened it . . . nothing had changed, she was astonished to find; the world outside looked exactly as it had done before he arrived. On the threshold he stopped for a moment.

'Why did you change your name to Curtis?'

Taken unawares, she almost gave herself away. 'I thought Ha— I thought it was time to abandon a father I never even knew.'

Still he lingered there, considering another question. 'Eleni Kladis mentioned a name to me once – Henry, I think it was. Am I allowed to ask if he still shares the house with you?'

Convincing delight suddenly glowed in her face. 'Of course – we love each other very much.'

'I'm glad,' Pierre said quietly, 'you deserve to be happy.' And with that he offered her a polite little salute and walked away.

She closed the door, found that her legs were trembling with the relief from tension, and climbed the stairs clinging to the banisters like an old woman. As she walked into Hal's room he woke up, and smiled sweetly at the sight of her – he was never cross if she was there. She caught him up and hugged him, and felt the racing beat of her heart gradually slow down. Now perhaps the day would become normal again.

Twenty-Two

Pierre drove back to Oxford, hesitated over how to fill the rest of a day that looked unbearably empty, and almost decided to catch the next train back to London. But a London hotel room would seem no less lonely than the one he'd booked into at the Randolph. He garaged the car, and then found himself walking along the High towards Rupert Whittaker's gallery. Rupert was just locking the door on his way out.

'You're off to a lunch date, I expect,' Pierre said quickly. 'I was only looking in to say hello.'

'*Cher collègue*, it's lovely to see you!' Rupert said with real pleasure. 'No lunch date – this is our early-closing day, and I was on my way home. Join me, please; it's only just round the corner.'

Pierre smilingly agreed, and matched his long stride to Rupert's shorter one as they fell into step together. His house *was* a stone's throw away, one of a pretty terrace of Georgian houses in Long Wall Street. The windows of the sitting-room on the first floor looked over the high wall opposite into the deer-strewn park of Magdalen College, and Pierre complimented his host on a charming house and view.

Busy assembling wine, paté, bread and cheese, Rupert agreed that he was fortunate; doubly so, because he also spent a lot of time with Anna and her mother in their country cottages. 'So nice for Anna,' he said casually, 'that dear Nicola decided to leave Rome and come back here. They're such good friends now . . . well, I think I can say we all are!'

'I've just come from Long Wittenham,' Pierre commented, sipping from the glass of wine he'd been handed. 'I went to congratulate Anna on her Greek book, among other things.'

'It's good, isn't it?' Rupert asked with pride. 'The best thing she's done. I don't know how she finds time to write . . . Henry's lovely, but he's a demanding chap.'

'He wasn't there,' Pierre said briefly. 'What does he do?' But the simple question seemed to take Rupert so aback that he had to try again. 'I imagine that like the rest of us he has to toil in the vineyard in some way?'

Still very puzzled, Rupert asked a question of his own. 'Why should he? Henry isn't anywhere near toiling yet – he's fifteen months old.' Then, as he saw Pierre's expression change, his own face crumpled. 'Oh God . . . you *didn't* meet him at the cottage? . . . Didn't realize that Anna shares her cottage with a child?'

Speechless for the moment, Pierre shook his head. Numbly, he tried to recall his visit, remembered that there'd been no hint of a masculine presence in the house . . . no sign of boots or stick in the porch, none of the clutter that most men couldn't help importing into the charming orderliness that a woman preferred.

'Henry's father . . . what about him?' Pierre demanded hoarsely.

Rupert lifted his hands in an expressive negative gesture. He was terribly afraid now of saying anything at all – for certain he'd say something else that Anna wouldn't want this gaunt and shaken man to know. But Pierre was now adding nine months to fifteen, and working out the answer. Two years ago they'd spent a day at Epidaurus, and a night together at a taverna on the way back to Athens . . . and they had loved each other.

'Pierre, my dear man, are you all right?' Rupert's anxious question penetrated the turmoil in his mind, and his stiff mouth achieved a sort of smile.

'There's a sketch of a child's head hanging in Anna's sitting-room . . . it's beautifully done. Is that Henry?' he asked.

Rupert hoped this was a question that it was safe to answer. 'That's him, my godson, only Anna calls him Hal. I'm not experienced in such things, but he seems a charmer to me, and she absolutely adores him.'

'Yes, I gathered that,' Pierre agreed more calmly now.

'Eat some food,' his host suggested. 'If I may say so you look as if you've been skimping meals lately . . . too many exhibitions to arrange in far-flung corners of the globe?'

Pierre nodded, and did as he'd been told. The food was simple but good, and Rupert's wine worth drinking; with its help he could pull himself together and carry on a coherent conversation about the subject they had in common. Then, after a reasonable stay he was able to thank his host and step out into the still-warm afternoon.

He walked at random, found himself at the entrance to Oxford's Botanic Gardens, and decided that it was as good a place as any to consider what he must do next. His strongest inclination was to drive straight back to Long Wittenham; but his deepest fear was that Anna would send him away. Since the moment of their parting outside the Phoenix Hotel in Athens she'd been at great pains to separate herself; he couldn't safely assume that she'd do anything else now. She'd been proudly bringing up her son alone, and maybe that was simply what she'd wanted from him all along, a child of her own.

But with his mind made up at last, he went back to find his car and drove out again to Long Wittenham. There was no answer to his knock at the front door, and he walked round the side of the house into the main garden. Anna was there, sitting on a rug on the lawn; beside her, intent on some tower of blocks he was building, was a dark-haired toddler who looked up from what he was doing to stare at the stranger. She lifted her hands in a little gesture of acceptance; it was too late for deception now.

'Meet Hal,' she said simply, 'he was asleep when you called this morning. I'm afraid you'll have to come down to our level.'

Pierre knelt down and held out his hand. After a moment of doubt, the child put his small fingers into the man's brown hand and smiled.

'He's mine, isn't he,' Pierre said quietly, '. . . I mean he's ours.'

'Yes,' she agreed, 'but there's nothing you need do about it; it was my mistake, getting pregnant. I meant you never to know about him because he's my responsibility, not yours. He's my joy as well, of course – I can't imagine being without him.'

As if aware that he was being talked about, Hal released Pierre's fingers and touched her skirt instead, but she smiled at him and, sensing no alarm, he went back to his building.

'I went to see Rupert Whittaker,' Pierre said in the same quiet voice. 'Quite by accident he explained that Henry was a child, not the man I believed you were living with. But for that I should have gone back to Paris not knowing the truth. Did Evgenia know?'

'Yes – she was afraid I'd be unhappy and I wanted her to know the treasure I had; of course, she promised not to tell, just as she promised not to tell the truth about you all those years ago.'

'There was something else she knew – that my marriage ended in divorce six months ago. Madeleine decided that Amélie needed to go away to school; once that happened there was no longer any point in my staying in the Rue Jacob.'

'But you still see your daughter . . . she's all right, Pierre?'

'She's very happy where she is. What the school in Lausanne will make of her I don't know for certain, but I *think* she'll leave it in seven years' time the very well-educated, highly sophisticate European that her mother expects. By then she may have become a stranger to me, but that's my problem, not theirs.'

At this point, bored with a conversation he didn't understand, Hal hauled himself to his feet and trundled across the grass to inspect something that had caught his eye. Pierre stared at Anna, whose face was slightly turned away from him.

'Look at me, please,' he insisted gently. 'What I've just told you need make no difference to you. I have no claim on Hal if you choose not to allow me any. But I would like more than I can say to be included in your lives to *some* extent at least.'

Anna's eyes skimmed his strained face and looked away again. 'Our lives don't coincide at all, do they? Well, only in that small scrap over there. You live in Paris when you're not roaming the world, we live *here*, in a rural corner of England, in a house, a village, a community that's made us very welcome. This is where we plan to stay.'

Her grave expression suddenly relaxed into the smile he remembered. 'If this were a Hollywood film or – God forbid – a television soap, having clapped eyes on each other we'd have fallen into an overheated embrace by now! The reality is that we met very briefly two years ago, and we've done a lot of separate living since then. Perhaps we're even different people from the man and woman who looked at *The Charioteer* together and loved each other for a little while.'

'Perhaps,' he agreed unsteadily, 'but may we at least find out? Will you let me visit you whenever I can, let Hal have the chance to decide whether he can accept me or not, and let me take care of you both a little?'

Her grave stare – just like her son's – considered him for so long that he thought she was going to refuse. He could begin to hear the door slamming, shutting him outside, and she'd never know – because this wasn't the moment to tell her – that he would love her until he died, that the need to try to persuade her was almost overwhelming.

'The answer's no, I think,' he said, to make it easier for her, 'so I'll just go and say goodbye to my son.'

She allowed him to get up and walk across to where Hal stood stock-still watching a ladybird walk across the palm of his hand. For moment man and child watched it together, then he stooped and kissed his son's dark head. When he came back she was standing up herself, and smiling faintly.

'I hope the goodbye wasn't too permanent – the answer was going to be yes!' She faltered under the sudden blaze of joy in his face, but swallowed the lump in her throat that made talking difficult and went bravely on. 'Evgenia had it all planned, I think. But she was hedged about with the promises she'd made and had to rely on us to sort things out.' It was hard to seem cautious even now, but she had to trust him to understand. Going without anything for a long while – warmth, food, and especially joy itself – meant that it had to be rediscovered slowly; lasting happiness insisted on that. 'Given time, we'll manage, don't you think?'

'Given time, there's *nothing* we can't manage,' he said with certainty. 'How shall we begin?'

Anna thought about this for a moment. 'By taking the good news to Clifton Hamden at least, if not to Ghent! It's high time you met Hal's grandmother.'

And so they scooped him up and, hand in hand, went out to Pierre's car. Somewhere, Anna thought, Evgenia knew, and for certain, now, she was smiling.